To Joan

ARCHER BOWS IN

Enjoy
Colin Easton

Also by Colin Eston

The *Saint and Czinner* books

Dying for Love

The Dusk Messenger

The Pepys Memorandum

The Seed of Osiris

COLIN ESTON

Archer Bows In

The first *Will Archer* mystery

Pickpocket

The pickpocket is quick - but I am quicker.

I have him.

He struggles madly - kicking, beating. I duck and jerk, avoiding flailing fists, sharp knees. We skid on squirming offal and rotting veg.

Bundling him past cursing stall-men and startled citizens I slam him up against the wall. He gasps, deflates like a stuck bladder and sinks into the filth. I tower over him, panting hard, a roaring sea-surf in my head.

A skinny thing, all teeth and scabby skin. Winded, but no bones broken. There will be bruises in the morning - for both of us.

Behind us the market mêlée has stuttered, glanced briefly. Now it shakes its head, decides we are none of its business, and flows on - our small rip in its fabric seamlessly stitched..

His puny frame rasps breath enough to croak, 'I'll give yer back yer purse - don't peach me to the runners, mate.'

I bunch a fistful of his greasy shirt and haul him upright. 'Don't 'mate' me, scab. I'm no mate of yours. A one-time fellow traveller, maybe, and a friend, though you don't know it. I'm not about to turn you in.'

His eyes, cunning, glitter and he sneers a gap-toothed grin. I catch his stable breath and his stink, stale as three-day offal as he whines. 'You ain't one of us - you smell too sweet.'

'I wash,' say I, 'occasionally.'

He's no more than eight years old, but shrewd. 'You ain't no 'prentice,' he says, 'nor skivvy. What are yer?'

'I serve a gentleman.'

'*Serve* a gennelman, do yer?' He sniggers through snaggled teeth. 'His bum boy are yer?'

I tighten my grip. 'Mind your lip! My master's none of your concern. But I am. I can be judge, jury and executioner to you .'

He catches my glance towards the horse-trough and cringes. 'I didn't mean nuthin'.'

It's late November. His rags are thin. He's seen his dipper mates ducked before. 'Don't souse me, mate,' he snivels. 'I'd sooner you shop me.'

'You'll shop yourself if you don't learn your trade better.'

''Snot my fault. Mi brother says get out and be a dipper, cos I'm grown too big for the basket.'

I know what he means. Boys concealed in baskets carried on another's head. Spy a rich man, snatch his hat and wig. The outraged mark clutches his head, glares about. Sees only a passing tradesmen carrying his wares.

I reach into my pocket. I hold a sixpence in front of his eyes. Greed flickers, then suspicion.

'You after my arse, mate? No way.' He considers. 'Shillin' at least.'

My lip curls. 'A midden like you?'

'I'd wash,' he says ingratiatingly.

'It's not washing'll keep you from the gallows,' I tell him. 'It's nous.'

I relax my hold on his crop, let his feet touch

ground. Shift my grip to his shoulder.

'This sixpence,' I say, 'is to buy knowledge. Today and tomorrow, do nothing but watch. Learn how to choose your mark. Silk or fine wool, wigs and canes. See how they walk, where they go, what they do. Take 'em when they're occupied, looking at a book, buying some trinket, greeting a friend.'

'Why you tellin' me all this?' He frowns. 'You ain't a taker, are yer?'

'No, I'm no thief-taker, luckily for you. The law wants to nab you. I want you *not* to get nabbed.'

An uncertain smile flickers. For a moment I see the eight-year-old he is - the boy I might have been.

'A rum'un you are, mister!'

'Believe it.' I hold out the coin. 'Learn - and prosper.'

He claws it into his grubby hand. I release him and he is away.

At a safe distance he looks back. His look is puzzled. Then he raises his finger obscenely and turns to run.

Straight into a bigger boy. The brother grabs him and smacks his ear. They gabble and the elder boy throws me a suspicious look. Another blow and the sixpence is surrendered.

Inwardly I sigh. Another lost boy. I didn't ask his name. There are too many.

The crowd absorbs them.

I turn and head back to Mr Garrick's lodgings. David Garrick, the famous actor.

And me? Will Archer. Nineteen - in this year of our Lord 1741.

Mutton Pie

The wine in David Garrick's glass winks ruby red in the firelight.

'Truly,' he says, 'we live in the best of times. An epoch of belief, a season of light, the spring of hope!'

'Nay,' grumbles Mr Macklin in his thick Irish brogue, 'the worst of times. An epoch of incredulity, a season of darkness, the winter of despair!'

His coarse features, already ugly, take on an even gloomier cast. Mr Garrick laughs.

'Why, Charles, you are liverish! With Cibber and Quin in retreat before us, you and I ride high.'

'Windbag Quin and simpering Cibber!' snorts Macklin. 'They are but pygmies. No, 'tis not our fellow actors we must look out for, but the managers. They will have us to hell in a handcart.'

With a sly smile, my master drains his glass. 'They must get us in the handcart to start with. What say you, Will Archer?'

The sound of my name jerks me from my daydream. I have been thinking of the nameless pickpocket and only half listening, lulled into reverie by the warm fire and the drone of fine words. Such verbal sparring is commonplace with the two actors, as if they expect their words to be preserved for posterity. Someday, indeed, they may be, but not by me. What words have found access to my head now jostle there with no more sense or purpose than fops at court.

Mr Garrick, noting my confusion, raises a mocking

eyebrow, 'Well, young Will?'

'Nay, Mister Garrick sir,' I reply with a shrug, 'such matters are beyond me. 'Tis as much as I can do to study my part for the next play. To study the ways of the world as well - 'twould addle what few wits I have.'

'Very diplomatic, Will,' says Mr Garrick with a smile. He nods, satisfied, as if I've passed some secret test.

Mr Macklin, on the other hand, twists round and favours me with a baleful glower.

Critics made much of his brooding brows and piercing eyes when he first played Shylock eight months ago. Indeed, the rumour ran that King George, after seeing his performance, passed a restless, sleepless night. The next morning, Prime Minister Walpole fearing rejection of a proposed measure by the Commons, remarked, "I wish it was possible, your Majesty, to find a recipe for frightening a House of Commons." "Seek no further," replied the king. "Send them to the theatre to see the Irishman play Shylock!"

I do not know about instilling fear into members of Parliament, but he certainly unnerves me!

'He's a deep one, this lad of yours,' snarls Macklin, jabbing a finger in my direction. 'I would not call that answer diplomatic; I would call it devious. I'll warrant he listens and takes all in, for all his protestations. I wouldn't trust him if I were you, Davey.'

'Away with you, Charles,' scoffs Mr Garrick. 'There's none more honest and loyal - or discreet, eh Will?' He gives me a confidential wink and holds up the empty bottle. 'Fetch us more wine, Will, and if Mrs Wiggins is not yet abed, a slice of cold mutton pie would not go amiss. Mr Macklin and I are not finished here.'

Relieved, I nod courteously and make my escape.

Mrs Wiggins will either be asleep or dead drunk this time in the evening. The kitchen will be left to Susan. I feel my spirits rise.

And not just my spirits. The very thought of Susan causes my little soldier to stir at the possibility of imminent action. Many a time, with Mrs Wiggins snoring in the rocker, Susan has pretended to resist, with much muffled giggling, as my little soldier has laid siege to her defences. Only once did he gain access to the citadel, but was routed before he could discharge his shot, obliged to waste it ignominiously upon the adjacent plains. The skirmish, far from deterring him, has rather whetted his appetite for further engagements.

Susan - about my age, plump and rosy, her body sour-sweet with sweat from the heat of the kitchen - that same heat which makes her greasy stays and petticoat the only needful garments to cover her charms. One Sunday a month she douses her head at the pump before donning her precious linsey-wolsey petticoat and sole pair of stockings, and the two of us walk in the park to stare at the toffs. For the rest of the time, the kitchen at Mr Garrick's lodgings is her home, her bed a straw mattress in the corner furthest from the food pantry to prevent it being too convenient a nest for vermin, though it still harbours more than its share of livestock - as I know to my cost.

Tonight, she meets me with sharp words. 'Mutton pie! At this time of night!'

'He has Mr Macklin with him,' I say, settling myself astride the corner of the great wooden table in the centre of the room and leaning back to watch her as she busies herself with carving-knife and platter.

'Aye, 'twill be the bog-trotter craves mutton, I don't doubt. Mr Garrick is more refined.' She slaps a plate upon the table and begins hewing off a hunk of pie. The aroma tempts me and I lean across to dip my finger in the gravy.

'Mrs Wiggins not about?'

Susan tosses her greasy locks towards the small closet off the kitchen where Mrs Wiggins sleeps. 'Started early on the gin today.'

The toss of her head and her sawing at the pie cause her breasts to quake most beguilingly above the battlement of her stays. Bending forward, I make to steal a chunk of mutton and receive a rap on the knuckles with the handle of the knife. I laugh and lick my fingers.

'Stolen meat is all the sweeter!' say I leaning back, letting her see that within my breeches, my impudent little soldier is already half at attention.

She takes the hint and dabbles her fingers between my legs with a mischievous grin. 'And this sweet meat,' she says, 'is this, too, ripe for stealing?'

Pushing aside both pie and pretence, I leap up and pull her to me, cupping her warm buttock. Breathing heavy, I rifle up her coarse petticoat until my fingers meet smooth, dimpled flesh. At the same time she deftly looses the flap of my breeches, whence the importunate ensign springs, ready for action. Then, as my right hand reconnoitres deeper into the narrow defile on her lower flank, our lips engage and rough fingers seize my resolute subaltern to begin briskly dressing him down.

Just as our encounter reaches crisis point, a clatter of footsteps on the stairs interrupts us. Outside the kitchen door a shrill voice cries, 'Master Will, Master Will - you must come at once.'

Susan giggles as, with a gasp, I involuntarily obey.

We have barely time to retreat to our original positions before young Charlie Stubbs bursts into the kitchen.

Tousled and half dressed, roused from sleep, Charlie seems not to notice our disarray in his eagerness to blurt out his message.

Running to me, he tugs at my sleeve and stares, wild eyed, into my face.

'Mr Garrick wants you, Master Will,' he says breathlessly. 'It's Harry Henderson. He's only gone and 'anged 'isself!'

Hanged Man

I follow Charlie at a brisk trot, tucking my shirt in as we go. Not upstairs to the room where, not twenty minutes ago, I left Mr Garrick and Mr Macklin, but out at the street door.

I wonder at this but decide he must be taking me to the theatre. I can think of no other destination that would draw my master and his friend away with such urgency at this time of night.

Charlie confirms it. A message from the night-watchman has clearly alarmed my master. He and Macklin have set off already, pausing only long enough to roust the lad from his bed to fetch me. 'Right worried they looked,' chirrups Charlie with relish.

Even on this cold November night the sour stink of the city dunghills hangs, almost tangible, in the air. The area round Goodmans Fields is known for wild nocturnal behaviour, so Charlie and I put our best foot forward, trying to remain as inconspicuous as possible and avoid the gangs of rowdy youths. No easy task when taverns along our route continually spill forth their noise and brawling drunks.

Avoiding one such eruption, Charlie collides with a drunkard relieving himself in the central channel. The churl spins round, cursing, and the steaming stream splashes Charlie's bare legs. Charlie retaliates with an oath and is all for following up with blows but I drag him away. A skinny boy is no match for a drunken lout, however irate the boy, however incapable the man.

With pressing business in hand, I'm not prepared to play the champion. We leave the drunkard posturing and growling, fists raised, lobcock bouncing at his flapping codpiece.

The night is dark and we place our feet with care. Every step could twist an ankle or land us overshoes in mire. Along these streets, taverns and stew-houses care nothing for their legal obligation to pave and light the way.

From the shadows in entries, brazen whores sidle forth, accosting us, bare-breasted, smiling with blackened teeth, soliciting for trade. 'Give you a good juicy ride for a shilling, mi buck - an' I'll do the lad for sixpence.'

I brush them aside contemptuously and draw Charlie closer. Not yet twelve, with voice still unbroken, he casts sidelong glances as I chivvy him along. Especially past the dark passages where furtive gasps and grunts of unseen men speak of harlots with skirts about their waists.

We pass under the smoky glimmer of a solitary light. Charlie looks up at me with a cheeky grin. 'You were at it, weren't you - you and Susan?'

I cuff him round the ear, 'No we weren't, you cheeky urchin.'

'So why was your prick a' bubbling?'

I make to cuff his other ear, but he ducks, causing me to curse as I stumble on a loose cobble.

'Mr Garrick wouldn't like it,' he taunts.

This time I get hold of his ear and twist it. 'Well, no-one's going to tell him, are they, maggot-breath? Not if you want to keep your ear attached to your grubby little head.'

He squirms and yelps, 'Leave off, you arsehole! Rest easy, I won't tell him!'

I let go his ear.

Charlie rubs it, then flicks his fingers towards my breeches. 'I won't need to tell him, will I? Sentry might not be on duty no more,' he laughs, 'but he's still peeping out of his box!'

I look down, mortified. Sure enough, in the rush I have mis-tied my breeches and half the flap hangs loose. Turning aside, I remedy the oversight. Red faced, I warn Charlie not to say a word.

'Why would I? 'Tis, after all, no great thing for comment!'

We turn from Prescot Street into the passage to Chambers Street and here the darkness is relieved somewhat. Light spills from the Ship Tavern hard by, and outside the main door of the theatre stands a watchman with a taper.

He is a surly fellow, but when we tell him Mr Garrick is expecting us he lets us pass, directing us to the back-stage door in the alley.

It is fortunate we're familiar with the place, for the alley is pitch black after the watchman's flare, and he thinks it no part of his duty to lend us a light. Together, Charlie and I feel our way along the rough bricks until our eyes adjust to the gloom and we discern the door in front of us.

Inside is no less gloomy but the smell of gluesize and paint is comfortingly familiar. Groping our way slowly, we know we've reached the wings when the narrow ranks of side-cloths loom darkly around us, and I stub my toe on one of the metal tracks along which scenes are pushed on and off. Following it, we come out on to the stage. The front cloth is down for there has been no performance the last two days.

But here on the deserted stage is an eerie sight. At the very centre flickers a ghostly column of light. Charlie starts and stifles a cry. Even I half expect a phantom to materialise at any moment. But then I realise the ethereal glow emanates from beneath, through the open stage trap.

Approaching cautiously, I look down into the under-stage area. Our arrival has not been silent, our feet upon the bare boards ringing hollow. As I kneel on the edge of the opening I see the foreshortened figures of Mr Garrick and Mr Macklin looking up at me, the dim flicker of a lantern illuminating their upturned faces and causing shadows to dance around them. My premonition of ghostly apparitions seems not so wide of the mark, for Mr Garrick's face is deathly white and Mr Macklin's wears a look of fearful horror.

'Ah, Will, at last. Come down, we require your assistance.' He shades his eyes as Charlie pokes his head over the edge of the hole. 'Leave Charlie there. This is no sight for the boy's eyes.'

Alarmed by the unwonted querulousness in my master's voice, I hush Charlie's grumble of protest. 'Stay here, as you're told,' I tell him. 'Keep near the main trap if you're afeard of the dark.'

The main stage trap has no ladder. It would impede the operation of the elevator platform and the sliding of the cover to and fro. It is not for climbing in and out of, but for spectacular revelations or disappearances.

Less showy descents use the smaller grave trap which has a staircase. I use it now to make my way under the stage.

At five-foot nine, I am accounted tall. But even I do not need to bow my head under the stage. There is a good yard of space betwixt the supporting beams of the stage and my head. It is gloomy enough by day, but now, at night, with dark wood all about, the clutter of properties and machinery, and dancing shadows cast by the feeble lantern, I feel the whole place press in on me. Carefully I make my way over to Mr Garrick.

'Henderson, sir?' I query.

'Over here,' replies Garrick in hushed tones. 'This is a fearful business.'

I follow him past the elevator machinery, ducking between the hoist ropes. The under-stage area of a theatre runs a man-o'-war a close race for rigging, and many a nasty scrape from hempen ropes can ambush the unwary.

Harry Henderson, however, is beyond ambush of any kind. As Garrick comes to a halt, I raise my eyes and in the dim light of the lantern, see a face unnaturally dark, suffused with blood. The dead eyes bulge and stare. They are, in truth, the most arresting part in a body limp as a child's moppet. The hands, once so expressive, now hang loose. The feet in lax *en pointe*, dangle eighteen inches from the ground. At a little distance, I glimpse an upturned three-legged stool. Looking at his suspended body, I remember him as being of a size with me, and think, irreverently, that he'd have had a job hanging himself in this confined space. The noose has nine inches or a foot at most of rope.

At several places, the underside of the stage boards is not in direct contact with the cross-work of beams above our heads. Some beams act not as supports for the stage, but as braces between the sturdy columns which forest the whole under-croft. Others have odd rectangular fillets cut away from their topsides for some long forgotten purpose. It is through one of these that the rope has been threaded. The far end is secured on a metal cleat half way up the wall.

'We must get him down,' urges Garrick. Then, in an undertone, 'You must help me, Will. There is only you and I.'

I follow his look and immediately take his meaning. Macklin has turned to stone. He stands at a distance from the body, staring at it in bleak horror, lacking the power either to move or to speak.

I retrieve the fallen stool and slide it beneath dead Harry's feet to take some of the weight but it barely reaches his toes. I kick it aside with my foot and steel myself to take his whole weight whilst Garrick unwinds the other end of the rope from its anchor at the wall.

I count myself lucky to have embraced a number of live bodies in my nineteen years on this earth, but never a dead one. As Garrick signals that he is ready, I bend my knees, take a deep breath and, turning my head away from his privy parts where a dark stain of urine and I know not what else soils his breeches, I stretch my arms about Harry Henderson's thighs and hug him to me.

Seconds pass as Garrick fumbles inexpertly with the rope. What do I expect? - he is a great actor not a stage-hand. All the while the dead cold of the corpse seeps into me, numbing my flesh and appalling my senses. In truth, it does not feel human at all. The limbs are icy and the flesh unyielding. When Garrick at last releases the rope end, it is a relief. But the sudden weight momentarily unbalances me. I stagger, regain my balance, then start lowering the body, slowly as I can, to the floor. Garrick hurries to my side, helping me support the dead weight, reaching up to close the tormented eyes. Gently he eases the noose from round the neck. Together, we lay poor Harry Henderson reverently on the ground.

My master stands looking down at the corpse. 'What is the cause?' he murmurs to himself, in echo of the fated Moor, as if his own poor words cannot suffice. 'What is the cause? What ills or troubles could be so dire, could have prevailed so monstrously, for him to take his own life?'

'If he did.'

I turn to see Macklin wild-eyed. Have I heard aright? His words come guttural, reluctant, almost as if forced from some secret vault of horror. He half crouches, arm upraised, pointing a bony finger. 'Thou canst not say I did it,' he hisses, 'Never shake thy gory locks at me!' His body shakes and his brow runs with sweat.

Garrick turns to me, distressed. 'His wits are turned. We must get him out of here. Help me, Will.'

Leaving the body for the moment, we both support Macklin up the steps, through the grave-trap and on to the stage. All the while, he shudders and whimpers like a wounded animal.

But once upon the stage, away from the confines of the under-croft, there occurs one of the amazing transformations that so astounded observers of his Shylock. The gibbering wreck becomes his usual irascible self.

'Unhand me,' he barks, shaking off our helping hands. 'Come, Garrick, the evening is wasted. Let us not waste the night as well.' He strides off into the wings.

Garrick looks at me with imploring eyes. 'Say nothing of this, Will, I beg you. Macklin is not himself. I must go with him.' Nervously he indicates the place from which we've just emerged. 'Set as much straight as you are able. Cover his face... There's no more to be done tonight. Tomorrow - arrangements will have to be made.'

In the wings Macklin is blundering about. 'A light, Garrick, fetch a light!'

Garrick gives me a look of resignation and mute apology. 'I am in your debt, Will.'

Then he is gone.

The cone of light still shines, spectral, from the open trap. Garrick has left a lantern for me. I am glad of it. I have no wish to be pursued by ghosts as I return to my master's lodgings.

But for now I have more immediate business. Loth as I am to descend once more into that cave of death, I know I must. The corpse must be covered and the place secured. So, with cautious steps, I return to pay what respects I can to Harry Henderson's remains.

As gently as I am able, I heave the body aside, away from the open space where we laid it. There is no reason to do so, I know, it means little enough to him now. But perhaps it is for my own peace of mind - to leave him so exposed seems an indignity. Not that he has much dignity now. For all our care in getting him down, his shirt and breeches are dirtied, ripped in places, and the toes of his shoes badly scuffed.

In a corner I find some trunks where old costumes are stored. From one of these, I rummage out an old woollen cloak, moth-eaten and spotted with mildew. I lay it reverently over the body. An inauspicious shroud, but one I hope a fellow actor would not find unfitting.

I didn't know Henderson well. No one did. He was reserved and kept himself to himself. Unusual in an actor, but not unknown. There are many in the profession, I for one, who prefer to keep their personal history private from the company.

Even Mr Garrick does not know all the circumstances which led me, a pale fifteen-year-old, to his door. Knowing Sir Francis Courtney, who brought me, he may guess at it but does not ask. 'I care not whence you came, or what you may have done at the behest of others,' he said to me shortly after he took me in. 'My only concern is for you and what, with my help, you may become.' And for the last three years, he has been true to his word.

I can sympathise, therefore, with Henderson's reticence, but I can't understand him taking his own life. He was a few years older than me, agreeable in person and in manner, with no sign of melancholy humour. Only three days ago I helped him con his part in the forthcoming performance of *The Changeling*, and we joked and were merry. Surely I would have sensed then if aught had been amiss?

This isn't the only reason I feel uneasy about his death. As I pause to recover breath after the exertion of lugging the body, I gather my thoughts.

I try to recall what I have seen. There's something not right. Something that's eluding me, making no sense.

Once I've stowed the body safe from prying eyes, I take up the lantern and examine the room again. The upturned stool, the rope now hanging loose.

Heaving a crate across, I climb on to it. I take the noose and begin to pull the rope through the aperture. Immediately, slivers and splinters of wood shower down on me. Cursing, I dash them away from my smarting eyes. Only when my eyes have stopped watering do I see why they were so numerous. With the weight of the body, the rope has chewed away both top edges of the dried-out beam, leaving them raw and splintered. On my side, where the noose has been, there are still copious splinters on top. On the far side they have cascaded down the face of the beam, where some few still adhere, but most lie on the floor, scattered by our feet.

Coiling the rope, I lay it near the wall and dust off my hands against my breeches. There is little more I can do tonight. It must be near midnight and though I do not believe in witches or such claptrap, I don't relish being here longer than is needful.

Besides, in every shadowy recess I still see Macklin's grimacing face, his accusing finger, and hear his hissing breath. What made him react so violently?

Hauling on the counterpoise rope, I slide the main trap shut and make my way to the grave trap. Suddenly, as I set my foot upon the first step, an eerie whining noise from above stops me in my tracks and turns my blood to ice.

For several seconds my heart plays chase within my breast until I realise with relief what this strange wailing must be.

I have forgotten Charlie!

Now, as I ascend the steps from the grave trap, he yelps with fright. Frantically he knuckles his eyes. Tired of waiting, he has fallen asleep. The thump of the closing trapdoor has disturbed his slumber but he is not yet fully awake.

'Keep away from me,' he whimpers, backing away.

'Peace, you noddy, it is only I. You're mazed with sleep.'

He rushes at me and starts pummelling me.

I pin him close and tousle his hair until his fright-fuelled rage subsides. At length, he calms and I am absurdly gratified when his arm snakes about my waist and he leans his head into my side. He mutters sleepily, 'You bugger, Will. You fair put the frights up me!'

For all his streetwise bravado, he is still a child at heart, and I am the nearest he has to a big brother. Or any family, for that matter, for Charlie was a child of the streets, abandoned by his drab of a mother and left to fend for himself. I found him begging feebly in the gutter, filthy and weak, and prevailed upon my master to have him as a pot-boy. That was nearly two years ago, and I have seen many in like circumstances since. But I have had to steel myself against pity. As with the pickpocket, there are too many.

Charlie was lucky. Fate decreed that I should chance upon him while I was still raw from my own degradation. It was shortly after Mr Garrick had taken me on. I suspect he only agreed to harbour a fellow sufferer because he saw the solace it would bring to me. As fast as Charlie's health improved, so did his impudence, but I know that underneath all the banter burns a loyalty so fierce that I am humbled by it.

I rest my hand on his shoulder. 'Stir yourself, cocker, 'tis time you and I were home and abed.'

Outside the theatre, the night is chill. The alley is just as dark as when we arrived but now we have the advantage of a lantern as we walk towards the light that spills from The Ship around the corner.

We have not gone more than a couple of steps, however, when that light is blotted out. I pause and feel Charlie stiffen at my side.

But it is no gang of roaring-boys intent on mayhem. It is a solitary figure, shrouded head to foot in a hooded cloak, a silhouette, black against the feeble gleam. Hidden within the shadow of the voluminous hood, it is impossible to discern either face or feature.

'Master Archer?'

The voice is light, refined. The voice of a woman.

'You have the advantage of me, madam,' I reply.

Around us, the world has fallen silent, no noises from The Ship, the night sounds of the city muffled, as if the very air attends upon her next words.

Beside me, Charlie shivers. My own spine creeps with apprehension.

'The body in the theatre,' she continues - not a question, but an affirmation of something already known - 'you have treated him with respect?'

I take a step towards her. 'What would you have with me, madam? Will you not make yourself known?'

She holds up a hand to stop my advance. 'Come no closer, Master Archer. I have one question for you and then I will be gone. Your master - Mr Garrick - he regrets the suicide?'

'If suicide it is, madam.'

'It *is*, Master Archer. There can be no doubt that Hendrik - Henry - took his own life. Make that clear to Mr Garrick.'

Then, in a swirl of dark velvet, she is gone.

Charlie and I run to the corner as fast as the night and treacherous cobbles allow and look both ways. Only to see the tail of black cloak flick around the corner into Chambers Street. I have hardly covered half the distance when the clatter of hooves and coach wheels affronts the night. By the time I emerge, breathless, into the wider thoroughfare, there is only the rear of a landau disappearing fast in the dark.

I lean against the wall, panting. Charlie comes bounding around the corner. 'Done a flit, 'as she, mate?'

'Showed us a clean pair of heels.'

'A fine lady, by the sound of her.'

'That's what I thought.'

'A rum do, and no mistake.' He yawns mightily.

A rum do, indeed.

Garrick Permits

After an eventful night, I sleep late. Mornings are dark as the year draws towards its end, and the panes of the casement in my attic room are feathered with ice. There is to be no rehearsal today, so I keep to my bed until someone knocks gently at my door.

'Will, are you awake?'

The sound of Mr Garrick's voice has me on my feet and pulling on my breeches in a trice. I can not remember another occasion when my master has summoned me in person. The matter must be serious.

I unlatch the door and Garrick enters, stooping to avoid the low beams.

'I'm sorry to disturb you in your own quarters, Will, but I have need of your assistance.'

Hastily I straighten the sheet and invite my master to sit, feeling awkward that I can offer no chair in my tiny garret. There is no space. In any case I have little need of furniture, my few belongings fitting easily into a trunk beneath my bed.

With a shake of his head, he declines the offer. We stand like two conspirators - whispering, shoulders bowed beneath the attic eaves.

Though my shoulders are bowed more than his. My master, at only five foot three, is the shorter by a good five inches. His success on stage arises from originality of performance rather than physical presence, which is slight and delicate. Were Macklin in my poor garret, he would overwhelm it with his bulk like a bear in a basket.

The only thing he and my master have in common is the way they have revolutionised the art of acting, bringing realism to the stage instead of bombast. In neither age nor character is there any other reason why they should be friends. Macklin is in his forties, whilst my master is only twenty-five. Macklin, broad Irish, has coarse manners and a fiery temper. Mr Garrick is soft-spoken, polite and even-tempered.

'I require you to accompany me to the Whitechapel Bridewell, Will. The Watchman apprehended a boy running from the theatre last night. It was he who discovered the body. They have him in the round-house still.'

'You think he may have seen Henderson die, sir?'

'I doubt it, but he may have seen something.'

I follow him downstairs. In the hallway, I help him into his outdoor coat. He hands me an old greatcoat. 'Put that on, Will. It is a trifle small for you, but it is raining hard and I would not have you brought low of an ague. Would you have this, too?' he asks, taking a tricorn hat from the peg.

'My thanks, sir, but I have no need,' I reply. The bulky coat with its muffler collar and large cuffs has me in enough of a straitjacket without imprisoning my head, too. Mr Garrick may have need of one to protect his side-curled wig, but my own hair tied in its habitual queue will take no harm in the wet.

We venture out into the pelting rain.

As we pause for a moment on the step, Mr Garrick says, 'Later today, I would have you go to poor Henderson's lodgings, Will. There may, amongst his belongings, be some clue to any family who should be informed of his demise. Mr Giffard is out of town at the moment, so it is up to me to see things done properly. I have given orders for the body to be brought here until arrangements can be made. I shall, if necessary, defray the funeral expenses myself if no relative can be found. It is unthinkable he should be buried in a pauper's grave.' He holds my gaze for a moment. 'Only you, myself and Macklin know the circumstances of his death...'

'What of the Watchman - and the boy we are going to see? Did he not discover the body?'

'The Watchman has been paid for his silence. And the boy may know nothing.'

As we set off, Mr Garrick appears troubled. 'I think it would be for the best if it were given out that Henderson died as the result of an unfortunate accident. Macklin concurs. Can I rely upon you to do the same, Will?'

This is what I've been dreading. I can't give Mr Garrick the assurance he desires.

Until exhaustion overcame me in the small hours I couldn't sleep for turning over my best course of action, for what I observed last night convinces me that Harry Henderson, far from taking his own life, had it taken from him. Mr Garrick must be made aware of my doubts. I know he holds the reputation of the theatre dear and would be loth to see it damaged. But his new style of acting proves, above all things, that he is a seeker after truth. Surely he will see the necessity of seeking the truth of this matter, too?

'I do not think,' I reply hesitantly, 'that Henderson committed suicide.'

But Garrick clearly mistakes my meaning, for he

breathes a sigh of relief. 'Good boy. I knew we could rely on you. Poor Henderson, tormented as he must have been, does not deserve the further indignity of being interred in unconsecrated ground.'

It pains me to disillusion him, but I know I must. I put my hand upon his arm, staying him. He turns to face me, puzzled.

'Mr Garrick, I do not think it was suicide, but nor can I agree it was an accident. It is my belief that Harry Henderson was murdered.'

Heedless of the busy thoroughfare, Garrick halts and looks at me aghast. He stands white-faced, unmindful of the irritation of pedestrians whose way we are blocking.

I feel for his distress. But I also see it as a sign of hope. In wishing to have the death regarded as an accident he is driven by noble motives - to protect the good name of the theatre and that of Harry Henderson himself, not to be branded a suicide and a sinner. This same compassion will surely see the dead man deserves justice as well as forgiveness?

Rain gathers in his hat and trickles unheeded from the corners.

I draw him gently out of the main concourse into the shelter of a shop-front.

I see his struggle only too clearly. An accident might reflect poorly upon Goodman's Fields Theatre. A suicide would bring scandal. But a murder could destroy it. Every member of the Company would come under suspicion.

For that, the absent owner, Mr Giffard, would never forgive him.

Following Macklin's Shylock in February and his

own Richard III in October, the theatre has been packed. A dozen noblemen a night have been drawn by the power of their performances to one of the most disreputable areas of the city. His own reputation and success are assured. So much so that he has written to his brother, George, to release him from involvement in their family wine business, so sure is he of his future as an actor.

Now Harry Henderson's death threatens to destroy all this.

'A grave accusation, Will,' he says at length. 'What grounds can you have for suggesting such a thing?'

I list all the things - the upturned stool, the wood splinters, the scuffed toes of the shoes - that explain my reasoning.

'When I put the stool under the feet, it did not reach them. He could not have stood on it, much less kicked it away.'

'Perhaps that was not what he used.'

'There was no other stool.'

'A chest, a crate? - the place was full of them.'

'But none near the body - none overturned as if kicked aside.'

'Very well - and of what import is the splintered beam?'

I hold out my forefinger stiffly. 'Imagine that is the beam, if you will.' I crook my other forefinger crossways over it. 'And this the rope. Now, if my hand is the weight of the corpse, which way would the rope be pulled?'

He tugs my hand downwards.

'Precisely - towards the weight of the body. And say the rope rubbed against the upper edges of the beam as it grew taut, in which direction would the loosened splinters go?'

'Those on the side nearest to the body would fall downwards, those from the other edge would rest atop the beam.' He adds hopefully, 'The splinters atop the beam are therefore inconclusive.'

'Maybe,' I concede, 'but if splinters fell on the body side, you would expect some to adhere to the rough side-face of the beam. There were none. But on the other side, away from the body...'

'I see. The inescapable conclusion being that the rope was pulled the other way across the beam?' he says despondently. 'In other words, it was not a body falling that caused damage to the wood, but a body being hauled up?'

'I cannot see how it would occur otherwise. Then there are the scuffed toes.'

'Any shoes may have scuffed toes.'

'I grant you that. But other parts of the shoe showed no discernible wear. A man being hanged may scrabble in desperation at the floor, but a man who hangs himself, having kicked away his support, has only empty air to kick – and air does not scuff shoes.'

Garrick is quiet, thinking, as we resume our walk towards the Bridewell. Eventually he says. 'You are persuasive, Will. Yet I remain to be convinced. So much is at stake here - the consequences, if your suspicions should prove true, are not to be thought on.' He puts a hand on my arm. 'Our first concern is that young Henderson's body be shown proper respect. To avoid the opprobrium of suicide, we shall abide, for now, by the story of accident. But, in the interests of truth and justice, I would ask that you to find out all you can about the manner, and possibly the reason, why he died. I need hardly stress that your inquiries must be discreet and circumspect.'

'And if my inquiries prove my suspicion correct?'

'We must meet that eventuality if it arises. In the meantime, our endeavour must be to ensure poor Henderson's soul is put to rest.'

We walk on in silence for a while.

'We may not be the only ones who know of his death,' I tell him. 'There was a lady - outside the theatre last night.'

I recount last night's mysterious encounter. He is as perplexed as I.

'And then there was Mr Macklin's strange behaviour, sir...'

'No more, Will,' he replies curtly. 'I know Macklin and will vouch for him. Turn your scrutiny elsewhere.'

His tone curtails conversation for the rest of our journey.

But it does not stop me thinking. Two warnings in as many days... First a mysterious lady insisting on suicide, now Garrick telling me to ignore Macklin's reaction. Much as I desire to see justice done, I cannot help but feel the stirrings of unease.

Bridewell

The Whitechapel round-house proves to be little more than a lock-up hard by Tower Hill. A rough, stone-built hut consisting of two cramped rooms, one of which is a cell in which vagrants, drunks or pestering whores arrested by the Watch are kept overnight.

The Watchman from the theatre last night answers our knock. His surliness, I notice, has not improved. It is not to be wondered at. Watchmen in my experience are old and decrepit, fit for little else than to patrol the streets with lantern and stave calling the hour and to be ridiculed by gangs of youths. 'Tis not a job to be envied, but the pittance they earn keeps them from destitution and the workhouse.

We follow him in to a small, cheerless room with barely space for the scarred deal table and two chairs that are all its furniture. In one corner a meagre driftwood fire splutters and cracks, occasionally filling the place with smoke as back draughts hit the chimney. In the far wall, a peeling wooden door with a metal grille leads to the cell. The table bears the greasy remains of a chop, presumably from the chop-house we've passed in the neighbouring street, and a half-empty flagon of small beer - remnants of the old man's breakfast.

'Be so kind as to recount the events of last night,' says Garrick with his habitual civility.

The churlish rogue is clearly put out. Evidently he's been expecting us to take the prisoner off his hands, not be asked to retell his story. 'I told all yesternight,' he grumbles. 'What need to rehearse it all again?'

Garrick brings me forward. 'This gentleman does not know all the circumstances,' he says evenly. 'I would be glad if you would recall it once again for his sake.'

I would not have been so polite to the old curmudgeon, but Garrick's amiability seems to mollify him.

'I were doin' my rounds along Prescot Street when this 'ere young 'un runs round the corner, screeting fit to raise the devil. Soon stops when I land him one and knocks him to ground, mind. But then 'e's a-blubbering and a yawling so there's no sense to be got till I hauled him up and threatened him with a beating. Tells me 'e's seen a dead 'un, so I goes with 'im to the playhouse - 'e won't go in so I leaves 'im outside. I seen enough just shinin' my lantern down the hole, so then I brings 'im 'ere and locks 'im up while I comes for you. The rest you know.'

My gorge rises at the contemptible way the old man's eyes glitter with self-satisfaction as he tells of his violence towards the youth. I wonder at Mr Garrick's continued restraint.

'May we see the boy?' he asks.

'For all the good it may do,' growls the Watchman. 'Lad's half-crazed, I'd say.'

He retrieves a bunch of keys from a hook on the wall and unlocks the inner door. The cell is windowless and cold with a sour smell of sweat and excrement. In the gloom, it is just possible to discern a huddled figure crouching against the far wall. In a pale smudge of face, the light from the open door picks out two wide, frightened eyes. I hear Garrick gasp in disgust, his patience cracking at last. He turns on the Watchman.

'Has this poor boy had aught to eat or drink?' he demands.

''Taint an inn,' retorts the churl.

Garrick reaches into his pocket and pulls out a sixpence. 'Go,' he orders the Watchman. 'Bring drink and victuals, and be quick about it if you value your job.'

Gone is the civility. His tone admits of no demur. The old man seems about to object but thinks better of it and scuttles out.

Garrick enters the dank cell and squats next to the cowering boy. 'Come,' he says gently, 'we mean you no harm.' With infinite patience, he coaxes the terrified boy out towards the fire and bids him warm himself.

In the light of the outer room, it is plain to see what a miserable wretch he is. Emaciated and sickly-looking, he could be any age betwixt twelve and twenty. Threadbare rags barely cover his decency and his arms and legs, caked in ingrained filth, are thin as sticks. The pale face, gaunt and sharp, is skull-like. Wisps of hair sprout in clumps between flaking sores on his scalp.

The urchin squats trembling by the fire. Mr Garrick unwinds his scarf and lays it round the puny shoulders. The boy shrinks from his touch, looks up fearfully. Realising Garrick means no hurt, he smiles, revealing blackened teeth, and pulls the warm wool about him.

'What's your name, boy?' asks Garrick gently.

'Joe,' whispers the boy. ''S what they call me.'

'Have you no other name?'

'Just Joe. Poor Joe.' Gazing into the flames, he

keens softly, rocking to and fro on his haunches.

Garrick looks at me, his silent message clear. Perhaps the boy is crazed, as the Watchman says. I doubt he'll tell us anything of use.

We let him alone for a while until we hear the Watchman returning. The old curmudgeon throws down a pennyworth of bread and a hunk of cheese on the table and places a jug of small beer next to them. He looks defiantly at Garrick, challenging him to ask for change. The whole lot amounts to no more than fourpence. Mr Garrick refuses to rise to the bait. Instead, he reaches into his pocket for another sixpence.

'Continue your round, sir,' he says. 'We would speak with the boy in private.'

'You may do as you please,' retorts the old man with ill grace. 'You have half an hour, no more, before the Parish Constable takes over. You must be gone before he comes. If the rogue goes with you, I care not.' He turns on his heel and leaves, slamming the door. The fire billows acrid smoke into the room.

The boy falls back, choking. Garrick and I help him to a chair next to the table.

'Eat, Joe. Then tell us what occurred last night.'

The boy looks frightened, but at a nod from Garrick he falls to, tearing at the bread, almost choking in his haste. We wait until not a morsel is left - he even mops the grease from the Watchman's chop with the last few crumbs - before renewing the question.

'Why did you go into the theatre, Joe?'

He shrinks away, his eyes becoming defensive.

'I never done nothing wrong,' he wavers. 'The door - 'twas standing open. It was cold - I was seeking somewhere to sleep.'

'No-one's blaming you, Joe. The door was open, you say? The door in the alley?'

Wide eyes slide from Garrick to me and back again. His tongue flickers over cracked lips.

'I followed the light,' he murmurs.

Garrick glances at me. 'A light inside the theatre?' he asks urgently. I catch his excitement and hold my breath. If there was a light, the murderer must have still been there. 'When you went in - did you see anyone, Joe?'

'He was dead - down in the hole.' His eyes cloud. He starts to tremble. 'And then he was right beside me - his face - like a - the eyes...' Burying his head in his hands, he sobs.

We wait for him to become calmer.

'Who was beside you, Joe?'

He turns a pleading look on Garrick and seizes his hand. 'But he was dead! I saw him.' His face crumples. Again he rocks backwards and forwards, keening, moaning.

'Be easy, Joe,' soothes Garrick, patting his hand. 'Calm yourself - no more questions for the present.'

Garrick turns to me. 'Come, Will,' he says, 'help me. We will take him back to my lodging. There, with proper nourishment and care, he may yet tell us more.'

Between us, we half support, half carry, the unfortunate Joe into the street. In truth, it is no great effort for he weighs nothing, being but skin and bone.

The rain has stopped and a watery sun plays chase with scudding grey clouds as we come into the main thoroughfare. Mr Garrick and I take it in turns now to support our charge. But, as victuals and daylight take their effect, he is able to walk unaided for much of the time.

I begin to find the greatcoat Mr Garrick has given me oppressive and unbutton it. The poor wretch beside me has greater need of it than me.

We pause to see a way through the traffic. I put the coat around Joe's shoulders.

It is a mistake. As we start across the road he darts away, ducking between two oncoming chairs, earning curses from the chairmen. Taken unawares, neither Mr Garrick nor I are quick enough in pursuit. A hackney intervenes. We barely escape with limbs intact. By the time it passes, Mr Garrick's hat lies in the mire, crushed by a wheel. His wig is askew.

Joe - complete with Mr Garrick's coat and scarf - is nowhere to be seen.

Bell Court

Returning home, Mr Garrick is in disagreeable temper, brooding on the loss of Joe and the affront to his dignity.

Nevertheless, he has me go at once to Henderson's lodgings, even though it's started raining again. Receiving no further offer of protective clothing for this next sortie, I despatch Charlie to the kitchen where he filches two squares of cloth, rank with old fat, to cover our heads.

The two of us set off for Bell Court, the address Mr Garrick has given me for Harry Henderson's lodgings. Hard by the church of St Mary le Bow in Cheapside, it is but a mile or so distant but, after all the rain, the streets are at their filthiest, mired in a festering mud, the product of household waste and chamber-pots, dung from market-bound cattle, the odd dead cat or dog. The stinking mess sucks at your feet and sprays your clothes when thrown from the wheels of passing carts.

Past Aldgate, as the way broadens into Leadenhall Street, the scurry of carts and coaches increases. Hooves and wheels clatter, carts rumble, chair-men shout and curse as they weave their way through the throng. The everyday cacophony of London, as ever-present as the ubiquitous dirt. Five years ago, a country lad come to the great city for the first time, it struck me as intolerable, but now it seems as natural as the teeming rain.

Our greasy cloth squares hold out some of the rain, but they don't stop the smoke trapped by the lowering sky assaulting our faces with smuts, or our clothes being pulled at by beggars and our ears being assailed by their cries.

Coming into Cornhill, a couple of bedraggled urchins tug at my sleeve. 'Long and strong, cotton laces, two a penny, mister,' chants the boy. His face is grimy and he uses his sleeve to brush snot from his nose as he runs beside me. They desist when I ignore them, latching on to an old gentleman in a bottle-green coat instead.

Three years ago, I'd have given the urchin a farthing, but since being in London I've witnessed so many a miracle as dusk gathers - bundles of rags shedding their infirmities, cripples getting up and walking, blind men's sight restored - that my pity has waned. All the same, I am tempted by a drenched and shivering waif huddled in a doorway selling tiny bunches of flowers. I consider buying some for Susan. But at the same moment a renegade trickle of water evades my stinking head-cover and sidles its way under my collar, so I think better of it.

At the crossroads from Cornhill into Poultry, I pay a ragged-arsed street-sweeper a half-penny to clear the way for us. Though not yet noon, there are plenty of chairs and hackney coaches about and I'd rather the lad brave the traffic first. Luckily a lumbering cart laden with animal carcases bound for Smithfield causes a temporary slowing of the rush so we are able to cross without mishap. An ambling horseman reins in his mare to allow our passage and responds good-naturedly to our gesture of thanks. A countryman, no doubt, for even when it is not foul weather, you're lucky if a city horseman gives quarter, let alone recognition.

Soon, the mighty square bulk of St Mary le Bow is here to the left of us, pinnacles at its four corners, the tall thin steeple atop its round cupola losing itself in the lowering clouds. Beside me, Charlie hoods his eyes against the rain and looks up.

'Sir Christopher Wren built that,' I tell him. 'The same cove as built St Pauls after the Great Fire seventy-odd years ago.'

'Think I don't know that,' replies Charlie scathingly. 'I've 'eard the bells many a time.'

'You're a true cockney, then,' I say, 'born in the sound of Bow bells.'

'S'pose,' he mutters gloomily, and I immediately regret my jest. To tell truth, Charlie has no idea where he was born, or who his mother was, having been abandoned almost before he could walk. His earliest steps were on the streets, his first words those needful to beg. He wasn't even sure of his real age or if Charlie was his given name, or simply what the other street kids called him. My finding him, he once told me, was his first good memory.

'Well,' I say, in an attempt to cheer him up, 'you're more like to be a cockney than a bumkin like me!'

Though at least I know my parentage and have a mother back in Yorkshire who I know loves me - even if she has no idea how she betrayed me.

Enough reminiscence! We have reached the turning from Cheapside into Bow Lane which runs along the side of the church. Somewhere off here is the entrance to Bell Court.

A gloomy enough entry it is, to a cramped alley of haphazard, toppling tenements. Like so many houses in the expanding city, these were erected fast and cheap by a speculative builder at the beginning of the century. Cracks and fissures in the front walls testify to shoddy workmanship. Many bricks, made from poorly fired clay mixed with the contents of refuse heaps and cesspits, are already crumbling.

The inhabitants of Bell Court probably live in daily fear of imminent collapse, yet still there is a faint remembrance of gentility. Respectable tradesmen once lived here. Now the houses are divided into rented rooms.

Harry Henderson's room is on the first floor of number five. It is a relief to get out of the rain, even into the cramped gloom and smell of mould that meets us inside the doorway. I leave the door ajar to provide some glimmer of light to see our way. Beside us, a door leads into the ground floor room and, at the end of the passage, steps disappear down into the cellar. On the top step, a pale-faced infant girl, half-naked in a grimy cotton shift stares silent and wide-eyed at us. How many more, I wonder, live in the dank hole below?

A staircase ahead of us ascends to Henderson's room. Cautiously, our eyes adjusting to the gloom, we make our way up. His door is half-way along a landing, at the far end of which twist the first few steps of the stair to the garret. It's well known that first floor rooms are best - the further up or down a staircase you live, the less money you pay. Henderson has - had - the best accommodation in the house.

The door is locked, but the door frame is rotten. No

match for a determined shoulder. Screws come out unresisting.

It is a simple room. A half-tester bed with flock mattress and bolster hung about with threadbare linsey-woolsey curtains that might once have been red. A single cane-bottomed chair beside a small table on which stand a pewter candlestick with a stub of candle and a small pile of books. On the bare floorboards, a scrap of rug beside the bed. White ashes in a small iron stove. Beside it a few billets of wood. Compared to my own attic room it is luxurious, but it is still the room of a single man with few possessions.

I look beneath the bed. It is clear that Harry Henderson, like myself, found a single trunk big enough for all his worldly goods. A trunk that Charlie and I will have to carry back to Mr Garrick's house. I pull it out and prise open the lid. On top are two shirts, one cotton, one fine lawn - expensive for a lowly actor. I lay them on the bed the better to investigate the remaining contents. And find yet more to surprise me.

For a jobbing actor worth forty pounds a year, in a rented room at two shillings and sixpence a week, this is unexpected finery. Laying aside one or two humble items I've seen him wear at the theatre, the rest of his clothes are those of a gentleman about town. Silk and velvet breeches, two coats, one of fine wool, the other of silk, a fine-embroidered waistcoat and all adorned with braid and buttons.

At my shoulder, Charlie whistles. 'Them's smart duds for a thesp, ain't they, mate?'

'Too right, my lad. Clearly there's more to mister Harry Henderson than we knew.' I lay more clothes on the bed. 'Hello, what have we here?'

Tucked beneath the coats in the bottom of the trunk is a packet of papers tied with ribbon.

'Love letters?' asks Charlie eagerly making a grab and holding them to his nose to sniff. 'Smells sweet. Come on, Will, read 'em out!'

'You're a smutty whelp,' I chide, knuckling his head and retrieving them from him. 'Even a dead man deserves some dignity.'

Charlie is unabashed. 'I thought we come 'ere to find out about 'im. Yer not goin' to discover nuffin if you play the pious ballocks, are you?'

He has a point. I undo the ribbon and scan the first letter.

'What's it say, then?' Charlie peers over my shoulder. 'It's a fair, neat hand - bet it's a woman!'

It is a woman's hand but the language is decorous and circumspect. Too cool for a love letter. Perhaps the relationship was clandestine and the writer feared discovery? Nor is there any way of telling if her correspondent, presumably Henderson, showed more passion in his letters to her. Possibly he did, for some of her replies urge restraint, reproach him, make excuses. How often they met, if at all, is not clear. What is clear is a request in the final letter to meet him 'in a place most secret, of your own choosing' - a letter dated two days ago.

Beside me, Charlie is almost jumping with excitement. 'Will, don't be a marplot - tell me - is there no choice bits?'

'None that would satisfy you, young 'un. 'Tis all chastity and restraint. As befits a gentleman and a lady.'

'But who is the lady?'

Who indeed? For the writer gives no name, signing herself only as an elegant initial - *A*.

'Here, bind them up again,' I tell him, handing him the letters and ribbon.

I turn my attention to the only other place in the room where anything of worth might be concealed - the drawer in the table.

It yields bills and tavern reckonings, items of little note until I reach the bottom and find two more letters. This time they are in a bold, flowing hand. And they are not in English. Which leaves me as illiterate as Charlie, able to identify the letters but unable to make sense of them.

'*Mijn ondankbare zoon,*' the first begins, '*Zoals zij in het Engels zeggen, u hebt uw bed gemaakt en u moet daarin liggen.*' It ends, '*Tot toen, ben ik niet meer uw vader.*'

The second is more directly addressed to '*Hendrick,*' and ends, '*U hebt twee maanden. Huw de vrouw of u zult niets van mijn geld erven.*'

Neither is signed.

Charlie is breathing over my shoulder again. 'Well?' he says expectantly.

'No, not well,' I reply. 'These are in a foreign language, Flemish or Dutch I think. I can make out odd words - *zoon* could be *son, vader* might be *father,* and *mijn geld* probably means *my money...*'

'You mean he's filched his old man's chink?' gasps Charlie, wide-eyed. 'I never had 'im down as a thief, no way!'

I pocket the letters and, going over to the window, rub away some of the grime to peer up at the sky. Patches of blue are beginning to show through the grey clouds.

'Look lively,' I tell Charlie, 'there's nothing more for us here. Help me put all this stuff back in the trunk and we'll have it back to Mr Garrick's.'

Assembly

Mr Garrick meets us in the hallway as we lug the chest into the house. In response to his questions, I tell him what we have found at Henderson's lodgings and show him the letters. He glances through them. When he comes to the two in a foreign language, he looks up at me.

'This would appear to be Dutch,' he says. 'Hendrick - isn't that what the mysterious lady at the theatre called him?'

He looks in the chest. Charlie stands hugging himself, shivering with the wet and the exertion of carrying the trunk all the way from Henderson's lodging. Mr Garrick looks up, notices his bedraggled state.

'Go, lad, tell Mrs Wiggins to give you a bowl of warm broth and sit you on the kitchen hearth to dry you out. You look like a drowned rat.'

Seeing there's naught else to hear and he won't be missing anything, Charlie obeys with alacrity, his stomach taking precedence over curiosity. My momentary pang of guilt for expecting too much of him turns to envy at the thought of the warm kitchen with its smells of cooking and of Susan's wanton smile.

'I regret no soup and warm kitchen for you, Will,' says Mr Garrick as soon as Charlie has disappeared.

Still displeased with me for losing his coat? No, Mr Garrick doesn't harbour grudges.

'We are to venture out again?'

He notes my lack of enthusiasm and gives me a sympathetic smile.

'I know I am asking much of you, Will. But believe me, I am grateful, and will show my gratitude in due course. In the meantime, there is clean linen airing by the fire. Once you are out of your damp clothes, we must to the theatre. I have called the company together for three-o'clock. We can keep Henderson's death a secret no longer, they must be informed of what has passed.'

Half an hour later, in the dim flicker of candle stubs from the last performance guttering in the sconces, we gather in the first few rows of the pit, subdued and anxious. In the mysterious way of rumours, word has obviously spread about Henderson's death.

The deserted theatre last night was eerie, today it is merely melancholy. With no audience to give it life, its glamour looks tawdry, the gold-leaf as thin and insubstantial as the dusty stage scenery. Sad ghosts seem to crowd the dark shadows of balcony and boxes, almost more real than the scatter of actors who look uneasy and out of place in the lonely stalls. Pale in the meagre candlelight, they appear somehow exposed, diminished. Gone are the strutting popinjays. In their place, mere mortals, uncharacteristically nervous and vulnerable.

Sitting on the front corner of the stage between the stage-box and the limelight trough, waiting for Mr Garrick to take the stage, I cannot help my eyes being drawn to the fatal stage-trap. With an effort, I wrench my gaze away and take the opportunity to observe my fellow players.

If Henderson was indeed murdered, his killer could well be here.

What should I look for? An unexpected expression? An unconscious gesture? A surreptitious glance? Any unguarded sign that speaks of guilt. Yet these are actors whose business is dissimulation. What chance of catching them unawares? My one trump card is that they don't yet know I'm observing them. I make the most of it.

Macklin sits apart from the others. Slumped motionless like a craggy outcrop on a blasted heath, he seems lost in thought, his scowl fixed, his gaze distant. Why did Henderson's death affect him so acutely? I know he has a fiery Irish temper, harbours grudges, is irascible and moody. But last night, in the presence of the body, he exhibited wide-eyed terror, and now his vacant stare suggests a deeply-troubled soul. Such reactions seem extreme even for him.

Of the fifteen others gathered in the first few rows, there is only one female - Kitty Blair. Her bright, roving eye and impudent tongue are attractive in a saucy, bar-maid sort of way. I, being only nineteen and a very junior member of the company, have so far been beneath her notice, though of late I've caught her glancing coquettishly in my direction. I'm not vain enough to think it's my looks. Rather, I suspect, it is because I'm in favour with Mr Garrick. Also, perhaps, the fact that she's already flirted with, discarded or been rebuffed by most other men in the company! Her dream, I think, would be to find some nobleman willing to indulge her and give her the luxurious life she craves. Until then she'll be happy to dally with whatever offers. At the moment, she's chatting merrily to Ned Phillimore, eyelashes a-flutter. Her hand rests lightly on his knee. He's accepting her advances with a knowing smile.

The other men, as in any theatrical troupe, range from those about my age to old stagers like John Garbutt and Septimus Drake. They sit together exchanging civilities, but in character they could hardly be more different. Garbutt is stout and coarse featured, his face and nose bearing witness to a love of strong liquor. Drink often renders him incapable. Any actor who shares the stage with him soon learns to be adept in improvising lines to cover his befuddlement. In contrast, Drake is lean, ascetic-looking, his face long, his look disapproving, ideal casting for stern fathers and aloof grandees.

A few seats along from them lounges John Aikin, supercilious and acid-tongued, whilst in the row in front Tom Parsons perches, wide-eyed and timid as a harvest mouse.

There's a clatter of footsteps. The subdued chatter ceases and all eyes turn to Mr Garrick as he climbs on to the stage. But just as he is about to begin there's a disturbance at the back of the auditorium It is Mrs Woffington. I noted her absence earlier but thought nothing of it. Late entrances are second nature to her.

'My apologies, Davey,' she chirrups as she hurries down the aisle. 'And to you all,' she adds as an afterthought. With a look of demure penitence, she arranges her skirts into a seat at the end of the second row and looks to Garrick with rapt attention.

I glance over my shoulder and see Garrick redden.

The rumour is that he and mistress Peg have an

'understanding'. She's a frequent visitor to his lodgings and often stays the night. And why not? He a newly successful actor, not yet twenty-five - she no older and with similar new-found acclaim, or rather notoriety, following her appearance in breeches as Sir Harry Wilder. They're ideally suited.

Garrick's momentary discomfiture does not pass unnoticed. A sour sneer clouds John Aikin's habitually disapproving face, whilst Ned Phillimore and mistress Kitty make no effort to hide their amusement.

If Mr Garrick notices, he gives no sign. In a cool, clear voice he informs the assembly of Harry Henderson's death and our discovery of his body.

'The cause of his death is still uncertain but we can only assume it to be the result of a terrible accident.' His eyes flick quickly between Macklin and myself. Macklin shows no reaction. I look down, not wishing either to concur or disagree with his fiction. He goes on, 'I have had his body removed to the cellar at my lodgings and my main endeavour over the next few hours will be to ensure that all due respect is accorded it.'

Part of that respect, I know, will be to have old Mother Hutchence come in to verify death and wash and prepare the body. As a Searcher, she will report the death to the parish without inquiring too deeply into the cause or circumstances. But that won't be the end of the matter. Since the Registration Act, five years ago, death has become a national, not just a local, concern. The registrar of births, deaths and marriages must be informed. He won't ask for a certificate from a licensed physician, but he'll want details of date and cause of death, the deceased's name, age, sex, rank and profession. And herein lies the problem. Normally the deceased's family provide these facts. But who were Henderson's family? All we have are letters, some from an unnamed lover and two, unsigned, which might be from his father.

Mr Garrick pauses and I sense the anguish in his voice as he resumes. 'For the past weeks Harry Henderson has been one of us, we have been his only family. If no blood relatives can be found, we owe it to him to see him buried with respect and dignity. To which end, I have sent to Mr Giffard to know if the theatre will fund the funeral expenses. I am confident of a favourable reply, but should that not be the case, I am sure that all of you will want to contribute to avoid the indignity of a pauper's grave.'

There are one or two murmurs of assent, yet at the same time I notice Aikin's look go sourer. It confirms what I often observed when Henderson was alive. There was little love between them. Hardly a day passed without some disparaging remark, some imagined slight or cool rebuff. Could such festering resentment lead to murder? If it happens that we all must contribute towards Henderson's funeral Aikin's offering will, I have no doubt, be small and grudging.

'It is my regret that I knew Harry Henderson only as an actor, not as a person,' continues Mr Garrick. 'In life, it seems this unfortunate young man chose to cut himself off from his family. His reason is not our concern. But in death, I believe they have a right to know, and I would like us all to strive towards that end. Perchance some of you who worked closely with him, who ate and drank and laughed with him, may have learned something of his life outside our little circle.'

His gaze roves over the upturned faces. 'I would ask you to share with me anything, trivial as it may seem, that could help us lay his soul to rest. Unfortunately, I shall have much business over the coming days and may not always be about, but Will Archer here shall be my delegate. Anything you would tell to me may safely be told to him.'

As he turns towards me, I feel all eyes light upon me. But rather than cast down my own in modesty, I control my embarrassment and glance swiftly along the rows. I see puzzlement in many eyes, acceptance in most and, in a few, suspicion and resentment that Garrick should choose me.

But most of all, my attention is caught by young Tom Parsons. He's a year or two older than me, yet with his slight build and delicate features he seems hardly more than a boy. Recently an affecting Prince in the Tower to Garrick's Richard III, he excels at simpletons and pathetic orphans. Earlier I paid little heed to his habitual nervousness, but as Garrick's speech progressed he appeared disconsolate, even grief-stricken, and now his eyes, already wet with tears, show unmistakable signs of fear.

Aikin

As the gathering breaks up, John Aikin saunters over to me. 'Well, Master Archer, you're the golden boy and no mistake.' His tone is bantering, insult lurking just below the pleasantry. 'The little lap-dog, running around whilst his master occupies himself with the bitch.'

He nods to where Mr Garrick is leaving with Mistress Woffington on his arm seeking to make me complicit in his lewdness. I disabuse him.

'If you have aught worthwhile to say, Mr Aikin, then I am willing to hear it,' I reply curtly. 'Otherwise I shall wish you good day.'

Aikin attempts a condoling smile which, with his habitually hooded eyes, appears merely cynical. 'Alas, poor Harry,' he says. 'Such a promising actor - so cruelly cut off. And by an accident, at that! Strange accident, don't you think, Master Archer? Alone, in the middle of the night, in the bowels of the theatre - what can he have been about?'

'That is something we may never know, Mr Aikin. And speculation on the matter is not profitable.'

Aikin nods slowly, appearing pensive. But his eyes don't leave my face.

'You were there,' he says.

'Ay - and Mr Garrick and Mr Macklin.' Accusation hovers in the air between us. 'Why? Would you make something of it?'

'Easy, Master Archer.' He retreats a step, holding up

his hands in submission. 'Be not so peevish, I mean no offence. Come, let us be friends - we have both lost a colleague when all is said and done.'

'One who deserves our respect - and heartfelt sympathy,' I remind him.

'Indeed, indeed,' he replies with every appearance of concern. 'He will be sorely missed.'

'He will.' I recall the relationship that had existed between him and Henderson. 'By most.'

He looks pained. 'A hit, Master Archer, a palpable hit! Of course, you are right. Our late companion and myself were not on the best of terms, 'tis true. No wonder Mr Garrick reposes such trust in you, you show perception beyond your years.'

'Do not patronise me, Mr Aikin,' I say impatiently. 'I can see you itch to tell me something, so why not put an end to prevarication and come out with it?'

'My, my, the puppy bites!' he says, amused. 'Very well, I shall be direct. As you are so much in Mr Garrick's favour, I would have you put in a word for me.'

I am puzzled. 'A word, Mr Aikin?'

He becomes unctuous, a transformation I recognise in his sort when they wish to ingratiate themselves. He makes to put his arm around my shoulders. I shift to avoid it. His is a confidentiality I have no wish to share.

'My dear Will, we both know that Mr Garrick undervalues my abilities as an actor. I am capable of so much more.'

I feel a chill of repugnance at his fawning. I know what he is about.

After the success of *Richard III*, Mr Giffard has

rewarded Garrick by allowing him to choose and mount a production of his own. Thus, whilst at night he performs as Jack Smalter in an adaptation of Mr Richardson's novel *Pamela*, by day he rehearses *The Changeling*, Middleton and Rowley's bloody tragedy of madness and obsession.

Garrick himself is to play Alsemero, the wronged lover. Macklin is De Flores, the deformed villain who blackmails Beatrice (Mrs Woffington) into loving him. In the comic sub-plot, set in a madhouse, Henderson was to play the principal role of Antonio, a nobleman who disguises himself to win the love of the doddering keeper's young wife, Isabella. Aikin and I take minor roles as Tomazo and Pedro.

'You would have me recommend you for the role left vacant by Harry's death?' I say coldly. 'Is your regard for his demise so scant that you view it only as an opportunity to step into a dead man's shoes?'

'I can excel as Antonio,' pleads Aikin pettishly. 'All you need do, Will, is suggest it.'

I cannot hide my contempt. 'You truly believe that Mr Garrick, great actor that he is, would heed advice from me? Your wits have gone astray, I think, Mr Aikin.'

He draws himself up. His heavy eyes go cold. 'You will not do this for me, Will Archer?'

'I cannot see how it would do you any good.'

'So be it.' He turns to go, but then pauses and fixes me with a shrewd look. 'No-one believes Henderson's death was an accident, you know, Archer. Mr Garrick may have persuaded you of that, but others aren't so easily fooled. You were there - I'll wager Macklin's face was a sight to behold!'

He sees me start.

'Yes, I thought so.' He laughs mirthlessly. 'You don't know his history, do you? Before your time.'

'If it is pertinent to Henderson's death in any way, it is your duty to tell me.'

'Duty, is it?' he sneers. 'Macklin's history is well enough known for you to discover it yourself. But he's not the only one. Ask yourself, little lap-dog, who else might have wanted to see Henderson dead? And why?'

I catch hold of his arm as he makes to leave. 'What mean you, Mr Aikin? What information are you withholding?'

For a brief moment, his hand rests on mine before he brushes it aside disdainfully. With an equivocal smile, he taps the side of his nose and whispers, 'Cherchez la femme, Will Archer, cherchez la femme!'

With a swirl of coat-tails, he sweeps up the aisle, singing to himself, ' - pity Missy Molly, not so pretty, nor so jolly...' Reaching the exit, he laughs mockingly, causing heads to turn. Then he is gone.

Phillimore

Hardly has Aikin departed than Ned Phillimore comes up to me. 'What have you done to ruffle his feathers?' he asks with a laugh. 'Not that it takes much. As Harry found out to his cost, poor devil.'

'Yes, I noticed often that he and Henderson were not on the best of terms.'

Phillimore raises a sceptical eyebrow. 'As good terms as curs fighting over a bitch on heat!' He sighs, 'Still, that's all done with now, though 'twould not surprise me if Aikin drove poor Harry to it.'

'You think he took his own life? But Mr Garrick believes it to be an accident.'

'Aye, that's what he says,' replies Ned with a broad wink, 'but you and I, Will, we know different, don't we?'

'Do we?'

He laughs aloud, an open, honest laugh quite unlike Aikin's mockery. 'Nay, Will, you've too much stubble on your chin to play the innocent! You were there, you saw. I charge you, look me in the eye and tell me you truly believe Harry Henderson died by accident.'

I cast my eyes down.

'No, I thought not,' he says. He sits and motions me to sit beside him. 'All of us in the company can understand Mr Garrick's desire to hush the matter up. It may be good for the company's reputation, but it's no good for poor Harry, is it? He might have been a secretive cove, but he didn't always keep himself to himself. He could be good company on occasions. He deserves better than to be interred hugger-mugger like old Polonius.'

'You knew him well?'

'Not well, but better than most.'

I believe him. Ned is open-hearted, honest and sociable. It was he who first welcomed me into the company when I was a green newcomer, put me at my ease and included me in conversations when others hardly recognised my existence. I've never known Ned to be downcast. A smile is never far from his lips, nor a ready jest to calm discord or puncture bombast. He rarely takes offence and seems not suffer from the insecurity or self-importance that beset so many of our profession.

'You hold to the notion that he took his own life? 'Tis a fearful charge, Ned. Have you cause to suppose such a thing?'

He leans closer, lest he be overheard, although there are few enough of the company still here.

Macklin, grim-faced, stumped out before Garrick and Mrs Woffington.

The petulant departure of John Aikin brought the flirtation between Ned and Kitty to an end. He is now with me. She, giggling, is leaving in the company of half a dozen others.

The two old men, Mr Garbutt and Mr Drake, are making their way sedately to the exit.

Only young Tom Parsons remains seated. He is the very picture of misery. Hunched at the end of a row, disconsolately chewing at his fingers ends, he looks forlorn and friendless.

'Two weeks since,' Ned says in hushed tones, 'I saw

a change in Harry Henderson. He took on a troubled look when he thought he was unobserved, a creasing of the brow and clouding of feature. In conversation, he was distant, preoccupied. Something was clearly weighing on his mind.'

'He did not divulge the cause?'

'It was not his way. You know how close he kept himself.'

'But you essayed to bring him from his gloom?'

'As much as was in my power, with jest and good companionship. But 'twas fruitless, he rallied but a while before becoming distant once again.'

'Was Aikin the cause, do you think? 'Twas common knowledge he coveted the roles that Mr Garrick gave to Harry.'

'His jealousy contributed, no doubt. But I sensed there was a deeper malaise, rooted more in his personal life.'

I recall the letters we found in his lodging. A secret amour? An unforgiving father?

'A woman?' I ask.

He laughs conspiratorially. 'Ah, Will - you betray your youth in thinking a woman the only cause of melancholy! *There are more things in heaven and earth*, as the doomed Prince says.'

I am piqued, but I do not contradict him. In my nineteen years I've experienced more than Ned or anyone could guess at, but if others choose to see me as naive, I won't disabuse them. They might, as a consequence, be more forthcoming, less on their guard. I feign an embarrassed grin and Ned recants somewhat.

'There may have been a woman, but...' He hesitates and regards me narrowly for a moment. '...yes, you're probably right.'

The hesitation and assessing look alert me. What is he not telling me? Something that might incriminate him - or another? Ned is a loyal friend.

'He did not mention a name?' I ask.

Ned shakes his head. 'I told you, he kept things close.'

I decide to reveal a little of what I know.

'There were some letters at his lodging, from a lady who signed herself just with the initial *A*.'

Ned seems genuinely surprised. 'Love letters?' he asks with a puzzled frown.

'They appeared to be, from what little I saw - I did not read them,' I lie. ''Twould have been an intrusion.'

'Well, well, who'd have thought it!' he murmurs. 'And those letters - they were all you found? Nothing else that might reveal aught about him - his history or where he was from?'

'Where he was from?'

He regards me uncertainly for a moment, then says hesitantly, 'I thought he had not the face of an Englishman.'

I laugh in astonishment. 'How can you tell? There is no paradigm that I can see - no colour of hair or eye, no cast of feature or complexion that denotes an Englishman!'

'True, we are a mongrel race,' he acknowledges, 'but others, less inclined to embrace all-comers, preserve a certain cast of feature - the pale Norseman, swarthy Spaniard or dark Frenchman. But Henderson was none of these. He had, to my mind, the doughy features of a Netherlander.'

I gape in amazement. 'There were indeed letters in

his lodging addressed to Hendrick, and written in a language which might be Dutch.'

Phillimore claps his hands together. 'Bull's eye! A Froglander! 'Twas the nose alerted me.' He thinks for a moment. 'Mayhap that explains his Sunday jaunts.'

I look at him inquisitively.

'Out towards the new developments up west. I went with him on occasion. At first I thought that when we reached Oxford Street we'd make for Rathbone Place and the fields and windmill beyond. 'Tis a pleasant enough walk through the country, where you can forget for a while the stink of the town. But no, we must go on, past Berners Street and through the market still smelling of fish and meat from the week. And all the time he had not the relaxed air of a Sunday stroller. 'Twas almost like he was on a mission, drawn against his will past Swallow Street and towards Cavendish Square. Have you seen it, Will? The houses there are mighty fine. Grander than you or I will ever see inside.'

I recall the fine clothes in Henderson's trunk. Such finery would not be out of place in Cavendish Square.

'That's where he took you, Cavendish Square?'

'Only because I was with him and would see it. But that was not his goal, for we'd return to Oxford Street and cross it. Hanover Square - that was his destination. It always struck me that he seemed in a mighty ill-temper when we got there, but circumnavigating piles of stone and builders' wares - there's several houses still a-building there - his spirits seemed to lift and by the time we came away, 'twas as if he felt he'd achieved some secret goal and he'd become quite content as we turned for home.'

He looks at me with satisfaction. 'If he was Dutch as you've just told me, it helps explain his shifting moods. Of those already in residence in Hanover Square, there be a number of merchants and businessmen, mainly Hollanders. Perchance he had relations there.'

'Mr Garrick will be pleased if we can find a family for him.'

Ned grins. ''Twill save him the cost of a funeral at all events.'

'Was there any particular house he seemed to study?'

'None that I took note of, though two thirds of the way round as we made our circuit he'd sometimes pause and the black mood seemed to lift somewhat and the spring returned to his step. 'Twas like an obstacle overcome, somewhere along the south side of the square.'

I rise. 'You've been of great assistance, Ned. Poor Harry may be reunited with his family yet!'

Coffee House

As Ned departs I resolve to have a word with young Tom Parsons. The abject misery, even fear, I observed in him during Mr Garrick's speech intrigues me. But I am disappointed, for by the time Ned goes, the seat where Tom has been disconsolately sitting, is empty. He has slipped away without me noticing. I debate the wisdom of seeking him out at his lodging, but decide against it. I do not want him to feel persecuted. I can see him tomorrow at rehearsal - if he does not seek me out before then.

In the meantime I must report to Mr Garrick and I know that, once he has bidden farewell to Mrs Woffington, he will go to the Bedford Coffee House on the south side of Covent Garden under the great Piazza. It is his custom to retire there late in the afternoon to read the papers and catch up with the latest theatrical gossip.

The up-and-coming place for writers, artists and actors to meet, the Bedford has the buzz of novelty which Button's, around the corner in Russell Street, has long since lost. There, the glory days when Mr Addison and Mr Steele set the pattern for the London scene are long past and the place is frequented only by self-important bores and jaded wits. For anyone wishing to rub shoulders with the newest and most exciting writers and artists, the Bedford is the place to be, and to be seen.

The doorman palms the coin I give him and lets me

in. He knows me now, but I must confess I was ill at ease upon my first visit. What should a young lad from Yorkshire be doing amongst the finest intellects of the time? How should I behave - and should I speak unless spoken to? But I need not have worried, for a coffee-house is the most democratic of institutions. Here all are equal, and none need give his seat up for another.

This doesn't stop the occasional literary or artistic grandee from holding court surrounded by adoring admirers. I regularly see Mr Hogarth, regaling his audience by dashing off a scurrilous cartoon upon a napkin, though on other days he repels all comers with a glare and a grunt, for his humour is as much composed of light and shade as are his drawings.

Today, it is Mr Fielding, whose novel, *The History of the Adventures of Joseph Andrews and of his Friend Mr Abraham Adams*, just published, is the talk of the town. Some of the more censorious condemn it for its salaciousness. They are shocked that a magistrate should not only so offend ideas of morality and taste, but also seek to parody the high-minded virtue of Mr Richardson's novel *Pamela*. I've dipped into both - and read parts of each aloud to Susan in the kitchen of an evening - and have found both works instructive, especially when the two of us act out certain scenes...

The air is heavy with pipe-smoke and the aroma of coffee. A short distance from Mr Fielding's admiring coterie, Mr Garrick is seated near the window, engrossed in today's newspaper. My heart sinks as I see Macklin with him, in conversation with an ill-kempt looking man of twenty-or-so whom I have not seen before. He isn't a member of the company for sure.

'Archer, my boy,' booms Macklin when he sees me. Faces turn towards the noise and he acknowledges their curiosity with a smile of condescension. They nod approbation and return to their reading and their talk. Macklin is in effusive mood. Gone is last night's terror, his recent dourness. 'Let me introduce you to Samuel Foote. As you are my friend Garrick's protégé, Mr Foote hopes to become mine.'

Garrick remains resolutely behind his paper. I bear the full brunt of Macklin's forced jocularity. I don't like it, it is demeaning. Still less do I like the simpering look that his pasty-faced companion gives me as he offers me his hand. A hand like a parcel of bobbins scattered in my palm.

'Pleased to meet you,' I say without conviction.

'Mr Foote has cast aside the dusty shackles of the law and intends to tread the boards,' Macklin explains, 'and I am endeavouring to prevail upon our friend Garrick here to enlist him in our company, now that we are a man down.'

With slow deliberation, Garrick folds his newspaper. 'I doubt that Mr Giffard will countenance it,' he says. 'You know affairs at Goodmans Fields are in a parlous state, notwithstanding recent successes. Rich and Freeman like not our success and would have us closed, and Walpole is on their side. He would revoke our patent tomorrow.'

Prime Minister Walpole, as anyone knows, is no friend of the theatre. Shortly before my arrival in the capital, Walpole was enraged by a production at Goodmans Fields of *The Beggar's Opera* which slandered him by linking him with the notorious thief-taker Jonathan Wild. The theatre was closed and Walpole brought in the Licensing Act of 1737. Theatres without parliamentary approval, or patent, are closed down and all plays have to be submitted for the Lord Chamberlain's approval. Mr Giffard was only able to reopen Goodman's Fields last year, on condition he present only musical entertainments. A restriction he has circumvented by presenting plays by popular demand - which is why he has fallen foul of Walpole once again. But for the moment he is thwarted, for Garrick and Macklin presently ride high and the crowds flock to Goodmans Fields to see them. Much to the envy of Mr Rich at Covent Garden and Mr Freeman at Drury Lane who would not only like to see Walpole close us down, but would also poach our actors.

Macklin snorts derisively. 'And for that Giffard would skimp our production of necessary actors?'

'Giffard might abandon it altogether,' retorts Garrick sharply. 'Our *Changeling* may not go ahead at all.'

'Giffard is a nincompoop! He forgets that it is we who have made his fortune. Or I, rather! For was it not I who taught you all you know, Garrick? Without me, he would not now be enjoying the profits of your *Richard III*!' exclaims Macklin, pushing back his chair with a clatter. 'Come, Foote, let us go. 'Tis time for me to guide your first steps in the noble art of acting.'

He sweeps out. The servile Foote trails after him. I catch his sneering grin, quickly hidden.

As soon as they have gone, Garrick exclaims in irritation. 'I despair sometimes, Will! So blinkered - as if Art can exist regardless of sound economy!'

'Is it true Mr Macklin taught you all you know?' I

ask mischievously.

Garrick smiles wryly. 'I do not deny the man's genius. His Shylock was a revelation and I learned much from it. But to say he taught me... 'tis to overstate the case somewhat. My Richard was my own - the product of many hours observing human nature. 'Tis not other actors, Will, but those around you in the real world that you must study if you seek the truth.'

'But Mr Foote did not impress you?'

He sighs in exasperation. 'I know Mr Foote of old! A satirical rogue, only just come of age, whose only skill is the frittering away of fortunes - fortunes which only came his way through murder and matrimony!'

He sees the curiosity in my face. 'His father is a Member of Parliament, a former Mayor of Truro in the county of Cornwall, and his mother one of the Gooderes of Hereford. 'Twas one of her brothers murdered the other. Do you not remember? The papers were full of it at the beginning of the year. The younger brother, Captain Samuel, along with two other ruffians set upon Sir John and beat him to death on a barge, the *Ruby*, at Marfleet.'

'I do recall it now - 'twas a dispute over the inheritance, was't not?'

'That's right. Sir John fell out with the rest of the family and threatened to leave his fortune to distant relations - one being his nephew, young Samuel Foote who was here just now. The younger brother, Captain Samuel, seeing his inheritance likely to be thus removed, resorted to murder. With little success, however, for he was arrested directly after the murder last January and executed in April.'

'So Mr Foote got his fortune?'

'Ay, and by all accounts has already spent it, which is why he has just married some unfortunate girl for her not inconsiderable dowry. I have no doubt he will have put both it and her behind him in very short time. 'Tis not the stage, but the Compter that beckons Mr Foote.'

I do not envy anyone the Compter, the debtors' prison. I know only too well how debt blighted my own family and steered the course of my own life into the dark waters from which Mr Garrick rescued me.

'But enough of the egregious Mr Foote,' says Mr Garrick, brightening up. 'How go your enquiries?'

I tell him what Ned Phillimore has told me.

He purses his lips in thought. 'Hanover Square, you say? And how should we discover if Henderson's family do indeed reside there? I have no contacts in that quarter.'

'You may not, sir,' say I, 'but young Charlie Stubbs has contacts everywhere. The street-boys of the city, in my experience, have unrivalled knowledge of what goes on. At the very least we'll discover the names of each and every resident - and probably much more that we might prefer not to know!'

'You trust him with this undertaking?' says Garrick doubtfully. 'He'll not break confidence?'

'He'll break all sorts of confidence,' I laugh, 'but none that will harm either us or his fellows on the street. He's a loyal fellow.'

Mr Garrick is satisfied.

A burst of laughter comes from where Mr Fielding is still holding court. Mr Garrick leans closer. 'And as for your suspicions about the manner of death - have you discovered anything more?'

'I have found no-one who believes it was an

accident,' I reply sombrely. 'Phillimore inclines to suicide, and talked of Henderson being somewhat melancholic the last two weeks. He was dubious that a woman might be the cause, however. His grief at Henderson's death seems genuine to me. Which is more than may be said for Mr Aikin, who sees it merely as an opportunity for self-advancement, which he would have me beseech you for on his behalf...'

Garrick's face clouds. 'You did not agree, I hope?'

'I told him no words of mine could sway your judgement. You are your own man and would do what you would do.'

'Well said, Will. And how did Mr Aikin take it?'

'He was not pleased.'

'I can well imagine,' says Garrick grimly. 'Does he, like Mr Phillimore, think Henderson took his own life? Or does he incline to your view?'

Recalling Aikin's sneering reference to Mr Macklin, I tread carefully. 'Tis only a few hours since Mr Garrick warned me off inquiry in that quarter.

'Mr Aikin insinuated there might have been foul play. That there may be some in the company who might wish to see him dead.'

With an effort I try to recall Aikin's parting jibe. My succeeding conversation with Ned has almost pushed it from my head but I remember it was in a foreign language, and I try to reproduce what it sounded like for Mr Garrick. '*Shershay la fam* he said, I think those were the words.'

'*Cherchez la femme,*' repeats Garrick. ''Tis French, Will - *Look for the woman*. We have but two women in the company - Mrs Woffington and Mrs Blair - he cannot accuse them, surely?'

He is silent a moment, shaking his head in perplexity.

But whilst Garrick may be at a loss, my mind has sparked into life. There is another woman – the one outside the theatre. Mayhap the same as also wrote the letters. But how could Aikin know of her?

'He mentioned no other names, I suppose?' says Garrick.

'Only one, sir.' There's no avoiding it now. I screw up my courage. 'Mr Macklin.'

Garrick's reaction this time is more exasperated than angry. 'Again! Why will not people let it rest? What's done is done.'

Having cleared this first hurdle, I persevere. 'Is there aught about Mr Macklin I should know, sir?'

Garrick sighs. 'It is no secret, Will. I thought the ghost was laid to rest, but it will rise, it seems, to plague us. Six years ago, before you came to London, Mr Macklin killed a man.'

He sees my shock, and goes on swiftly. 'It was a foolish matter - a quarrel over a wig of all things! Macklin came into the dressing room to find a younger actor, Hallam, wearing his wig. An argument ensued and Macklin thrust at him with a cane that pierced his eye. The young man died the following day and Macklin straightway gave himself up. He was arraigned for wilful murder. The court, fortunately, saw sense and he was convicted of accidental manslaughter, for which the punishment was branding on the hand, which in compassion they performed with a cold iron. And there the matter should have ended, were it not for the spitefulness of men like Aikin.'

'This goes some way to explaining why Mr Macklin

acted as he did on seeing Henderson's body,' I say.

'He thought he would be blamed again,' says Garrick sadly. 'I had much ado to convince him otherwise. But I would stake my life upon his innocence, Will. Charles Macklin may be hot-headed, but he is not malicious.'

'Besides,' I say, 'he was with you all evening, thus exonerating him from any possibility of blame. The testimony of the vagrant, Joe, suggests that the killer was in the theatre that night. The light that lured Joe in belonged neither to you nor to the watchman. If it was not Henderson's, it must have been the murderer's.'

Mr Garrick regards me dubiously. 'Can we truly give credence to what he said? A boy who, at the first opportunity, made off with a valuable coat. He is a thief - why should he not be a liar, too? Besides, he said he saw poor Henderson alive - yet we both know he was dead, for he also said he saw him hanging. How do you reconcile that contradiction?'

I shake my head. 'I confess, I do not know. We need to find him again. Tell him we mean him no harm. Get him to relate more calmly the events of that night.'

A waiter appears beside me. 'Sorry to trouble you, Mr Garrick, sir, but have you done with the newspaper? There's another gentleman would like it.'

'Of course, James,' says Garrick, handing it to him, 'and welcome to it - the news is all of the Austrian war, or the Whigs trying to bring down Walpole. And if not war and politics, 'tis crime.'

James nods towards where the group about Mr Fielding is dispersing. 'I've heard Mr Fielding is urging the powers-that-be to consider some better method of policing the city. 'Tis well-known that thief-takers are often greater criminals that those they send to the gallows.'

'I doubt our Honourable Members will countenance it, James. They'll maintain 'tis against the liberty of the individual when what they really mean is that it threatens their authority. Parliament and a Police Force would make uneasy bedfellows.'

'All the same, 'tis a shame. It's only the rich what gets justice, it seems.'

James the waiter's radical sentiments, however, are cut short by a man staggering into the room, white faced. 'Come - someone - help...' he babbles. His wild eyes appeal desperately to all who listen.

Garrick starts up, as do I, but we are stopped in our tracks by an authoritative voice that rings out behind us, 'I am Henry Fielding, I am a magistrate, fellow. What is the matter?'

'He's dead, Mr Fielding, sir...' blurts the man.

Fielding strides across to him, his full bottomed wig flying. 'Show me!' he commands.

The crowd of Fielding's admirers follow him eagerly out into the street, myself and Garrick among them.

Turning from the Piazza into a narrow lane and the gloomy entry into a yet narrower alley, we jostle to see what lies in the shadows.

Fielding kneels beside a shapeless heap of rags hard by the wall. The alley stinks of urine and offal. One or two of delicate sensibility hold handkerchieves to their noses, exclaiming at the offence. Yet they still press forward to take in the scene more avidly.

The man who burst into the coffee-house is now stooping over, beside Fielding. 'I thought he was asleep, guv'nor, till I tried kicking him out of the way...'

'Silence, fellow. Help me move him.'

Together, they roll the body over. Beside us, two or three ladies gasp and hurry away, reluctant to witness further horror. A portly gentleman in front of us turns aside. 'Nothing of any consequence,' I hear him drawl dismissively, 'a street urchin merely.' He saunters away with his companion.

Garrick and I now have an unimpeded view. We see Fielding open the coat and dab the chest of the corpse with a linen handkerchief. It flowers red.

Fielding rises stiffly. 'Stabbed through the heart,' he pronounces, for the benefit of the remaining onlookers 'A thin blade, I'd say, the hole in the coat being hardly noticeable.' He reaches into his waistcoat pocket, extracts a florin and turns to the man who discovered the crime. 'Stay here, fellow. I shall send to have the body collected.'

As the magistrate stoops and spreads the bloodied handkerchief over the upturned face, I turn to Garrick. Our eyes meet, and I see that he, too, has recognised his stolen coat and the unmistakable features of Joe, the street boy.

Tom Parsons

Drawing me aside before rehearsal, Mr Garrick tells me he's promoting me from the minor role of Pedro to that of Antonio, the part that Harry Henderson was to have played. Tom Parsons will take over my original role.

I express misgiving that Aikin may see this as a mortal slight.

'Take it as he may,' says Garrick, 'that is my decision.'

Once all the company are assembled, he announces the changes. I cannot help but notice Aikin's sharp intake of breath and his frustrated glance in my direction. But his resentment does not concern me overmuch at the moment as, not appearing until the second act, he will not be needed at this morning's rehearsal. Nevertheless, as Tom and I retire to the back of the theatre to con our lines - (we're not on until scene two) - Aikin makes a point of reproaching me before he leaves.

'I see, Archer, you prefer to advance yourself rather than help one who accounted you a friend,' he says in his usual disdainful manner.

His supercilious tone, as offensive as ever, seems nevertheless to conceal something, some feeling unspoken and unreadable. Unsettled, I inject as much coolness as I can into my reply. 'A *friend,* Mr Aikin? A strange word from your lips, who in the past have scarcely deigned to acknowledge my existence. And, for your information, I did not request the role; Mr Garrick gave it to me. My advancement, as you perceive it, is unsolicited.'

His lip curls with indifference 'Well, I give you joy of your good fortune. Enjoy it while you can, Archer. It may be short-lived.'

'How so, short-lived? Do you threaten me, Mr Aikin?'

'Not me, but Fortune is a fickle whore.' He glances contemptuously at Tom. 'Ask your little milksop companion there. Lucky at cards, unlucky in love, 'tis said. Though some have not much luck at either, eh, Parsons?' Beside me I sense Tom wince and I turn to see his face crumple.

Aikin laughs mockingly. 'I wish you well of him, Archer. But beware, he is a mopy mouse who craves attention. I hope you don't regret it - you deserve better!'

Once he has gone I lead Tom, who is trembling, to a seat near the back and sit him down. For all that he's my senior by at least five years, his pale complexion and slight build give him an air of vulnerability. At the moment I feel myself the elder.

'Take no heed of Aikin, Tom. He does not merit it.'

Fine words for me to say, considering the way Aikin's insinuations have wormed their way into my own head – that hint of a threat and suggestion of words unspoken...

Tom quivers with suppressed passion.'He is a devil, Will! 'Twas he who killed poor Harry.'

The accusation, uttered with such quiet vehemence, shocks me and sets my thoughts a-racing. Could Tom have the information I've been searching for? I rein in my excitement, waiting for his passion to subside.

'You do not mean that, Tom?' I strive to keep my voice level, gently chiding.

He seizes my hand and faces me defiantly. ''Tis true. He hounded him with sneers and taunts and insinuations till Harry could bear it no longer.' He pauses for breath, then sobs, 'It was all my fault!'

'Easy, Tom, calm yourself,' I say gently. ''Tis plain Harry's death affected you greatly, but how can you be to blame?'

Even in the dim candlelight at the back of the theatre, I can see the glitter of tears in his eyes. I glance towards the front of the auditorium where they have reached the first encounter between Beatrice and the villain, DeFlores whose thwarted desire for the woman he can never have will lead him to murder and their mutual destruction. Across the rows of empty seats booms Macklin's resonant voice:

Will't never mend, this scorn,
One side nor other? Must I be enjoin'd
To follow still whilst she flies from me? Well,
Fates do your worst, I'll please myself with sight
Of her, at all opportunities,
If but to spite her anger. I know she had
Rather see me dead than living.

Even in rehearsal, Macklin acts as if an audience is present. No wonder, for he was brought up in a tradition where leading actors conned their roles in private and did not rehearse with the minor characters. His famous interpretation of Shylock was as much a revelation to his fellow actors on the first night as it was to the audience. But Garrick, like Giffard, insists on methodical rehearsal, steering a production in the direction he wants rather than leaving it to individual actors to do as they like. I can see Macklin resents it, but he acquiesces out of friendship.

Engrossed in such high tragedy, no one heeds our smaller drama being acted out here in the shadows at the back of the auditorium. Tom and I are not required for some while yet. Time enough, I hope, to discover if his wild accusation against Aikin has any substance.

I lay a hand upon his shoulder. He starts, an unreadable emotion flickering in his eyes. But then, as if assured of my sympathy, he calms.

'Can I trust you, Will?' he whispers.

'Only you can decide that, Tom,' I reply. 'But be assured that I have Harry's interests at heart. I believe it best the truth about his death be known.'

Seconds pass as his eyes waver over my face. But I have the impression he is not looking at me, rather at some inner conflict. At last the turmoil within him seems to resolve.

'Aikin spoke true,' he mutters. His voice is so low I have to lean closer to hear him. 'I am cursed with ill-luck.'

I remain silent, unwilling to interrupt this confessional mood. In a moment, he raises his eyes and continues.

'I was not always as you see me now,' he says almost defiantly. 'When my father died, he left me tolerably well-off. I was young - about your years, Will, but without your level head - and I fell prey to gambling. I had no confidence with women, drink made me nauseous, but then one day I chanced upon a crowd in the street gathered round a trickster with three cups. Under one, he placed a coin then shuffled them about, inviting any who could to say where the coin was and, if they guessed aright, to keep it. I found I had a facility for guessing aright - and thus began my ruin. I began buying lottery tickets. The less I won, the more I bought, certain that my luck must soon change. Finding myself one day in the lottery office in Whitehall with no money about my person, a gentleman offered to pay for me...'

He stops suddenly and looks at me with alarm, as if he has said too much. But I am already there - such generosity on the part of strangers usually comes, in my experience, with provisos. Tom, however, has no intention of enlightening me as to the nature of what bargain, if any, was struck.

Looking away, he continues, 'He introduced me to gambling hells - the one atop of Golden Square, another hard by the turnstile in Holbourn - and it was there I first encountered Aikin.'

'He is a gambler?'

'No, he was simply there in company of another. Mr Samuel Foote.'

'I have met him.' I recall the plump young man that Macklin deemed his protégé. I recall, too, what Mr Garrick told me of his profligacy. 'He did not impress me favourably.'

'Aikin and he are two of a kind - sneering, satirical rogues, the pair of them,' says Tom bitterly. 'Yet when we first met, Aikin was charm itself, advanced me cash when I was on a losing streak and when he learned of my love for the stage, offered to introduce me to Mr Giffard. Which he did...' His voice trails away and he sinks his head upon his hands. 'If only I had known the price he would exact!'

'I take it Aikin wanted more than gratitude by way of repayment?'

'He wanted things I could not give,' murmurs Tom, avoiding my eye.

I guess at what he is unwilling to tell me and understand his reticence. Have I myself not been in a similar case?

'So now he scorns you, and you are afraid of him?'

'I am not afraid of him. I detest him!' His knuckles whiten with tension in his clenched fists

'And Harry?' I enquire gently. 'Did he know of this?'

At once, he relaxes. 'Harry saved me,' he murmurs fervently. 'He stood up to Aikin and protected me from him.'

'With the result that he, too, became a subject for Aikin's malice?'

'Yes,' replies Tom crestfallen. 'I couldn't bear to see him suffer so - and all because of me...'

It is at this moment that we are called for our scene. 'Come, Tom, brace up. We are on.'

By the time we reach the stage, Tom has composed himself and our roles reverse. He becomes the staunch friend, Pedro, and I the dissembling idiot, Antonio.

While Ned Phillimore, as the tormenting buffoon, Lollio, quizzes me, his new charge in the madhouse, I fumble my lines, earning a frown from Mr Garrick.

But my thoughts are not on Antonio's dissimulation. They are upon Tom Parsons. I feel he has more to tell about his late friend - information which may have more direct bearing upon his murder.

Hanover Square

Charlie does not disappoint. He returns just after noon, his grin both triumphant and impudent.

'Harry Henderson, my arse!' he tells me. 'You were right, mate. Them letters *was* Dutch. Hendricksen's the name.'

Then, in the evident belief he's said enough for the time being, he helps himself to a hunk of my midday bread and cheese and flings himself into a chair, where he sits cross-legged, wolfing the victuals for all the world like a voracious goblin.

'Well?' I ask when I can control my curiosity no longer.

He wipes crumbs from his lips and raises his eyebrows. 'What's the information worth?' he asks cheekily.

'That depends on how useful it is,' I reply. 'A clip round the ear if you're lucky!'

'What!' he whines, with an aggrieved grin. 'Prime information, this! Straight from Sniffy the jumper.'

'Sniffy? A jumper - who climbs in windows to rob decent folk? Nice friends you have!'

'Don't get arsey - gen'lemen of the street, they are - jumpers, faggers, dippers, knuckle-boys. 'S an honour to call them my friends. When you're on your uppers, you still have to put bread in yer mouth. Speaking of which, are you goin' to eat that or not?'

I toss him the last crust. 'Are you telling me your friend Sniffy robbed Mr Hendricksen's house?'

'Not hexactly,' he mumbles, mouth full. 'Give it the once-over, but decided that crib wasn't for cracking. Tight as a green jill's cunny! But Natty knuckled the old man's wipe a while back.'

'Natty stole a handkerchief - from Mr Hendricksen? How can you be sure it was him?'

'Initials embroidered in the corner. Followed him right from his front door to the 'Change and done it while he was a-jawing with another swell. Liberated it from his pocket sweet as you like. Any beer left in that bottle? All this spying's made me mighty thirsty.'

I hand it to him. 'So you know which house Mr Hendricksen lives at, and that he has business at the Exchange?'

'More than that,' says Charlie, wiping his lips with the back of his hand. 'Mynheer Jan Hendricksen of 43 Hanover Square is a highly respected banker, very rich by all accounts. He has no wife - she died a while back - but two sons who are a sore disappointment to him.'

'All this from a stolen handkerchief?' I say sceptically.

'Nah!' he scoffs. 'Sniffy told me that Cocker - he's nigh-on eighteen and a bit of a lady's man - has been living up to his name, and playing a bit of the blanket hornpipe, dipping his sugar-stick in the biddy from under-stairs at number 43. Glad to have someone to talk to, she is, for being pretty low down, none of the other servants speak to her, save to order her about.'

'You've done well, Charlie. I'll put in a word with Mr Garrick. There may be a crown in this for you.'

'Only a crown!' he retorts scornfully. 'A sovereign at least!'

'You overvalue yourself,' I laugh, ruffling his hair.

'Are you up for taking me there this afternoon?'

He agrees readily and within the hour, we are ready to set off for Hanover Square.

I'm wearing my very best stockings and shirt and my hair, newly combed, is tied back neatly with a black ribbon. With polished buckles on my shoes and the plain blue waistcoat and fine wool coat that Mr Garrick lends me, I look quite the swell. Not a full-blown gent, perhaps, but a very respectable servant worth at least £8 a year.

Before we set out, I hold Charlie's head under the pump, scrubbing his face, ignoring his outraged protests. No boy of his age should know, let alone use such language! I drub him soundly, then attempt to call his hair to order with a dab of goose-fat begged from Susan. By the time we set out, he's tolerably presentable, though mighty sulky.

The day, fortunately is fine. A cold autumn sun and a biting wind have iced some of the puddles in the street and powdered dung-heaps with frost. But at least it is not raining or foggy, and as we weave our way amongst the crowds of Oxford Street and draw near Hanover Square, Charlie's sulkiness evaporates. His constant stream of excited chatter shows he's feeling as nervous as I.

Parts of Hanover Square, as Ned Phillimore said, are still under construction. A number of artisans' carts stand about in the open space in the centre, the horses placidly chewing the spiky grass. The sound of sawing and hammering comes from various quarters. Workmen move among piles of bricks carrying planks of wood or trundling barrows, and shouts echo from the scaffolding at the far side of the square But on the south side, which is our destination, all work has long since been completed and all the houses are inhabited.

Number forty-three, like the houses on either side is a three storey building, with large windows on either side of an imposing front door. An elegant lantern, supported by a wrought-iron bracket above the portico matches others on the finials of the railings that front the house and flank the steps to the front door. Residents of Hanover Square, unlike the publicans of Goodmans Fields, clearly take seriously their civic responsibility to light their area of pavement. And, like many of the wealthier developments, Hanover Square actually has a pavement, separate from the roadway, on which pedestrians might walk without fear of being run down. Charlie's mouth is agape with the luxury of it all.

It's not only the plaster dust in the air that makes my throat dry as I raise my hand to the brass knocker. Although Mr Garrick agreed to my coming here, the enormity of the task ahead suddenly hits me with full force. I have only the word of Charlie and his disreputable cronies that this is Hendricksen's house, and no guarantee that the family living here have any connection with Harry Henderson. Even if these both prove true, how am I to broach the subject of a prodigal son - a son, moreover who is now dead, and died in suspicious circumstances?

Beside me, Charlie nudges my leg and says, 'Go on, then - stop standing there like a great booby!'

I take a deep breath, swallow, and knock.

A footman answers the door. His coat and breeches are bottle-green plush, with gold braid round lapel and cuffs, his stockings and cravat spotless white. With his polished buckled shoes and tightly curled white wig he's an impressive sight. He clearly doesn't think the same of Charlie and me. He looks us up and down disdainfully.

But I'm an actor, too. If he can do haughty, I can do bold. 'I have business with Mijnheer Hendricksen,' I tell him.

'May I enquire the nature of the business?' Although his tone remains civil, I see the contempt in his eyes. We're not the class of callers his master usually receives at the front door. But at the same time, I sense he hasn't the courage to refuse us out of hand. I seize on his uncertainty.

'It is personal - for the ears of your master only,' I brazen it out. 'I doubt he will take kindly to any delay in receiving my news.'

I've hit home. 'Who shall I say is calling - sir?' The hesitation is fractional, just enough for the deference to ring false.

'You may tell him a friend of Mr David Garrick, the renowned actor, would speak with him on a highly confidential matter,' I announce with as much dignity as I can muster. 'My name is Archer, and I would esteem it a courtesy not to be kept waiting on the step any longer.'

He admits us with scant grace into the hallway and bids us wait.

'Right smirking princox he is!' mutters Charlie at my elbow. 'Needs taking down a peg or two.'

'Peace,' I reprimand him, 'show some respect.'

'Didn't show us none, did he, the starched screw-jaw?'

Minutes pass. Long enough for the twitching in my

guts to remind me once again of our temerity in being here at all. The footman returns.

'Mijnheer Hendricksen has agreed see you.' His tone is sour, leaving no doubt that his master's condescension is in spite of his best efforts at dissuasion. 'But your boy must wait below stairs. Children are not allowed in the best rooms.'

At the far end of the hall, from a doorway that presumably leads to the servants' quarters appears a timid-looking girl in a plain smock. She stands with head bowed. 'Go with Lizzie, boy,' orders the footman.

Charlie obeys with suitable meekness but his face is thunderous.

'He'll be sent for when you leave, Master Archer.' The lackey pauses, to let this further slight sink in - my youth and social standing don't merit the address of Mister. I let it pass. It's a petty enough victory. One which, once I concede, he does not hesitate to build on as I follow him up the stairs to the reception rooms on the first floor. 'My master is a person of considerable standing, Master Archer, both here and in his home country. You must show appropriate respect. You will not speak unless spoken to and you must address him as Mijnheer at all times. It is the Dutch equivalent of Milord. Do you understand?'

'I bow to your instruction,' I say, matching my words with a slight inclination of the head.

Unable to tell if I'm mocking him or not, he coughs dryly. 'This way, Master Archer.'

The room into which he shows me is large and airy, with late winter sunlight streaming in through large windows. It is elegantly furnished, the walls a dark green, relieved with lighter plaster mouldings, which I believe is the latest fashion. Gold-framed mirrors opposite the windows, a crystal chandelier and gold sconces are eloquent of wealth, all a-shimmer with reflections from the great fire in the hearth.

Mijnheer Jan Hendricksen sits in an armchair beside the ornate marble fireplace. Plainly dressed in a brown velvet coat and breeches, he looks oddly out of place amongst this ostentation, like a yet to be completed afterthought in one of Mr Hogarth's paintings. He is shapeless, stocky, with a solid, square face on which the features seem only pencilled-in, atop which sits a dun-coloured slab of wig.

He does not get up. Nor does he invite me to sit. This is to be an interview where I must be made aware of my place. An audience reluctantly given and to be concluded quickly.

'You say you have personal business with me Master Archer?' His voice is low, heavily accented. His eyes are fixed on my face. They show curiosity but no warmth.

'My news may not be welcome, sir - Mijnheer.'

A sudden rustle of material behind me tells me we are not alone. I turn, startled, as a young woman, tall and dark-haired, rises from where she's been sitting at a small table in the corner near the window, hidden from me by the door. She walks slowly across the room to stand beside him.

As she rests a hand on the back of his chair, he raises his arm and covers her hand with his. A casual gesture of intimacy.

'My apologies, milady,' I stutter, 'I had thought your - er, husband...'

'This lady is not my wife, Master Archer,' he says

icily. A smile plays on her lips as she casts down her eyes.

'Your daughter...?'

Whoever the lady is, she is arresting. Not beautiful, but with an assurance that attracts. She wears a gown of cream cotton, embroidered with bright flowers, which, for all its simplicity, outshines her surroundings and contrasts all the more sharply with the square, dun-coloured man beside her. I can hardly keep my eyes off her. My insides feel empty and I am lost for words.

'Who the lady is does not concern you, Master Archer,' he snaps. 'Proceed to your reasons for coming here.'

I reach into my pocket for the letters I found in Henderson's lodgings, the two written in a foreign language. Taking a couple of steps forward, I hand them to him. 'Would you be so good as to peruse these letters, Mijnheer?'

Without relinquishing his hold of the lady's hand, he scans the papers. If they affect him in any way, he does not show it. He raises his eyes to mine once more and his voice hardens. 'How came you by these, Master Archer? These are confidential letters written by me to my son.'

'They were among his belongings in his rooms, sir.'

'In his rooms? - what business had you in his rooms, Master Archer?'

'For some months, your son, whom I knew as Harry Henderson, has been one of my fellow-actors in Mr Garrick's company.'

He waves aside my explanation brusquely. 'This is of no interest, Master Archer. I know nothing of it, nor do I wish to know. Tell me how you came by these letters and why you bring them to me now.'

'I am sorry to inform you, Mijnheer Hendricksen, your son has been - has had an accident.' It is lame, but even in face of Hendricksen's hostility, I cannot come out directly with the bold fact of his son's death.

My reply exasperates him. But it has a very different effect on the lady. She notes my hesitation and perhaps guesses its cause, for her face shows momentary alarm. She bends forward and whispers in his ear. Forewarning him, I hope, to contemplate worse news.

But the question, when it comes, is not what I expect.

'And did you find aught else of note in his belongings?' he asks.

No concern for his son, just an enquiry over bits and bobs! Is the man completely without feeling?

'Some papers, sir - and clothes...' I stammer.

I look to the lady for help and see merely anxiety. I am disconcerted, but then the cause of her alarm suddenly becomes clear. It is not the possibility of Henderson's death that is distressing her, but fear for herself. She asked him to question me about other possessions because she is concerned what may be among them - letters which the obdurate banker does not know about, but she does... She must be Harry Henderson's enigmatic lover!

I cannot deny the notion excites me. I envy Harry Henderson's good fortune in capturing the heart of such a woman. With an effort I gather my thoughts. It is not my place to betray her. My business is with the man - a man whom I am beginning to detest.

'Would you not have news of your son, sir?' I say somewhat testily.

'He had an accident, you say?' he says disinterestedly. 'Is he badly hurt?'

'Very badly, sir. I regret to tell you, Mijnheer - your son, Hendrick, is dead.'

What do I expect? Some exclamation of grief, or even anger? But all he does is become very still, his expression hardly changes. Yet in his eyes I see that my words have had an effect - a momentary flicker of pain, rapidly snuffed.

For several moments the silence hangs heavy, broken only by the crackling of the flames in the hearth. Then, tonelessly. 'How did he die?'

I choose my words carefully. 'He was found hanging, sir.'

He looks at me keenly. 'No accident, then? You are telling me he died by his own hand?' For the first time, I think he might have feelings after all. His brow creases in pain.

'The circumstances are not clear, sir.'

Hendricksen looks up at the woman and she places her hand on his shoulder. As their eyes meet, some silent message passes between them.

'Mijnheer is not well.'

It is the first time she has spoken. A clear voice, controlled and authoritative. A voice which shocks and chills me. 'Please leave us, Master Archer. We will send for Hendrick's things in due course.'

I bow and leave the room.

I am hardly aware of the imperious footman showing me out, hardly aware of waiting on the pavement for Charlie to emerge from some dark recess under the front steps, hardly aware of his importunate curiosity. My heart is beating hard. Not from the tension of the encounter, nor from the callousness of the father's response, but from the fact that the voice I have just heard was that of the hooded lady outside the theatre on the night of Henderson's death.

Understairs Gossip

Leaving the house in Hanover Square, I have great ado to gather my thoughts. It is clear that the self-possessed young woman - for she is young, not much above five and twenty - not only wrote those love letters, but also knew of Henderson - or Hendricksen's - death and, for reasons I can't comprehend, didn't pass that knowledge on to old Hendricksen. In him the news, for all his control, elicited the shock of the unexpected. But she remained cool to the point of disinterest - strange behaviour for a lover.

Also I can't begin to fathom what she's doing in Hendricksen's house. What is her relationship with this stony-faced banker who is easily twice her age?

The two seem intimate. Is she the old man's mistress? The thought of his old flesh on hers repulses me but it makes perfect sense of the clandestine nature of her correspondence with his son and her failure to communicate the news of his death. She won't want the old man to know of her relationship with his son.

Or perhaps she is not the old man's mistress but merely a poor relation, or a governess, no fit match for a son and heir? If the old man suspects the relationship it is unlikely to meet with his approval. This could explain the secret letters, but it makes her presence in the house more puzzling. What sort of man harbours under his own roof the presence of an unsuitable wife for an out-of-favour son?

Such questions revolve in my head as I leave the

house, and it is some time before Charlie's insistent badgering penetrates my consciousness.

As we weave through the Oxford Street throng, he has further excited revelations for me. He tells how the Cook below stairs took one look at his skinny frame and decided he needed feeding forthwith. And as he ate she gossiped. So did Lizzie, the maidservant who guided him to that underworld and who, it turns out, is the lusty Cocker's grateful conquest. The topic of their gossip was, of course, 'them upstairs'.

'Once they started, I had all on to stop 'em,' Charlie tells me. 'Funny what they'll tell a young 'un like me that they wouldn't dream of telling a grownup. Finks, because I'm a nipper, I don't understand the doings of my elders and betters. They didn't 'alf blub when I told them you was upstairs telling old Hendricksen that Master Hendrick was dead...'

'You didn't tell them the manner of his death, I hope?'

'Nah - what d'you take me for? I may be young, but I'm not green. Give 'em a sprat and get a mackerel back, that's me. I told them like Mr Garrick said, that he'd had an accident, but I didn't know no more. And then they started - how since he left, the life had gone out of the place. He'd always been the cheery one, always ready to have a laugh and share a joke. Got on with the servants, treated the boots and the under-butler like brothers, didn't take advantage of the maids like what some young masters would've. Then he'd had a blazing row with his father.'

'What about?'

'Didn't want no part in the family banking business - the only parts he wanted were ones he could play on the stage. Well, the old man showed him the door - told him not to come back until he'd seen sense. Once he'd decided to lead a respectable life and marry the young lady...'

'What young lady?' I interrupt.

'The lady what's living there now, with the old man. Not with him in that way - she's still affianced to Master Hendrick. Her family's all dead, so she's been living in Hanover Square since the betrothal was all arranged. Has 'er own quarters, of course - nothing shady going on.'

So this explains her presence in the house: she's Hendrick's intended bride. But that only makes her behaviour yet more unfathomable. Why was she outside the theatre? Why warn me off? Why didn't she tell old Hendricksen about his son's death before my visit? Because she'd been forbidden to have contact with Hendrick while he persisted in his madcap scheme? But the language of those letters didn't suggest thwarted longing - it was cool - just like her behaviour today. Not at all that of a prospective bride who's just lost her husband-to-be...

But Charlie is still chattering, raising his voice above the noise of the busy thoroughfare.

''Twas a severe blow to the old man, they said, after the business of Master Nicklaas.'

'Master Nicklaas?' It seems that Charlie has learned far more than I during our visit to Hanover Square.

'Aye, Master Hendrick's older brother - only older by a year, mind you. That's what Lizzie declared had done for the mistress, having two babies in such quick time. Went mad, she did. Had to be put away, then died within the year, so the two boys never knew their mother.'

'And what happened to Master Nicklaas?'

Charlie draws closer and lowers his voice. In the frosty air, his breath steams. 'You may well ask.' He assumes an air of mystery. 'They didn't exactly clam up, but they went real cagey, like they'd let their tongues run away with them and regretted it. I got the impression he was a bit of a roaring boy, Master Nicklaas - drink, fights, doxies - not at all the sort of son a dry old Calvinist like Mijnheer Hendricksen could stomach. They wouldn't tell me what happened to him - got all shame-faced and fussed around giving me more victuals to change the subject. But I gathered he was still alive - though where is anybody's guess.'

Back in Holland, most likely, sent to look after the firm's business and keep him out of trouble. Yet the existence of an elder brother poses another riddle - why should a wife be sought for the younger brother if the older one remained unmarried?

By this time, we're nearing home, but Charlie is still rattling on.

'Since Master Hendrick left, the old man's been even more crusty, they say. But he brought it on himself as far as they're concerned. It's the lady they feel sorry for. Been quite ill with worry, she has these last few weeks - sick every morning. Kept to her bed till noon most days.'

Within an hour of our return to Mr Garrick's lodgings a carrier arrives to collect Harry's body, together with a message that one will come later that evening for his effects. They put him into a plain wooden box and load it onto the cart. The driver is wearing a black cloak and all is covered respectfully with a black pall. Due, if simple, ceremony to mark his return home.

How he would feel about it, I don't know. Considering the trouble he took to cut himself off from his family, mayhap he'd prefer an anonymous interment, a simple £15 affair with rented pall and cloaks, his fellow actors carrying a plain coffin. What he will, no doubt, receive will be black horses and sable plumes - an ostentatious funeral designed to gainsay any hint of family estrangement, and one to which none of us, his companions for the last months of his life, are likely to be invited. The obdurate banker may make amends with lavish ceremonials of death, but I doubt he will be prepared to countenance what made his son happy in life.

As I watch the cart trundle over the cobbles in the fading light, my thoughts turn to hapless Joe whose body may even now be being tipped into the poor pit along with other unfortunates too impoverished to merit a private resting place. Joe lived with nothing and dies with nothing. Mr Garrick's scarf and second-best coat will now be gracing some parish undertaker's shoulders, unexpected recompense for washing, shrouding and carrying the corpse. There will be no inquiry into why Joe was killed or by whom. As a poor child of the streets, such an end is only to be expected.

At my side, Mr Garrick says softly, 'Well, that's the last we'll see of Harry. Would we could lay his memory to rest as easily as his body. But suspicions, once roused, cannot be so easily allayed.'

As we turn to go in, he continues, 'I have been thinking, Will, of all you've told me and I am now of your opinion. However repugnant the idea of its being one of our number, if we do not find out the truth of Henderson's death, uncertainty will eat like a canker into our company. How shall we trust anyone again? How go about our everyday business without insidious doubts poisoning every relationship?' He faces me and, says with quiet vehemence, 'You must find who did this, Will. Whoever meant harm to Henderson may well intend harm to others.'

'I fear, sir, that he has already proved that - in the death of the vagrant, Joe.'

'You think the two deaths are connected?'

'I am sure that Joe was killed to stop him telling what he saw. It was by sheer good fortune that we got to him first.'

'For what little good it did us,' says Garrick with a heavy sigh. 'A half-mad boy who thought he saw a corpse alive.'

'It was dark. I am convinced he saw something - some person. Seeing the hanged man's face in the lantern light must have affected him greatly. It was probably then that he ran, and encountering another in the shadows of the stage, he thought it was the dead man come to life. For certain, the other person must have been on the stage, for how else could he have vanished so swiftly in the time it took Joe to run around the corner and fetch the Watchman?'

'And you believe this person to be the murderer?'

'I cannot think otherwise,' I reply gravely, 'and if it is so and if it becomes known that you and I saw Joe before he died, I believe that may put both of us in danger.'

'In that case,' says Garrick with a nervous laugh, 'we had best keep with others at all times - and only be alone with those we can completely trust. I shall have a truckle bed put in my room. You and I shall be each other's bodyguard!'

Agnes

Later that evening, just as Charlie and I are setting up the temporary bed for me outside Mr Garrick's door, my master shouts up the stairs.

Leaving Charlie to sort the bedding, I obey the summons. I knock gently on the parlour door and Mr Garrick calls me to come in.

He is not alone. Seated by the fire is a woman, veiled and dressed in black. Garrick starts to introduce her, but I need no introduction. The moment I enter, I catch that unmistakable perfume. The scent evoking the embroidered flowers I saw on her dress earlier today.

'This is Miss Agnes Mayer,' Garrick says. 'She has come to collect Harry's - sorry, Hendrick's - things. Miss Mayer, this is my - er...'

I see him struggle with how he should classify me - servant? protégé? In one word he must sum up all our shared history since I was brought to him when he was still in the family's wine business, an aspiring actor only, contenting himself with amateur dramatics in the converted upper room of Mr Edward Cave's house.

I am gratified by the way he resolves his dilemma. 'My young friend, Will Archer.'

With a swift but elegant gesture, she lifts the veil from her face. 'We have already met, Mr Garrick.' She favours him with a sad smile, eloquent of grief before turning to me. 'Master Archer.' She holds out her hand.

I take it briefly. Her skin - so soft! I bow to hide the

unwonted heat that suffuses my cheeks. 'Miss Mayer.'

When I raise my eyes, her smile has subtly changed. Do I detect the merest flicker of warning in her eyes? Warning - and entreaty. It is gone, as quickly as it appeared. She turns back to my master.

'Mijnheer Hendricksen sends his regrets. He would have come in person, but he is quite prostrate at the news of his son's unfortunate death.'

Mr Garrick nods sympathetically.

'As of course am I,' she continues in hushed tones, 'for he and I were to be married.' Her voice wavers and she chokes back a sob. Mr Garrick steps forward solicitously, but she waves his sympathy aside as she takes out a pretty lace handkerchief, with which she dabs her eyes. 'Forgive me this weakness,' she says. 'You may wonder at my coming here, tonight, while still afflicted by the grievous news. I, too, find it hard to comprehend my own actions, but though I grieve, as does his father, I felt that if I might just see something of Hendrick's - touch with my lips the clothes he wore...'

She raises anguished eyes to Garrick's face. 'Does this sick fancy, shock you, Mr Garrick, that I should crave this last contact with one who is lost to me forever?'

'Madam, I - er - not at all - I understand...'

I have rarely seen my master thus lost for words. Her entreaties are clearly affecting Mr Garrick. He clears his throat and turns to me. 'Will - go fetch the trunk, would you?'

She rises quickly and prevents me. 'Do not trouble yourself, Master Archer, to bring the things here. Pray take me where they are.'

Garrick makes to protest, but she cuts him short with most engaging demureness, resting her fingers upon his arm. 'I have troubled you too much already, Mr Garrick. I cannot say how much I appreciate your consideration. But I can trespass on your kindness no longer. I require only to view what few, precious possessions my dear Hendrick left, and perhaps have them taken to my coach. Master Archer here will serve my turn perfectly well.'

Garrick melts in her liquid gaze. I take a candlestick. I lead her to the dining room where we have put the trunk to await collection. I busy myself lighting the wall sconces, the better for her to examine its contents.

Having provided her with light, I apologise for the dying embers of the fire - the dining room is little used at this hour - and ask if she prefers to be left alone.

'That is most considerate of you, Master Archer. I will not be long.'

I leave her kneeling by trunk and, once out of the room, take the stairs two at a time up to my garret.

Here, spread upon my bed, are the love-letters I found in the dead man's lodgings. If Mr Garrick knew, he'd no doubt reprimand me severely for such a breach of confidence. But where murder is concerned, there's no place for secrets. Before I returned the two written in Dutch to Hanover Square, I took the precaution of making copies, and am already some way through copying the love letters. Only two or three remain. It takes but a few minutes to commit their contents to memory. I bundle the copies under my mattress. The originals I gather together, tie them about with the ribbon and place them inside my shirt. I make my way back downstairs.

I tap softly upon the door and enter. The trunk lies open, empty, upon the floor. The clothes from it are spread haphazardly about the table. Miss Mayer is searching through the pockets.

But I know that what she seeks is nestling at my breast!

She has not heard me come in. I cough. She turns at the sound.

I can not but admire the adroitness with which her mask slips back into place. She must know I have seen her frantic search, yet her smile is ingenuous, her words civil. Used only to the exaggerated humours of actresses and Susan's brazen desire, this self-assured subtlety of concealment is new to me. It is unsettling - and fascinating.

'Master Archer, you are soon returned.'

'I can retire again,' I say, taking a step back, 'if you are not yet done?'

'No, stay.' She waves a hand at the scattered garments. 'I confess myself mistaken, Master Archer. These things - they are not Hendrick. They do not speak to me of him. I find not the comfort that I sought.'

'I am sorry, Madam. Shall I return them to the box?'

'You may do with them as you like, Master Archer.'

She gives me a look of such deliberation it sets my skin a-prickle. I feel myself redden as her gaze travels from face to feet and slowly back again. The letters burn hot against my chest.

'You are of his height and build, Master Archer. You may have these garments. They are no use to me.'

'Madam, I...'

Suddenly she is very close, laying her finger upon my lips. 'Do not protest. They are my gift to you.' Her breath is warm on my cheek. Her perfume all but overpowers me. She slips past me and across to the parlour once more. In a daze, I follow. Through the open door, I see Mr Garrick rise as she enters.

She extends her hand graciously. 'I am done here, Mr Garrick. Alas, these meagre belongings bring me no comfort. I thank you for your kindness once again, and take my leave.'

Garrick takes her hand and bows politely. 'My condolences, Miss Mayer. Would you have Will carry the trunk to your coach?'

She shakes her head. 'Thank you, but no. I have made Will a gift of all that is therein.'

Garrick raises his eyebrows at me over her shoulder. 'That is most generous. You will not take it amiss if I say I think him truly worthy of such generosity? He is a remarkable young man. Your kindness gratifies me as much as him.'

She turns to me as I stand, uneasy in the doorway.

The expression on her face is a mixture of triumph and challenge. 'A remarkable young man, indeed, to merit such approbation. Hendrick was fortunate in having such a friend.' She pauses, finger to lips, thinking. She turns to Garrick again. 'Might I borrow him for a while longer, Mr Garrick? I would talk with him about Hendrick. Mayhap Master Archer's words can do what Hendrick's few possessions could not - help raise the spirit of my poor, dead love one last time?' She gives him a smile of compelling sweetness. 'I shall return your friend unharmed, Mr Garrick.'

How can he resist her charms? How can I?

Within two minutes, I am stepping into the landau that waits at the door. The same landau I had seen disappearing on the night of Henderson's murder. Any intimation of alarm, however, is entirely vanquished by the closeness of Agnes Mayer. What possible harm can she do me? She a fragile woman, I a strapping youth?

She speaks in Dutch to the driver, a burly, stone-faced man of fifty or thereabout, as he helps her into the carriage. 'I have ordered him to drive - anywhere but back to Hanover Square.'

'Won't he...?'

'Menninck does as he is told. He will not talk, for he is dumb. Even if he overhears what we say, he will not understand for he has no English. Mijnheer prefers it that way. He does not like his business known.'

Both hoods of the Landau are up as the year is late and the weather cold. She sits opposite me. Menninck shuts the door, confining us in an intimate space that smells of leather and polish. As the horses quicken into a brisk trot over the cobbles, I can not ignore her closeness - her heady perfume, the occasional brushing of our knees. Despite the November cold, my skin prickles with sweat and I rub my damp palms covertly along my breeches, giving silent thanks to the darkness within the carriage for hiding my growing discomfiture.

'You have not been honest with me, Master Archer.' Her voice is a soft purr of accusation from the shadows.

'How so, Madam?' I reply, as levelly as I am able.

'You forget, I have known Hendrick for a long time. He was a hoarder, Master Archer. He did not throw things away. Especially not letters.'

'Letters, Madam?'

She tuts in annoyance and sits back in her seat. Her foot comes tantalisingly close to mine.

'Oh, Will,' she sighs. Her use of my first name clips my heart. 'This verbal fencing is pointless. I know you have the letters that I sent him. I would like them back.'

I breathe slowly. 'If we are to trade honesty, Miss Mayer, you must first put my mind at ease. We have met before, have we not?'

She pauses, uncertain. 'This afternoon at Hanover Square, yes.'

'Before that,' I reply.

In the gloom of the carriage I am aware of her turning away. 'I don't know what you mean.'

'Come, Miss Mayer, I think you do. Your voice is one that is hard to forget - in an alley, at night, near the theatre where your fiancé had just died?'

I am ashamed at the pleasure her consternation provokes in me. My heart goes out to her. I tense as she leans forward and puts her hand on my knee.

'You have told no-one of this, Will?'

'Others know there was a woman outside the theatre. None but I know it was you.'

'No-one must know,' she says in deep distress.

The carriage is on a relatively smooth road. Suddenly she moves to sit beside me. I feel the heat rise to my cheeks, as one hand presses my thigh whilst the other grasps my arm. 'Can I trust you, Will, to tell no-one? It is a matter of the greatest importance.' Her face is very close to mine. I almost feel the soft brush of her lips, see the faint gleam of her eyes.

How easy to assent...

But the vision of Harry Henderson's hanging body flashes before my eyes and I steel myself.

I shift away. 'You knew he was dead when I came to Hanover Square, yet you gave no sign.'

'You are right, Will. But you must believe me when I say I had no choice but to dissemble.'

'Why?'

'To answer you, I must tell you something of my history. In doing so, you will see how I trust you, Will Archer. You have seen that Mijnheer Hendricksen is an obdurate man. And yet he allows me to stay in his house.'

'I own your presence there confused me.'

'My family is of Austrian descent. My father and Mijnheer Hendricksen did business for many years until my father fell ill of a fever and died, leaving my mother and me, their only child, to fend for ourselves. Much of my father's supposed wealth was in loans and bills of exchange, which on his death, the creditors reneged on, leaving my mother and me almost destitute. The strain was too much for my mother, who died shortly afterwards. It was then that Mijnheer Hendricksen took me in.'

'An uncommonly kind act, if he is as obdurate as you say.'

'Oh, do not believe it was through any feeling of philanthropy! In matching me with his younger son - making me one of the family, whilst at the same time recognising that my impoverished status did not make me a suitable match for the elder son - he saw a way of calling my father's debtors to account, thereby increasing his own fortune. I was collateral merely.'

'But then he and Hendrick fell out?'

'Hendrick was a dreamer, ill suited for a world of accounts and figures, debentures and debts. His father put him to work, but he fared so ill and earned so many reprimands that at last he broke. The quarrel is fixed in my memory. I was on the stairs when I heard raised voices from the withdrawing room. I was rooted to the spot, unable to move. And, as the dispute grew hotter, I knew there could be no resolution. So many hurtful things said, so much intransigence - oh, Will, the violence...!'

Distress at the recollection deprives her of words. I summon the temerity to reach for her hand and take it in mine. After a few moments she regains her composure, and continues, but she does not withdraw her hand from mine.

'Of course, with Hendrick gone, I thought that I must needs follow. With no son, there would no longer be necessity for a wife. I resigned myself to a return to my impecunious existence, forced to become a paid companion or a governess.'

'Yet he didn't cast you off?'

'No. It seems that under that cold carapace, he still harboured hopes that Hendrick might come back. He was the favourite son.'

'He did not favour his elder son? That is unusual, surely?' The question is disingenuous. Charlie has already hinted at the reason. But I am curious to know where that other son is now.

'Nicklaas. The elder by a year, but most unlike his brother. He fell into bad ways, gambling, drinking - until, in the end, he killed a man.' She sighs, her voice full of pity.

'What happened?'

'He was with several others, all young, all rich, all rakes about town and a quarrel arose over cheating at cards, or some such. There was a fight and blows were struck. One of them was pushed or punched - none could recollect the incident, they were all so drunk - and he fell, striking his head. Nicklaas was implicated and was like to go to prison – or worse. But Mijnheer intervened.'

'He sent him abroad?'

'Would that he had! But Mijnheer Hendricksen is a stern moralist. To have a son imprisoned would bring disgrace. To evade justice by sending him abroad would cause scandal. No - he chose a course that would not reflect upon him, the father, but would rather bring him sympathy. He had Nicklaas committed.'

'To a madhouse?' I exclaim in horror.

'Aye. To have his son cured of his profligacy, an affliction that, in his eyes, could only be the result of lunacy. And there was precedent - the boys' mother had been committed shortly after they were born. She died in the madhouse... '

'And Nicklaas - he is still there?'

'He is in Bethlem Hospital - Bedlam,' she says sadly. 'He was first committed to a private madhouse at Clerkenwell, but Hendrick, visiting one time found him so restrained and weak from lack of food and ill usage that, notwithstanding his estrangement from his father, wrote letter after letter begging he be removed. Mijnheer relented only a few days ago. But he himself would have no part in it. Hendrick was authorised to make all arrangements. It was the last thing he did before...' A catch in her breath. Then she resumes, 'I visit him, without Mijnheer's knowledge, of course.'

She grips my hand. 'You must not tell him, Will. If he were to find out, I would certainly be cut adrift.'

I assure her that, even were I in a position to tell Mijnheer Hendricksen anything, I would protect her confidence. Yet, affecting as her tale is, there are still matters that puzzle me. Before I return the packet of letters which still nestle in my breast, there are things I want resolved.

'Did you love Hendrick?'

'We were to be married, Will.'

'That does not answer my question,' I say, but I can't admit to reading the letters with their distant, formal tone.

I change tack. 'You haven't explained why you were at the theatre on the night of his death. Nor why, at Hanover Square this afternoon, you gave no indication that you knew of it. And though you expressed affecting grief earlier tonight at Mr Garrick's, I have seen little sign of it since. Strange behaviour for a lover.'

She looks away and sits back in the corner of the carriage, silent for a moment. Then, 'I would do well not to underestimate you, Will Archer. I see you know me only too well. You are right, I do not - did not - love him. Nor did Hendrick look upon the prospect with relish. It was one of the reasons why he quarrelled with his father. But Mijnheer Hendricksen is an obdurate man and he had decided the match was appropriate...'

'That explains your coolness, but it does not explain why you were outside the theatre the night he died.'

'We had agreed to meet, Hendrick and I, in some place of his choosing to - er - discuss matters. The subject of our discussion can be of no concern to you, Will. In any case, it did not take place, for when I ventured into the theatre, I found him dead. It was horrible, I could not comprehend how it had happened, I didn't know what to do. But then I heard a noise...'

'There was someone else there?'

'A beggar boy, he came creeping in.'

'Did he see you?'

'I don't know. I hid among the scenery at the side of the stage until he ran out screaming. Then I left. But I could not just go - I had to see what ensued, who came - so I waited out of sight. And as I waited, I began to gather my thoughts. I realised that I must deny all knowledge of being there, that I must not seem to know of Hendrick's death before we were officially told. Suspicion might fall on me else. Oh, Will, you cannot know what relief it is to unburden myself at last!'

'So why did you accost me?'

'As I waited in the cold to see what transpired, it came to me that, with his son dead, Mijnheer Hendricksen would have no further reason to harbour me. But if I could persuade the old man that Hendrick had committed suicide in a fit of remorse for his betrayal of family and father, he might regret his cruelty in casting off his son and come to see me as a substitute... A desperate hope, I admit, but it was all I had. And when I saw you and the boy come out of the theatre, I seized the opportunity. Was that so foolish of me, Will? Hendrick had mentioned you so often in his letters - you have no idea, Will, what high regard he held you in...'

The relief of confession opens the way for tears. I

draw closer, reach uncertainly towards her, wishing to put a comforting arm around her, yet afraid. I am all too conscious of the disparity in our rank.

Perhaps she sees my dilemma, for she knocks upon the roof of the carriage as a signal to Menninck to head back towards Mr Garrick's lodgings. She fumbles in her reticule for that same dainty lace handkerchief she'd used earlier with such effect on Mr Garrick, and dabs her eyes.

I withdraw the packet of letters from inside my shirt and hand them to her.

'My thanks, Will. I would not have these fall into Mijnheer's hands.' She holds them to her cheek. 'Still warm from your heart, Will. A heart which has shown me such consideration and kindness this night. I am for ever in your debt. I see now why Hendrick had such regard for you. My affections would have been more surely engaged, had he been more like you.'

'You do me too much honour, Miss Mayer.'

'Agnes,' she whispers reprovingly. 'I have confided more in you than in any other person. We know each other better, I hope, than for me to be still Miss Mayer.'

'Do you know - Agnes - of any reason why Hendrick should have taken his own life?'

She considers for a moment. 'Hendrick had secrets, Will, as do we all. Perhaps he had intended at our last meeting to reveal them to me - but then decided he could not. The fate of Nicklaas was always in his mind. As brothers, they were close, but not alike. Hendrick was not addicted to cards or drink or women - but some secret there undoubtedly was.'

'The brothers were close, you say? Might Nicklaas know?'

'You would trust the word of a madman?'

I laugh, embarrassed. 'It will amuse you to know that I am shortly to play a madman. Mr Garrick wishes me to take on Hendrick's role in *The Changeling*.'

Suddenly, unbidden, the image of John Aikin's reaction to Mr Garrick's decision, announced this morning, flashes into my mind - an expression eloquent of dislike hardening into loathing. And for a moment I wonder if my stepping into her dead fiancé's shoes might have similarly offended Agnes, for her next remark comes cool.

'And you would observe the reality for yourself?'

I hasten to make amends. 'I am not so crass to affront your regard for him thus. Besides I very much doubt if Nicklaas is truly mad. I don't believe that libertines are of necessity lunatic. And you, yourself, said his incarceration is more expedient than needful.'

'It was. But that place at Clerkenwell has worsened his condition. He is much changed. As I told you, Will, I visit him without Mijnheer's knowledge, and there are days when I do not recognise the Nicklaas I first knew.'

'Could you, nevertheless, arrange for me to see him?'

'I will send you word.'

The carriage comes to a halt. We must be near Mr Garrick's lodgings. I take her hand in farewell and shiver with delight as she lets me raise it and hold it momentarily to my lips.

A shiver of a different kind possesses me, however, as Menninck opens the door and I step out into a night that is not only dark, but also thick with fog.

The coachman takes me none too gently by the arm and points silently towards the street sign on the wall. We are on the Whitechapel High Road at the southern end of Somerset Street. A warren of tortuous lanes and alleys lie between me and Mr Garrick's lodgings. I know them to be hazardous enough in daylight and can understand Menninck's reluctance to negotiate them in a carriage on such a night. I nod my acceptance of the situation and turn my face towards home.

The fog has done little to quell the habitual night inhabitants, however - whores and drunks loom out of the mist and gather in the small pockets of misty light around inn doors. But in between these havens it is all but impossible even to see my feet, for the fog reduces visibility to little more than a yard in every direction.

Keeping close to the wall, I feel my way through streets which, though I have walked them a hundred times in daylight, are now a labyrinth of unfamiliar turns and obstacles. The fog muffles the night noises and alters the smells of the streets. The individual stinks of dung-heaps, cattle, fish and meat that usually act as indicators of location all blend into one, cloaked by the all-encompassing acrid smell of smoke that swirls in the fog and creeps into my lungs.

I lean against a wall coughing and that is when the blow falls.

I am struck hard on the back of the head.

The bricks blur in front of my eyes and I fall into blackness.

Distantly I am aware of my body thudding to the ground. Of air being punched from my lungs. Then blows - side, ribs, back...

I slide into deeper blackness.

In the silence I dream a figure stoops. Mutters, uneasy. Arms wrench. Scrape and heave, dragging. A foot pushes. My inert body rolls over. Stench of a dung heap...

Time passes.

Then birdlike chattering. Fingers which pull and probe. The skitter of feet. A catch of breath...

Again, blackness.

I am floating – jogging – arms and legs flopping loose and heavy...

Blackness.

Awakening

I come round to find Mr Garrick standing over me, his face lined with concern.

I try sitting up. Immediately a thousand smiths start hammering in my head, obliging me to sink back on to soft pillows. I realise I am in a bed and I ache all over.

'Where...?' I try to say, but only a croak emerges. My throat feels caked with dust.

'Will, you're back with us! What a relief, we thought we had lost you.'

He busies himself at a side table and after a few seconds, he touches a glass to my lips. Water has never tasted so good.

'You may drink with confidence, Will, it has been boiled.'

As the liquid hits my dry throat, a coughing fit sets my head a-pounding once more. Pain jabs my chest and back.

Mr Garrick supports me. 'There, there, my boy. Carefully! Sip it, gently'

After a while I lie back and try to take in my surroundings. The pillows are soft, but the bed is hard, and somewhere to my left, watery sunlight is streaming through a window. With an effort, I try to make sense of it. I must be in the parlour, on the settle. Under the blanket I am aware of wearing a shirt, but nothing more. I raise myself gingerly on one elbow, feeling the ache of bruises all over my body.

Mr Garrick is straightway by my side, supporting

me. 'Easy, now,' he smiles. 'Susan would not forgive me, after all her good work over the last two days.' He sees my puzzled look and explains 'She and Mrs Wiggins washed you when we brought you home - I'm afraid to say you stank, Will, and we had to burn your clothes. Since then she has been anointing your bruises with arnica morning and night.'

The thought of Susan at loose on my naked body without me knowing anything of it is vaguely troubling in my present state.

But Mr Garrick seems not to notice. 'You've been badly beaten, Will, and had a severe concussion - you might be dead now, if not for your thick skull, and Charlie.'

'Charlie?' I murmur.

'Mindful of our resolution, that we should be wary and not be alone with strangers, I had him follow when Miss Mayer took you off in her carriage.'

'But...'

'But you thought Miss Mayer would be no danger?' Mr Garrick tuts sorrowfully. 'Oh, you are young, Will, and too apt to let your heart rule your head! I could see how she charmed you. Those downcast eyes, the tremor in her voice... Such winning deployment of her handkerchief... Did you think I had not noticed? Miss Mayer is an accomplished actress, but she did not fool me. Which is why I set Charlie to look out for you.'

As if on cue, there's a timid knock and Charlie's head appears round the door. His black hair stands in greasy spikes.

'Come in, lad,' says Garrick. 'He's awake - but not making much sense, as yet.'

'Naught new there, then!' He bounds over with a

broad grin on his face. 'You're a rum 'un, and no mistake - we all thought you were a goner!'

'Which well you might have been,' adds Garrick seriously, 'if you'd been left where you fell, prey to the damp fog and night-time felons. Fortunately, you were attacked at no great distance from here, and Charlie is a swift runner.'

'Near enough didn't make it, though,' adds Charlie. 'That carriage what you got in set off lickety-split. I had all on to keep it in sight. But then he had to slow down at a crossroads and I hitched a ride on the back. Damned uncomfortable it was, too. Fair jounced my bones, and near deafened me with the clatter. Had all on to hear you and your lady-love.'

'She's not...' My head rings with the effort, and my protest gets no further.

'No, of course she ain't,' he replies scathingly. 'You didn't see me when the coach stopped - I nipped down smartish and out of sight - but I eyeballed your lovey-dovey slobbering... Kissing her hand - ugh!'

Mr Garrick smiles. 'You're lucky Charlie didn't desert you there and then.'

'Don't think it didn't cross my mind. I was near done in with all that shakin' about. I 'ad ter rest. 'Ow was I ter know you was still in danger arter you trotted off into the fog? If it 'adn't been for Natty doin' night-shift...'

'Natty?'

Charlie lowers his voice and leans close. 'You remember - 'im wot lifted old Hendricksen's wipe. Got a soft spot for you has Natty - Lord knows why.'

My head spins. I have lost track. 'I don't know anyone called Natty...'

'Well, 'e knows you. Tells me you offered to gi' 'im a ducking a while back...'

The pickpocket in the market-place!

'Any'ow, he sees you gettin' orf the coach – don't recognise yer, mind, but figures you're a toff - so 'e follers yer, thinkin' there might be some pickin's. But then this 'ere cove jumps yer, so Natty - not bein' wot yer might call the bravest - 'e lies low while the feller kicks yer about a bit and dumps yer on a dung-heap. Then, when 'e's confident the bloke's scarpered, Natty creeps up to see wot 'e can find in yer pockets and discovers 'oo you are - and that's when I come up...'

'He was going to rob me when I was insensible?'

Charlie scoffs at my indignation. 'Don't get arsey, mate. 'E 'as ter earn a livin', don't 'e? An' 'e did save yer life arter all. 'E were proper upset when 'e saw 'oo you were an' 'e stayed with yer while I ran for Mr Garrick.'

Mr Garrick laughs. 'Charlie's right, Will. Urchin he may be, but this boy, Natty, seemed truly distressed. I gave him half a crown, and it was as if I'd bestowed upon him the riches of the Orient, so great was his gratitude. Still he helped us carry you home.'

'I tell yer - Natty thinks you're the goods, Will - says you saved 'im from the law, give 'im good advice. "Well, that's a first!" I told 'im.'

I manage a weak smile. 'I can't thank you enough, Charlie...'

His face splits into a grin. 'Oh, you can - I'll think of a way, don't you fret!'

All this talk is exhausting. I lie back on the pillow. But there is still one thing I need to know. 'The person who attacked me...?'

'Put your mind at rest, 'tweren't the lady. 'Twas a cove in a cloak and hat.'

I close my eyes and sigh with relief. Agnes is not implicated!

Mr Garrick takes my sigh to mean they have overtired me. He draws the curtain to darken the room.

But Charlie is not so easily deflected. 'Could have been the coachman, though. He could have doubled back on her orders...'

Mr Garrick takes Charlie firmly by the shoulder. 'Come, lad, your friend needs rest. And such speculation is profitless.' He turns to me. 'Sleep, Will. We need you fully recovered.'

He propels Charlie out and closes the door softly behind him.

But the damage has been done. Charlie's words have sown the seed of doubt. After all her assurances of confidence and trust, has Agnes Mayer deceived me?

Sir Francis Courtney

I awake several hours later, feeling much restored. My headache has gone and my body, though still stiff and bruised, is responding more readily to my demands. I sit up as Mr Garrick enters.

'You have a visitor, Will.'

For one joyful moment, I hope it might be Agnes, but the look on Garrick's face warns me to expect no such happy encounter.

And he is right. For the person he ushers in is someone I hoped never to see again. Sir Francis Courtney.

He who brought me to Mr Garrick three years ago. The epitome of my degradation - and yet also my saviour.

That night is etched in my memory as the moment my redemption began - being taken I knew not where in Sir Francis's carriage, but fearing the worst. Arriving at Mr Garrick's door... Deference for Sir Francis's rank sufficiently overcoming Garrick's abhorrence of his person to invite in a licentious libertine and a shivering boy.

I remember the warm parlour, in which I now lay abed. Sir Francis's high, affected, fluting voice. 'He is simply destined for the stage! Such heart-rending simplicity and pathos, such poignant sincerity - I tell you, Garrick, I was hard put to't not to weep! You really must take him and train him up. That is,' he'd simpered, wagging a bejewelled finger at the actor, 'if you can abide another traveller along the path whereto your own aspirations lie.'

At that time, my master had yet to achieve his fame. He was but lately come to town to run the London branch of the family wine-business. But it was no secret that all his interest lay in a theatrical career and his theatrical enterprise at Mr Edward Cave's house had attracted the attention of many, including Courtney, which was why he had brought me to him.

What Mr Garrick saw in me that night, I do not know. In truth, I was a sorry enough wretch, pale and shivering. He cannot have seen the great actor that Courtney promised. Rather, I believe, he saw only a poor abused boy who, out of compassion, he felt he must rescue from Courtney and his like.

Undoubtedly it was out of charity that Mr Garrick took me as a fetcher and carrier in his wine business. But it was necessary economy that, apart from my board, kept my labour unpaid. Nonetheless, he had my undying gratitude. Whether, even now, he appreciates the full extent of my degradation at that time, I do not know but, since that night, he has never asked and I have never told.

Mr Garrick may have suspected Sir Francis to be a patron of Mother Ransom's molly house, but he knew better than to refer to the fact. Such knowledge is dangerous.

I, for one, before I was brought to London, had no such knowledge. As a callow country eleven-year-old, I was beginning to have vague glimmerings of what went on between grown men and women. At the same time, I was aware that one of my fellows had little interest in girls, and that another pleasured himself with animals on his father's farm. They were a subject for gossip, wagging fingers and bawdy jokes, but in general were regarded as harmless and left to themselves. Only when I was brought to the city, at the age of fourteen, and put with Mother Ransom was my innocence finally confounded.

Her establishment - which, as far as I know, still thrives - is frequented by sodomites with a wide variety of tastes. Some desire just other men, but others dress as women, and flirt and dance, and bounce upon each other's knees like hussies at a city rout or country merrymaking. A few go through mock marriage ceremonies and even pretend to give birth, producing from under their skirts, after much panting and shrieking, a wooden moppet which is then handed around and cooed over by all present.

When I first observed such a ritual I found it laughable until I saw the seriousness of those participating. Such men are rather to be pitied than scorned, shunned as they are by society at large, liable to hang if apprehended, but compelled in spite of all to seek satisfaction with others like themselves in such a place.

As a boy barely on the verge of manhood, I was one of Mother Ransom's most sought-after assets. With my still smooth face, I might easily pass as a woman, though with the attributes of a man, as yet only slightly furred, ready to be discovered beneath - a combination which excited many of her clients to fever pitch. For the most part, I saw it as harmless fun, parading and primping for their delectation - perhaps that was the start of my acting career! - and prettily protesting when they allowed their hands to wander. But as time passed, and I grew from pretty boy to tolerably handsome youth, Mother Ransom would have me go further to satisfy the gentlemen. Though little inclined, I knew that, to avoid a hand to mouth existence outside Mother Ransom's walls, I must become adept with those very organs within them. And so, for many months, I toyed and teased and winningly deflected the ardour of those who would use me more carnally.

Until Sir Francis Courtney came - a gentleman of such influence that Mother Ransom was unable to deny him. No matter that I pleaded and protested, the old harridan was adamant - either I obeyed her or she'd cast me out on the streets.

But when it came to it, I could not submit to the degradation. I fell on my knees before him and pleaded, most piteously, to be spared the humiliation - I was but a country boy, wrenched from my mother's love, alone in the world...

I hardly recall all I said, but it had its desired effect. He raised me to my feet. 'Remarkable,' he said in an awed whisper, 'truly remarkable!' He might even have had tears in his eyes. Proof that even such a degenerate libertine had a heart that could be touched.

Which is how I came Mr Garrick's door, three years ago.

And why Sir Francis Courtney's presence now is so unwelcome, reminding me of a part of my life that I thought had been buried for ever.

Standing in Mr Garrick's unpretentious parlour, Sir Francis seems out of place, a gaudy creature tricked out in silken frills and curled wig, a beauty spot and reddened lips unnatural in his white complexion.

'Will, my dear, how are you? Still so pale! Mr

Garrick has told me all. Such a fearful ordeal!'

'I thank you, sir. But already I am much recovered thanks to Mr Garrick's care and the good offices of his cook and her wholesome chicken broth.'

Sir Francis looks perplexed. I doubt chicken broth figures highly in his world. He waves his hand dismissively.

'By your leave, Garrick,' he says. 'I would speak with Master Will in private.'

Garrick glances at me, but I nod acceptance. Sir Francis poses no threat to me now I am a man.

As soon as the door closes, he arranges himself on the chair that Mr Garrick set beside my couch. Though I am his only audience, he carefully displays his white-stockinged leg, ornate shoe buckles and peacock-blue silk breeches to advantage. He completes the effect by resting his chin on folded hands atop a silver handled cane. His eyes are soulful.

'Ah, Will, what a loss you are to we men of sentiment! Where is that beautiful boy? Gone, alas, gone forever.' He sighs dramatically. 'Tis he should be on the stage! He cocks his head on one side. 'Yet you have grown into a tolerable handsome young man - firm chin, fine eyes - yes, yes, a pleasing mien. You might do well still with some of my acquaintance.'

'I am sorry to disappoint you, Milord,' say I with firm civility, 'but those days are behind me. It was never my choice to be where, or what, you found me. I was forced into that life and am now most heartily glad to be away from it.'

'Such a waste!' he says sadly. The curls of his wig tremble with regret. He extracts a comfit box from his waistcoat and pops a sweet dragee into his mouth.'You know I have attended every play in which you have performed? You have an air about you, a definite presence! You might go far were you to catch the eye of some discerning man of taste.'

'I am quite content in my present situation, I thank you.'

He leans closer. I smell the perfumed powder in his wig, his sugared breath. Then the affected manner falls away and I glimpse a worried man, looking suddenly old and afraid.

'I am the bearer of ominous tidings, Will. I have been ordered by Sir William Hervey to bring you to him.'

'Sir William Hervey? I do not know him.'

'He is a distant cousin of Sir John Hervey, the King's favourite, and one of Mr Walpole's most trusted men. Know him or not, Will, he is not someone to be disobeyed. He may have risen through their influence, but he is like to be powerful long after they are gone.'

The change in Sir Francis's demeanour alarms me. This is clearly not just a request from one of his companions wanting a catamite. Sir Francis is afraid.

His fear stirs unease in me, too. 'What business can he have with me?'

'That I do not know. I am merely his messenger and must do his bidding. I am to take you to his office in Westminster at three-o'clock tomorrow.' He looks around, then puts a hand upon my arm. 'You must tell no-one of this, not even Mr Garrick.' With genuine anguish, he strokes my cheek. 'Oh, my dear boy, what have you got yourself into?'

'Truly, I have no idea...' I am by now thoroughly unnerved.

Sir Francis rises and with visible effort resumes his effete manner. 'Well, then, adieu, dear boy.' He raps his cane upon the floorboards, for all the world like a directeur in a French play announcing a change of scene, and Mr Garrick enters as if on cue. 'I take my leave, Garrick. Our reunion has been altogether delightful. My carriage will call tomorrow at two.'

In reply to Mr Garrick's expression of concern as the peer sweeps out, I smile and give a slight shake of my head to tell him all is well. He seems reassured as I assume a nonchalance I am far from feeling.

Sir William Hervey

Sir Francis's coach arrives promptly at two-o'clock. Considering the character of its owner, it is a modest affair, with only four horses and no liveried footmen or gilded coronets on the corners. The door panels, however, are enamelled in bright colours, unlike the sombre landau belonging to Mijnheer Hendricksen.

Sir Francis himself is more soberly dressed than usual in dark red plush and black stockings. His waistcoat is one of the least flamboyant I've seen him in and the buckles on his shoes could be those of any modest gentleman. A plain black bob-wig replaces his usual extravagant curls. Such dressing down should reassure me that we'll avoid curious glances. Instead, it increases my anxiety about the forthcoming encounter.

He surveys me up and down, seems satisfied with my attire - the same blue suit I wore on my visit to Hanover Square - and I climb into the carriage beside him. The carriage sets off and we trot along in silence, Sir Francis uncharacteristically pensive and subdued. At the end of Leaden Hall Street, instead of continuing on into Cornhill and past the Royal Exchange, we turn left into Grace Church Street.

In answer to my interrogative look, Sir Francis tells me we are to go by river to Westminster as it is Sir William Hervey's express wish that we be circumspect. Arriving by coach in front of all eyes would be anything but.

He lays a hand upon my knee and I prepare to rebuff

any further advance. But this is not the habitual lecher. His eyes are heavy, his voice grave. 'Sir William is a Yorkshire-man, like yourself, Will. But do not be misled by his open manner. He would appear straightforward, but his mind is devious. He notes everything and forgets nothing. He would not be head of Mr Walpole's secret service else.'

From Grace Church Street into Fish Street and, as the overhanging tenements of London Bridge come into view, we veer right, down Thames Street with its noise and bustle of traffic bound for the wharves, and thence down Ebbgate Lane to Old Swan Stairs.

Having bid his coachman hail a wherry, we alight and wait at the top of the steps. Below us, the Thames is a-jostle with barges, some laden with coal from Newcastle, others with wood for the nearby timber yards. To our left the river, swollen by winter rain, churns and roars between the sterlings of London Bridge and even as I watch, a boat pitches through on the torrent. The boatman plies his oar deftly to avoid the stone arches as his craft bobs like a cork in the swirling water, while his hapless passengers cling on for dear life.

'An experience to be avoided at all costs,' shudders Sir Francis. As if to confirm his view, a green-faced passenger leans over the side of the boat and vomits copiously into the foaming waters.

The wherry draws up and I help Sir Francis in. Once securely settled as far from the sides as possible, he orders the boatman to take us to Westminster. His apprehension makes him generous, promising a crown for a swift and smooth passage. The boatman sets to with despatch, weaving in and out of lumbering barges, colliers and fruit-boats to attain the clearer water midstream.

Being thus on the river is a novel experience for me, and I gaze with awe at buildings I've never before seen from this elevation, amazed at the number of church spires on every side. As we draw away from London Bridge, the breeze wafts the overpowering fishy stink of Billingsgate from behind us, mingling it with the stench of the Skin Market on the north shore. How do the fine tradesmen in their guildhalls, the Fishmongers and Vintners with halls new built at the water's edge after the Great Fire, endure it? Are they as inured to the smell of the river as I am accustomed to the reek of the city? At least the river current carries away the effluent from tanners, dyers, fish and meat markets, unlike the festering heaps of domestic waste that clog every street and alley.

Towering high above the bustle of the river, serene amongst the warren of cramped streets at its foot, the noble dome of St Paul's shines in a cold winter sun. Where but in London can such majesty exist side by side with such squalor?

Past the great cathedral, the north bank changes. Wharves give way to open gardens around the Temple and the Inns of Court, whilst on the south shore, past the timber yards, I glimpse flapping sheets on the tenter grounds, the dyers taking advantage of a fine day to dry and stretch their fabric.

Rounding the bend past Somerset House, the bulk of Whitehall looms. The temporary calm afforded by curious observation begins to drain away. My stomach knots up again. Beyond Whitehall is Downing Street, where Mr Walpole, the King's first minister, lives. Mr

Walpole, who is no friend to actors or to Goodmans Fields.

And Sir William Hervey is Walpole's man.

Looking across at Sir Francis, I see that he, too, is nervous. Picking at the lace about his cuff, his face is set, impervious to the scatters of spray sent up by the oars. More used to travelling by water, he has found little diversion in the novelty of passing buildings. Unlike myself, he seems to have spent the past minutes brooding on the impending encounter. Now, as the shadow of Westminster Hall casts a chill on the water, my own apprehensions return in force.

The boatman pulls in to Parliament Stairs, wielding his oar to cleave through slushy ice which, with the onset of Winter, clogs still water even at noon. Though, from what I can see, there's not much still water here. Wherries are constantly pulling in and departing. Our small craft jostles others, tossing us from side to side, causing Sir Francis to call out, 'Have a care, fellow!' He pitches forward as our prow thumps against the jetty. Slinging a rope around a wooden post, the boatman steadies the boat for us to step out.

Sir Francis, dignity restored now there's firm ground beneath his feet, draws the promised reward from his waistcoat and hands it to the man. The boatman pockets it, knuckling his cap with calloused fingers, and glances pointedly about him at the mêlée of craft.

'D'ye want me to wait, milord?' His voice is husky, weathered by his river life.

'We do not know how long our business will detain us.'

The fellow, loth to lose a generous fare, persists. 'I'm yours till dusk, your lordship - for another crown?'

Sir Francis hands him a shilling. 'Wait for an hour. Affairs will, I trust, be concluded by then.'

The boatman knuckles his forehead again. Looking at the constant procession on the steps, I suspect he'll take another fare or two before we return. He turns aside with a satisfied smirk. I wish we could exchange places for the next hour!

But Sir Francis is signalling impatiently for me to follow. We make our way up the steps and into the building. No one heeds us, all being intent on their own business. And why should they, for we are unremarkable. There are numerous gentleman much more flamboyant than Sir Francis in their attire, MPs most likely, and numerous others like myself, bearing neither hat not wig, their clerks or servants.

Sir Francis leads me through a maze of dark panelled corridors. By the time he pauses outside one door and knocks, I have quite lost my bearings. If Sir William Hervey is indeed the head of Mr Walpole's secret service, he hides himself as tightly as any state secret.

A sharp, dry voice bids us come in. We enter a small ante-room, gloomy and airless, smelling of dust. Huge tomes teeter from shelves which cover every wall.

In the middle of the room, a slight, grey-wigged man looks up as we enter. He is sharp featured with hard, bead-like eyes. A look too penetrating to be welcoming.

Sir Francis bows. 'Sir Francis Courtney and Master Will Archer for...'

'Yes, yes, I know,' snaps the fellow with no like courtesy. 'Sir William is expecting you. Wait here and I will inform him of your arrival.' He disappears between the bookshelves and I hear the murmur of voices from an inner room.

'A sharp-tongued fellow,' I whisper nervously to Sir Francis.

'Nathaniel Grey,' he replies, with evident distaste. 'Clerk to Sir William, and a man with neither manners nor refinement. I would advise you not to trust him. His malice is as sharp as his tongue.'

Grey reappears. 'Sir William will see you now, Master Archer. You, Sir Francis, may depart, Sir William has no further need of you.' His tone is peremptory, disrespectful. 'Wait below for Master Archer if you must, but Sir William would speak with the young man alone.'

I cast an alarmed glance at Sir Francis and he starts to protest on my behalf.

The hard eyes glitter, cut him short.

'Alone, Sir Francis.' The thin lips split in a condescending smile. 'Do not fret, Sir Francis, no harm will come to him. He will be returned in good order. Now, be good enough to do as you are requested. Sir William grows impatient.'

Giving me one final helpless look, Sir Francis departs.

Grey's black-button eyes turn on me, flick briefly over the bruise from my night-time encounter that is ripening on my cheek, and coolly dismiss it. 'This way, Master Archer,' he says

I follow him past the bookcases into a large room where the sudden light causes me to blink and shield my eyes with an upraised hand. One wall is entirely tall windows looking out upon the River Thames and the low afternoon sun. Against the glare, a shadow resolves itself into a tall, broad-shouldered man. Sir William Hervey comes towards me and grasps my hand firmly, taking my elbow in his other palm. I try not to wince as the pressure revives the ache of my recent beating.

'Master Archer, so pleased you could come.'

The voice is hearty, and I recognise the flat vowels of my home county. Had Sir Francis not already warned me that his bluff manner was a ruse for the unwary, I might easily succumb to his open smile and welcoming tone. As it is, I incline my head and reply politely, 'I count it an honour, Sir William, to wait on you.'

'Well said, young man,' responds Sir William. His eyes assess me. He also takes in my grazed features but makes no comment. He nods to Grey and the ferrety little clerk slips out, shutting the door firmly behind him. Motioning me to sit, Sir William takes the chair opposite me, for all the world like two old friends by a fireside.

'You strike me as a sensible young man, Master Archer,' he begins affably. But he offers no explanation of why I am summoned. 'I would know you better. Tell me about yourself.'

'There is little enough to tell, sir. I am a country boy come up to town, and work for Mr Garrick.'

He laughs companionably, 'And what might this work involve?'

This is not the sort of question I was expecting - but what *was* I expecting? I hear myself stammering. 'Er - acting, of course - if Mr Garrick feels I am good enough. Apart from that, I - er - make myself useful -

doing jobs, running errands...'

'You have Mr Garrick's confidence?'

'I think - I hope - he finds me reliable and trustworthy.'

Sir William nods in approval, 'I am sure he does, Master Archer. The question is, will I find you equally so?'

'Er - I am not sure I understand you, sir.'

He looks directly at me. 'What business had you at Hanover Square, Master Archer?'

The suddenness of the question, allied with surprise that he knows of my visit, unnerves me further 'I - er - I was there on a matter of - er - some personal delicacy, sir.'

'You were there to inform Mijnheer Hendricksen of the death of his son.' The friendly smile is still in place, but his tone has hardened. 'Is that not so?'

'It is, sir.' Aware that I am mumbling, I look up at him directly. 'That was the purpose of my visit.'

'Yet the young man had assumed a different identity amongst you actors, I believe. Harry Henderson, was't not? How did you connect him with Hanover Square?'

'There were letters, sir, in his lodging.'

'Letters?' He is interested. 'You read them, clearly. What did they say?'

'I don't know, sir. They were written in a foreign language.'

'So how did they lead you to Hanover Square?'

'I found the address amongst his belongings,' I lie.

No need to mention Ned Phillimore's Sunday jaunts with Harry, nor the investigations of Charlie's low-life associates.

He regards me narrowly, then gives a sly smile and

a dismissive nod. My explanation clearly does not convince him, yet his smile seems to approve my dissimulation. He does not pursue the matter. Instead, he asks, 'How did Mijnheer Hendricksen receive the news?'

I hesitate, unsure of how close the relationship between Sir William and the Dutch banker may be. I decide on the truth. 'To my mind, he appeared unconcerned. I received the impression that he and his son were estranged.'

'Very perceptive of you, Master Archer,' murmurs Sir William. 'And have you any thoughts as to the reason for such an estrangement?'

'I supposed the gentleman did not approve of his son's choice of a career upon the stage. I, myself, come from humble stock, where a life in the theatre might be considered an advancement. But Harry - Hendrick - clearly came from a wealthy family who might regard his life as an actor very differently.'

Again he nods in a satisfied manner. I feel I have passed some secret test.

'Do you know the source of Mijnheer Hendricksen's wealth, Master Archer?'

'How would I, sir?'

'Aha, a question answered with a question!' He slaps his thigh, delighted. 'Equivocation or genuine ignorance, Master Archer?'

I assume a puzzled look and remain silent.

'No matter.' He regards me for a moment, almost as a doting father might regard his son. Then he performs yet another of his unnerving changes of tack. 'And the young lady, what did you think of her?'

He sees me redden at the mention of Agnes and

smiles broadly. 'I see she cast her spell on you as, I am reliably informed, she does on all who meet her. Attractive, is she?' He raises a complicit eyebrow.

'She is a lady of a class well beyond my own, sir.' I reply somewhat stiffly. 'It would be presumptuous of me to express an opinion.'

He laughs out loud. 'How very gallant! Tell me, Master Archer, did you find her as persuasive as she is alluring? What did you talk of, the two of you, when you took your little ride together?'

I cannot help my jaw dropping. I stare in disbelief.

'There is little escapes my notice, Master Archer. I trust you will not waste my time by pleading gentlemanly honour - by your own admission you are but a country lad like myself. Therefore, I ask you again, what did you talk of?'

I pretend to have some difficulty recalling the conversation, of which every detail is, of course, enshrined in my memory. I give merely a bare summary. Any more would be a betrayal.

'Miss Mayer talked of Har - Hendrick, naturally. You know they were engaged to be married? And she talked of her life, and how fortunate she was to be taken in by Mijnheer Hendricksen after her father's death.'

'So you do know that Mijnheer Hendricksen is a banker?' interrupts Sir William smoothly.

'Miss Mayer merely said that her father and Mijnheer Hendricksen had done business together.'

'Very well.' Sir William rises. Is the interview at an end? 'Time presses, and diverting as I find your company, Master Archer, the moment has come for me to tell you why you are here. Sir Francis gave you no indication, I suppose?'

Little as I like Courtney, I cannot malign him. 'Sir Francis told me nothing, sir. Merely that you wanted to see me.'

'Excellent!' He claps his hands together. 'I am glad Sir Francis knows where his interests lie. Though it is, of course, his *other* interests which ensure his co-operation - you understand what I am saying, Master Archer? You being, not so long since, one of those interests?'

I understand all too well. He is referring to my time with Mother Ransom. I stand before him, hands behind my back, head bowed, feeling like a chastised schoolboy. 'The circumstances in which I first encountered Sir Francis were not of my choosing, sir. That life is behind me now. I would prefer to forget it.'

Sir William nods sagely. 'There is much in our lives that we might prefer to forget, Master Archer. But the past is like pitch - the stain lingers and, like a phantom shadow, we never know when it will come back to haunt us. That is why I thought it well for Sir Francis to be my messenger today - as a reminder to you that we are all hostages to fortune. With that in mind, I come to the business that brings you here today. Mijnheer Hendricksen is a very influential man. I do not want him upset.'

'Has he complained to you of my visit?' I ask in alarm.

Sir William is displeased at the interruption. 'I do not know the man. All I know is that he is important to His Majesty's Government. Therefore, you will not go near Hanover Square again. You will have no further contact with Mijnheer Hendricksen, or with anyone associated with him. Is that clear, Master Archer?'

Anger begins to burn inside me. Who is this man to threaten me with my past and to give me orders? His prohibition on seeing Hendricksen does not worry me, but what right has he to prevent me seeing Agnes again?

Looking him directly in the eye, I say coldly, 'Abundantly clear, Sir William.'

Again he gives me that assessing look. 'Have a care, Master Archer,' he says softly. 'You have impressed me as a personable and intelligent young man, yet it is clear that not everyone shares my view.' This time his gaze lingers unmistakably upon my injuries. 'You may deem your present discomfort irksome, but believe me it is as nothing compared to what may befall should you ignore my advice. Affairs of state take little note of individuals. It is never wise to get in their way. Remember that.'

Behind me, the door opens softly and I turn to see the sharp-faced clerk slide into the room.

'Conduct this young man back to his companion, Nathaniel. It would not do to leave Sir Francis pining.'

With a complicit smirk at his master, Grey ushers me out.

Unlike Sir Francis, who conducted me privily through deserted passages, Nathaniel Grey escorts me through bustling halls and lobbies, threading a way past MPs locked in conversation, skirting groups of petitioners waiting to plead their case, and dodging scurrying clerks laden with papers. At first I take it that, on his master's orders, I am to be made aware of my own insignificance in this world where great men decide the fortunes of the realm. But gradually I suspect his purpose to be more sinister. For amidst all those so engrossed in their own business, our passage, whilst not attracting attention, does not go unnoticed.

Many, as we pass, cast covert glances at Grey himself. Looks of respect but also, I note, of fear and contempt. I begin to understand the ambivalence of his role - a man reviled, a man not to be trusted but also not to be crossed. I am also aware of curious glances being cast at me. Uneasy with such scrutiny and beginning to feel the taint of his company, I several times endeavour to meet the watchers' eyes, only to have them quickly look away. By the time we reach the main door, however, I don't doubt that my every lineament has been noted, my character assessed. By showing me thus to the assembled throng, Grey is indelibly linking me with his master, Hervey.

By the time Grey debouches me into Old Palace Yard, I have the feeling I have been in some mysterious way marked as someone to be wary of – and I am inwardly fuming.

Sir Francis hurries across to me, his relief evident.

'My dear boy...' He stops short, seeing my fury. He looks across to where Grey is disappearing, smiling, into the shadowy interior of the building. His face as he turns back to me clouds with anxiety. 'The affair has not gone well?'

He attempts to lay a consoling hand upon my shoulder. I shake it off, unable yet to articulate the fury which arises in equal measure from Hervey's proscription on my activities, Grey's sullying of my character and my own continuing incomprehension. How can inquiries into a humble actor's death have attracted the attention of one of the most powerful and feared men in the land?

But Sir Francis is not to be denied. 'Will, you alarm me mightily, my dear.' He clutches my arm once more. 'For the love of God, tell me what transpired in there? Is Sir William angry?'

I face him as he cringes beside me and see fear in his eyes. I brush his hand angrily from my arm. 'Is it for me you ask?' His cravenness makes me cruel. 'Or do you fear for your own already irretrievably tarnished reputation? I doubt it is concern for my safety that exercises you thus. Rather the loss of Sir William's favour, which leaves you open to scandal and disgrace as a sodomitical pederast.'

It as if I have physically struck him. He falls back, his mouth working but with no sound coming out. I feel a qualm of pity, but am still too angry to give it rein.

'You need not fear,' I tell him coldly, 'I said nothing about you that Sir William did not already know.'

'You are too cruel, Will.' Sir Francis extracts a linen handkerchief and applies it to the corners of his eyes. 'I own I fear Sir William, and with just cause, but you do me great injustice in not believing my concern for you is genuine.'

Our animated conversation is beginning to attract the attention of passers-by. Several coming out of Parliament and down the steps to summon wherries are those who have seen me in company with Grey. I am loth to have their opinion of me tarnished further by seeing me also with Sir Francis.

'Pray compose yourself, sir, and let us walk awhile. 'Tis but half-an-hour since our arrival and I do not see our boatman. The rogue has taken another fare, I'll be bound. Let us take a turn about the gardens and I will tell you what has put me in such a choler.'

Sir Francis follows me gratefully to the tree-fringed lawns bordering the riverside before the House of Commons. There, out of earshot of the crowds on Parliament Steps, my ire gradually subsides as I tell him what has passed in Sir William's rooms.

When I have done, his face creases in perplexity. 'He warned you off this Hendricksen fellow?'

'And anyone who has aught to do with him. He said His Majesty's government had an interest in the old man.'

'And he is a Dutchman, say you? Could he, perchance, be a foreign spy? Someone that Hervey is watching?' He pauses, a be-ringed finger idly tapping his lip. 'Or mayhap he is one of Hervey's own agents?'

'Hervey denied knowing him.'

'In that case, Hervey may merely be obeying orders - and it is Walpole himself who would not have Hendricksen disturbed.' He is thoughtful for a moment. 'You say he knew of young Hendricksen's death?'

'Yes, but his concern was not the manner of his death. Rather how I made the connection with Hanover Square.'

'Suggesting perhaps that he already knew how young Hendricksen died?'

I look at him with horror as the significance of his words sinks in. 'You think that Hervey had poor Harry killed?'

'It is possible.'

'For what reason?'

'Men such as Hervey do not give reasons - only

commands. He gave you no reason why you should not approach Hendricksen, just that you should not do so. Take my advice, Will - for your own safety leave well alone. Give up any attempt to bring Harry's murderer to justice.'

We return to Parliament Steps to find our boatman waiting. A cold drizzle sets in as he rows us back towards London Bridge. It inhibits further discussion, but we are in any case not inclined to talk, both Sir Francis and I being engrossed in our own thoughts which chill us more than inclement weather.

I see clearly that to continue my investigation into Harry Henderson's death will be to invite danger. But I'll be letting him down if I abandon him now.

Besides, Hervey did not directly forbid my enquiring into the death - only to avoid upsetting old Hendricksen further... Sir William Hervey's interest in the older Hendricksen might have naught to do with the son's death. Agnes told me how young Hendrick was estranged from his father, and therefore from his affairs. When I informed him of his son's death, he knew little and cared less. It won't be any hardship to obey Hervey's command with respect to Mijnheer Hendricksen. I can't foresee any necessity to contact the old man again.

With Agnes, though, it may be a different matter...

By the time we reach Old Swan Stairs I am feeling more sanguine. I decline Sir Francis's offer of riding back in his coach to Mr Garrick's lodgings, pleading that a walk in the air will help clear my thoughts. With relief I watch it trot away along Thames Street and turn my steps towards home, casting frequent looks over my shoulder. The knowledge that my previous activities have been observed has so unsettled me that I am determined never to walk unsuspecting through London's streets again.

Bethlem

Returning to Mr Garrick's lodgings, I find a note waiting for me.

My heart leaps as I think I recognise the hand, and Charlie vanquishes all doubt as to the identity of the writer.

''S from her ladyship, I bet. 'Twas Lizzie, the maid from Hanover Square wot brought it. Ran after her, I did and we had a good old chinwag afore she went. Seems her ladyship's in a fine tizzy cos the old gennelman's acting right peculiar.'

'In what way?'

'Well, the young master's funeral is set down for two days time. The old man wants it to be a grand affair. To make up for the shameful way he treated him when he was alive, Lizzie says. And there's been letters going pell-mell backwards and forwards ever since he heard of the death. Letters to Holland and letters to big-wigs in Parliament. And fine gentleman a-calling at all hours, leaving the master looking like thunder when they've gone.'

Considering where I've just been, the mention of letters to Parliament is intriguing. 'Strange, indeed,' I agree.

Charlie nods at the paper in my hand. 'Ain't you gonna open it, then?'

'Yes I am - once you've gone about your business.'

My tone brooks no dissent. Shrugging his shoulders sulkily he slouches away, muttering under his breath as he goes.

I carry the note up to my garret room, holding it to my nose the while to breathe in its perfume.

But my delight at receiving a note from Agnes is tinged with apprehension. Hervey has just warned me off further contact with the Hendricksen household. The reprisal for disobedience, although not stipulated, promises to be worse that my present aches and pains ...

But what can I do? It is *she* who has contacted *me*. To ignore her would be churlish, and to reject her would be a gross breach of manners.

I recall Hervey's sly smile as I told him of my conversation with Agnes, his assessing look as I lied about finding Harry's address. As if he saw my deception - and silently applauded it... Can it be that he will *expect* me to disobey his commands...?

With trembling fingers, I open the letter.

Master Archer, she writes, *If your purpose to see Nicklaas still holds, meet me at the Dutch Church in Austin Fryers at noon tomorrow. Take every care, I beg you, to avoid notice. Forgive the subterfuge, but discretion is necessary. A.*

My throat feels tight at the prospect of meeting her again and as evening drags on, I can not settle. But her exhortation to avoid notice causes me unease. Does she too suspect that we were being watched? Amongst all the visitors to her house, has one perhaps given her the same warning as Hervey has delivered to me?

I try to divert myself by learning the lines for my next scene in *The Changeling* where the disguised Antonio reveals himself to a startled Isabella. But rather than distracting me from thinking of tomorrow's destination, the hospital for the unfortunate deranged at Bethlem, and of whom I am to accompany there, the words seem strangely relevant.

This shape of folly shrouds your dearest love,
The truest servant to your powerful beauties,
Whose magic had this force thus to transform me.

Is it folly to go against Hervey's interdict? Has Agnes worked some magic to make me her truest servant? Alone in my garret, straining my eyes in the candlelight to peruse my script, it is not my fellow actor Kitty Blair's flirtatious face I see, but the dark eyes and tempting lips of Agnes Mayer. Only for them, in their turn, to be replaced by the mocking features of Sir William Hervey.

At last, realising that the words are merely jostling in my head without imprinting themselves on my memory, I snuff the candle and make my way down to the kitchen.

A brisk, uncomplicated encounter with a compliant Susan will be the ideal antidote to my growing tension.

Next morning is crisp with frost. I excuse myself from rehearsal - I am not required anyway - telling Mr Garrick I am following another trail that might lead to information on the murder. His mind on the forthcoming rehearsal, Mr Garrick does not press me, merely warning me to be careful and to take Charlie along as a precaution.

Mindful of what happened the last time I met Agnes, I heed his advice. I do not want to add more bruises to those that are only now yellowing around the edges.

But nor do I want Agnes to see me with Charlie, so I give him stern instructions to keep out of sight. Feeding him just enough information about my visit to Westminster, and the mysterious Sir William Hervey to fire his imagination, I urge Charlie to keep an eye open for anyone who might follow me. When Agnes and I enter the hospital, he is to wait outside until we come out again. Inside Bethlem, I reason, there will be folk enough about to preclude any possibility of harm. He enters with wholehearted enthusiasm into the subterfuge.

Bethlem Hospital for the insane is out beyond the city boundary at Moorfields. I saw it once from the outside not long after I first arrived in the city and, not at the time being aware of its purpose, thought it a very fine building. It was Mother Ransom who enlightened me. As a little girl, she had accompanied her parents, just a few years after it had been built, to visit an uncle who had been incarcerated there. Prone to fits and violent rages, he had been in the ward for curable patients and had been released some while later.

The story ran, so she said, that Robert Hooke, the architect, believing lunatics might be recovered by noble and beautiful surroundings, had based his design upon the Tuileries Palace, one of King Louis of France's royal residences. The French monarch was insulted. So, when his new palace at Versailles was a-building, he had ordered the necessary-house to be modelled on our own king's St James's Palace. At this point Mother Ransom would collapse into fits of laughter. 'So them blessed Frenchies shit where English nobs parade themselves!' She was no respecter of authority.

My only other intimation of what may await me inside Bethlem is gleaned from Mr Hogarth's salutary paintings of *The Rake's Progress* wherein Tom Rakewell suffers the same fate as I presume befell Nicklaas Hendricksen - a career of gaming and debauchery leading to crime and the threat of prison, moral insanity eventually landing him in the madhouse.

As I make my way to my assignation at the Dutch Church, I wonder quite how mad I will find Nicklaas Hendricksen. If gambling, drinking and wenching are signs of insanity, half the young men of London should by rights be in Bethlem. Besides, he is in the curable ward and I cannot believe those inmates to be so very hopeless if Mother Ransom's uncle is typical. Nor dangerous, for, as Mr Hogarth shows, it is quite the thing for the gentility to visit the hospital, seeking to divert themselves by observing the lunatics' antics. These same visitors, so I've heard, pay a few pence to view the incurable patients through the grilles on their cell doors and hire sticks with which to poke and aggravate them.

My way to the Dutch Church takes me to Grace Church Street once again, where I rode in Sir Francis's coach. But this time I head north towards Bishopsgate and Threadneedle Street, taking care to cut circuitously through the little lanes and byways away from the main thoroughfares in case Hervey is having me followed. I know Charlie won't have any trouble keeping me in sight - such rat-runs are his territory. But, unless Hervey's man is very skilful, I am confident that I will have shaken him off long before I reach Old Broad Street and unlatch the wicket gate into the churchyard of the Dutch Church.

I have no trouble recognising the hooded figure at one of the graves. She is wearing the same cloak she wore the night outside the theatre when she attempted to influence my view of Henderson's death. Rather than approach her directly, I pace slowly about the gravestones as if paying respect to those resting beneath, coming little by little in closer proximity to her. As I draw near, she rises and moves gracefully away as if unaware of my presence. But I see her twitch aside the hood for a brief moment, catch the glance she directs at me before turning away towards the church.

She is waiting for me in the porch. 'You have come alone and were not followed?' Her voice is anxious, its soft insistence robbing me of breath.

'Of course,' I lie. 'Your note was very clear.'

She smiles. 'Then you may give me your arm, sir.'

Together we walk up Bell Alley and into Winchester Street, like any couple out for a morning stroll. At London Wall, we cross into Little Moor Gate and soon the wide gardens at the front of Bethlem are before us. Along the walks, strollers like ourselves take the air. Only the presence of a number of women in plain grey gowns and starched caps suggests that this is anything different from the fashionable parade of Vauxhall Gardens.

'The curable patients are allowed to roam within the grounds,' says Agnes. 'It is a step towards releasing them back into the world.'

'And Nicklaas?' I ask, searching among the figures. 'Which is he?'

Her brow clouds. 'He is inside,' she says

despondently. 'He was doing so well, to the extent that I was allowed to take him out on occasion, but he has been seized with a melancholy of late and they have been obliged to restrain him. It is so sad.'

Boldly, I take her hand to comfort her as we approach the gateway and feel no small pleasure when she does not withdraw it.

Atop the gate arch on either side, wrought in stone, are two recumbent figures. On the left a prone, near naked man, resting leisurely upon his elbow, his face a picture of pensive sadness. This must be a representation of melancholy madness. His companion, on the right, presents a much more disturbing mien. Entirely naked, chained, with muscles bunched, he strives to break free, his expression one of wild-eyed desperation - the very image of raving madness. A fearsome sight indeed for the unfortunates about to be committed and salutary for we who visit them!

Agnes hurries me under the archway with a shudder, and within a few moments we find ourselves within the chilly entrance hall, where a warder, a large bunch of keys at his waist, appears so suddenly he might have been on the look-out for us. Her glowers insolently at me.

'Your business?'

'We would visit a patient, sir,' says Agnes gravely. 'I have been before. Mr Sampson, is it not?'

The turnkey makes show of scrutinising her features as she casts back her hood. His face is too close to hers. She does not flinch, but I sense her repugnance at his unmannerly proximity. I feel my blood rise. After an unconscionable time, he appears satisfied.

'Jack Sampson at your service, ma'am,' he says,

with a sideways look at me. He palms the coins that Agnes gives him and agrees to conduct us to Nicklaas Hendricksen's cell.

He is a burly fellow with a day's growth of beard and a contemptible fawning manner, who persists in talking as we enter the labyrinth of corridors.

'Is it only the Dutchman you've come to see? We've many to divert you. 'Twould be a shame to miss Kurt, our own mad Heracles. Takes four warders to tame him when he's in a rage. Or we've Ned down there who dug his mother from her grave and warmed her by the fire, complaining all the while why did she choose to go to that cold hole. He has a straw dummy in his cell which he scolds and plies with tea. Or there's a well-set young man who can't abide clothes, but rips them off and displays himself naked as the day he was born. He's a favourite with the ladies. Two have fainted clean away at sight of him.'

His lascivious sideways glances at Agnes are insupportable.

'Enough, sir,' I reprimand him. 'This is no way to talk to a lady.'

'No harm meant, master,' he sneers, giving me a scornful look. 'There's plenty gentlefolk who're grateful to hear of new attractions.'

We emerge from gloomy corridors into a large hall where a great many ladies sit around tables drinking tea. Were it not for rows of barred doors along each side and the hectic bursts of chatter from the all female assembly, it could be any tea-garden in town.

At length, the warder unlocks another door which, as with all the others, he locks again once we have passed through. We are in another hall where the occupants are all men. Some sit in groups, smoking or conversing. Several, solitary, rock back and forth whilst yet others walk desperately about debating animatedly with themselves. Here, too, the hall is flanked by rows of stout doors with metal grilles, some open, but others closed, from behind which occasionally erupt violent shouts or bursts of unnatural laughter.

Coming to one of the open doors, the warder thrusts his head inside. 'Visitors for you, Closh,' he calls, using the cant name for a Dutchman. 'Look lively now.'

The hurt look that clouds Agnes's brow prompts me once more to reprimand the oaf. 'Show some respect, sirrah!'

'Respect is it?' he scoffs. 'There be no lords or gentlemen here, young master. All are equal, as I am sure the young lady has cause to know. Madness is a great leveller. See for yourself.'

I follow Agnes into the cell. It is bare with but one barred window. A ledge along one side serves as both seat and bed with only a rank straw mattress for comfort. Over Agnes's shoulder I see a figure rise to greet us. Dressed as any young gentleman, but his clothes sadly crumpled and soiled. Foetid body odour wafts as he moves. The hopeful expectancy as he sees Agnes is almost that of a sane man, but catching sight of Sampson and myself it transforms into the petulant snarl of a lunatic.

'Another doxy!' he rasps. 'Have they not done for me already?' I recoil involuntarily as he makes to shoo us from his cell, hearing Sampson snigger behind me. But Agnes does not flinch. With great bravery she grasps his outflung hands and holds them.

'Claas,' she says, her voice breaking with emotion, 'it is I, Agnes. Do you not know me?'

It as if, somewhere in his bewildered mind, a memory stirs. He frowns uncertainly.

Behind me, the warder says coarsely, ''Tain't no use reasoning with him, ma'am. He don't know you from the whore o' Babylon!'

I see Agnes stiffen. Without turning round, she snaps, 'Leave us, sir!' Her voice rings with cold authority.

'None of that, milady, you know full well it ain't allowed...' he begins, but I cut him short.

'Do as you're bid, sir. The lady has my protection. She has no need of yours.'

Amusement flickers briefly in his eyes, then he holds out his hand. A couple more shillings suffice. 'Bawl when he gets too much for yer,' he growls as he goes.

'Push the door to, Will,' says Agnes softly once he's gone. 'Claas is no danger to you or me.' She sits beside him and, relinquishing his hands, takes his face gently. 'My poor, dear brother,' she croons softly, stroking his cheeks.

I hover awkwardly just inside the door of the cell, like an intruder upon their tenderness, yet feeling unaccountably jealous. I sense his eyes upon me. I know not how a madman should look, but his gaze, fluctuating between boldness and subservience, one moment looking directly at me, the next flicking aside, unnerves me. After a moment, a sneer twists his lips. 'Your gallant, doxy? Your beau?'

Agnes laughs lightly. 'My friend, Claas. His name is

Archer.'

'An Archer - but no beau!' he cackles. 'How shoot you then your shaft, sir?'

I redden at the impropriety of the obscene gesture which accompanies his taunt. But Agnes is unabashed, dismissing the offence with sparkling laughter.

'Be not cruel to Will, Claas. He is a friend. He is here to help.'

Again the madman giggles, looking at me crazily. 'Will he, won't he? Only Will - helpful Willie, but no beau! Poor Archer! Woulds't have me lend you my dart, sir? 'Tis a proven shaft.'

With no regard for the modesty of the sweet creature beside him, he starts to fidget about and touch himself, making to unbutton, but Agnes stays his fingers. It's clear the sexual excesses that caused his incarceration still prey upon his mind. Agnes sees my discomfiture. 'Take no heed, Will. 'Tis but his delusion that speaks. See, he is calm again.'

And, in truth, his frenzy has abated as swiftly as it came. He sits now gazing at her, docile as an infant. For the first time I see in his distracted features a similarity to his dead brother, Hendrick. Aware of my gaze, he becomes agitated again.

Agnes clasps his hand more firmly and turns to me. 'I fear your presence inflames him, Will. Perhaps you could give me a few minutes alone with him?'

As I make to protest, she says, 'Fear not, he knows me now, don't you, Claas,'

'Agnes,' he says simply. 'Sister.'

'I shall talk to him, calm him. Give me but ten minutes and he shall be as lucid as you or I. Go, Will, find the warder and tell him we would walk in the garden. The fresh air will do him good. Then you may put to him any questions you may have concerning Hendrik.'

Loth as I am to leave her, her serene certainty convinces me and I go in search of the warder.

Hardly have I set foot back into the hall when there is a sudden uproar among a group of inmates at a table in the far corner. Raised voices are quickly followed by shouts of encouragement and hoots of derision as separate bodies in the group tangle in a flurry of flailing limbs. Within a matter of seconds, all but the most distracted in the hall have risen in a clatter of falling chairs and toppling tables and are surging towards the source of the commotion.

I am thrust aside, none too gently, as a warder pushes past me. Flung back against the wall, I watch half a dozen of them charge into the mass of jeering bodies, laying about them with stout cudgels, clearing a path to the centre of the disturbance.

Such a riot in the outside world would have ruffians in the crowd fighting back against the upholders of law and order, but here the throng parts as easily as the Red Sea, casting demented bodies back to all corners of the hall. They howl and set up a shrieking which turns my blood cold. Some flee to their own cells. Others, like flotsam at the tide's edge, fetch up against the walls where they scrabble their fingers raw, or huddle on the floor, moaning most piteously, their faces masks of anguish.

At the far side of the hall, where the disturbance first began, two warders are with great difficulty pinning down a burly man who writhes about yelling obscenities. Even above the clamour of the inmates, I can clearly hear his frantic cries. He curses those who lay hands on him, he screams of the beast that blasphemes against God, of the Antichrist, of the angels of the Seventh Seal... One of the warders clubs him, but he does not let up his railing. At last they subdue him enough. Four of them pick him up bodily, restraining his arms and legs, whilst a fifth takes a vice-like grip upon his head, wrenching his neck backwards to prevent further resistance.

With great haste, they carry him past me from the hall. I am borne along with a straggle of cowed and curious inmates to see him cast, none too gently, into a cell some six feet square its walls padded with thick straw mattresses. I watch in horror as they strip him naked and force his arms into a kind of canvas waistcoat with elongated sleeves. Wrenching these sleeves behind him, they tie them securely, then strap him down upon the pallet bed. All the while there is no abatement in his ranting.

Dusting off their hands, still panting from their exertions, the five warders slam shut the cell door and begin rounding up those who have followed them to witness the drama.

'Seen enough, have you, young fellow?' Sampson is at my shoulder. 'Our bible-mad strong-man, Kurt, as I told you of. We'll let him cool his heels in the Hole till his ardour's abated. Happen then he won't kill anyone.'

'Has he killed someone?' I ask in horror. The experience of the last few minutes has considerably shaken me.

'Oh, yes,' he gloats, revealing blackened teeth, 'killed one man outright by breaking his neck, and mutilated several others, gouged eyes, broken limbs -

doesn't do to handy-dandy theology with our Kurt!'

'A religious maniac?'

'A monk - 'til they got tired of him in Prussia and shipped him over here under the guise of a seaman. Arrested at the docks for murdering a whore. Neck so thick, he survived hanging three times. Can't try a fourth time, that's the law - so we got him here.'

'And yet you let him mingle with the other patients?'

'Most times, he's as reasonable as you or me. Chats as pleasant as pleasant. We even lets him out occasionally. Then, a stray remark puts him in a frenzy and he ends up in the Hole. Very penitent he is afterwards, stays in his cell muttering the Bible to himself for up to a week sometimes, no trouble to anyone.'

On a sudden, I think of Agnes alone with her supposedly reasonable brother-in-law, and recall my errand. 'You must take us to the gardens,' I blurt. 'The lady would walk out with the Dutchman.'

The churl raises his eyebrows in a mocking smile. 'Left 'er alone with him, have you? Tsk, tsk! So much for being under your protection, eh? I hope you're not looking to me to take the blame for aught that might have happened.'

With what I consider infuriating slowness, he conducts me back to Nicklaas's cell. In the uproar, I realise I have completely lost my bearings and cannot tell one cell from another. Arriving, I see with dismay that the door is firmly shut. Did I not leave it ajar? Fearing the worst, I fling it open without ceremony.

Agnes rises in confusion at my precipitate entrance. Her back towards the door, she has been crouched before Nicklaas, who now cringes back, cowering on to the straw mattress.

She turns on me, flushed and startled, annoyance clouding her face. 'Why, Master Archer, why such haste?' she rebukes me. 'See how you have affrighted poor Claas.'

Indeed the madman is curled almost into a ball, looking fearfully at me. I stammer an apology as she coaxes him to his feet, standing between us, shielding him with her own body. I watch, mortified with remorse, as she pats and consoles him, solicitously smoothing his disordered dress, stroking his cheeks. She puts a delicate lace handkerchief to her lips to moisten it, then smoothes his brow.

'There now,' she says at last, standing back to survey him. 'Master Archer means no harm. He has come to take us out into the gardens.' She turns, fixing me with a severe look that calls the blood to my cheeks. 'Is not that right, Will?'

Behind me, I hear Sampson cough and resign myself to further depletion of my purse.

'Indeed, ma'am,' I reply, standing aside to let them pass. I slip a florin into a grinning Sampson's palm. He revels in my discomfiture all the way to the gardens, where with a mocking bow, he leaves us.

Agnes puts her arm through that of her brother-in-law and strolls nonchalantly along the gravelled paths, chatting pleasantly of the weather, birds and the sparse stunted winter plants which she points out to him with as much earnestness as if they were gorgeous summer blooms.

I trail, chastened, a few steps behind them. Even from behind, I see that Nicklaas responds favourably to the open air. His stooped, shuffling gait becomes more confident and, by little and little, his responses to her chatter become almost those of a normal man.

After a while, she leads him to a seat within a little arbour with a view over the expanse of lawn. She motions me to sit on her other side.

Now that we are in good light and he is calmer, I notice for the first time how like he is to his late brother. More dishevelled due to his lodging, and with a look of troubled uncertainty in his eyes due to his condition, but in cast of feature and lineament, almost identical. I recall the bare twelve months between them that sent their poor mother to a place such as this...

For all his appearance of normality, however, his discourse still shows his delusion. In response to Agnes's gentle prompting, he speaks of his family. His father, one moment an admirable man, then in almost the same breath a tyrant. His brother and he playing childish games of hide and seek. But now he says he has no brother and never had, yet at the same time he believes his brother is here in this place, one of his gaolers, intent on tormenting him.

'Is there aught you would ask him?' says Agnes to me after she has patiently endeavoured to unravel his tangled memories into a semblance of order, bringing him to some realisation that his father has committed him here and that his brother is truly dead.

'How long have you been confined, Nicklaas? Here, and before at Clerkenwell?' I ask.

He looks to Agnes, his brow furrowed. She nods in encouragement.

'Under a year,' he says hesitantly, 'but more than a six-month.'

'And do you recall why you were committed?'

He looks aside and a slow, secret smile spreads across his features. 'I was a roaring boy,' he replies with a giggle. 'I spent my father's money. On gambling and on ladies of pleasure.' He bites his lower lip and sniggers, cupping his privates and glancing up mischievously. 'I made them squeak!'

'And your brother - did he accompany you on these jaunts?' I ask, realising too late how great offence this may give to Agnes who was engaged to him. I glance at her, mortified, but she seems unperturbed.

Nicklaas becomes animated. 'My brother, pah! He died, you know, hanged himself.'

Agnes takes his hand in hers to calm him. 'I think that is enough questions for now, Will. I shall take Claas back now. You will not take offence if I do not ask you to escort us back?' The chilliness of her tone shows I am not forgiven.

I bow low, hiding my mortification. They stroll sedately away, for all the world like two lovers, leaving me bereft. How could I have been so stupid! Bursting in to the cell like that - questioning her dead fiancé's morals! And I have learned nothing! Once they are out of sight, I punch my fist hard into the side of the arbour, bloodying my knuckles.

Nathaniel Grey

As soon as I emerge from Bethlem Hospital, Charlie appears apparently from nowhere. He makes a show of looking about .

'No lady? Kept her in, 'ave they?' He nods his head sagely. 'Understandable I reckon - they'd think her wits are addled to be seen with such as you!'

I aim a half-hearted cuff which he dodges. 'Hold your clutter, you sapscull. I am not in the mood.'

'In the dumps, eh? The mad man gave you nought but babble and taradiddle? Or is it the lady's put you out of humour?'

This time, my hand connects with his ear, but with little effect. He's wearing a woollen muffler against the cold. All the same he yelps and falls to rubbing his head, giving me mutinous looks the while. But at least it puts an end to his unwelcome inquisition. He trots along beside me sniffling and muttering under his breath of 'love-sick scrubs'.

I stride on, lost in my own melancholy, heedless of the fact that I'm obliging Charlie almost to run to keep up with me. Thus we turn eventually into Cornhill where the bustle of chairs and carriages and the throng of those on foot slow our pace somewhat. A constant procession of carriages comes and goes under the pillars of the Royal Exchange across the way. Weaving amongst them, risking life and limb, flows an unending stream of bodies, braving the hubbub betwixt its noble facade and the mean-looking entry into 'Change Alley on this side of the road. Most are on their way to Jonathan's Coffee House where jobbers and brokers deemed too ill-mannered and raucous for the hallowed halls of the Exchange, conduct their business.

This whole area is the haunt of bankers, investment-brokers and stock-jobbers. Seekers out of marvellous schemes and fantastical projects. Like the notorious South Sea Bubble three years before I was born, which promised swift and untold riches only to bring the stock market crashing, plunging many into penury and despair. I have every reason to detest such charlatans, for it was they brought ruin to my family. Without them, my mother and I would never have become beholden to Rev Purselove - and I would not have ended up at Mother Ransome's.

But I have little enough time to dwell upon the past for, as Charlie and I pass opposite the Royal Exchange, a slight, black-clad figure scuttles from 'Change Alley a short distance ahead.

I thrust out my arm and draw Charlie close. In reply to his curious look, I put a finger to my lips and lower my head. Carried along by the throng, we cannot hope to avoid him. The most I can hope for is to pass unobserved.

But I should know better. The bead-like eyes of the scurrying beetle in the dark greatcoat and the nondescript grey wig miss nothing. He pounces.

'Why, Master Archer, is it not?'

We stop dead, Charlie genuinely bewildered, I pasting a look of surprise upon my face.

Two business-men, deep in conversation find their way blocked by our sudden pause. One, florid-faced and heavy jowled, opens his mouth to remonstrate but, catching sight of our black-clad companion, claps it shut and hurries his startled companion away.

'Not rehearsing today, Master Archer?'

'I am about Mr Garrick's business, sir.'

Nathaniel Grey fixes his button eyes on me. 'Mr Garrick's business?'

'Aye, sir. What other business would I have?' Then emboldened, I continue, 'I did not expect to see you here, sir, so far from Westminster.'

'I, too, am about my employer's business.'

'At the Exchange? I had not thought you a man of commerce, sir?'

'I am many things, Master Archer, in many places,' he returns suavely. He cocks an eyebrow. 'Like yourself, perhaps. Did I not see you but an hour or so ago hard by London Wall? And in company with a lady? The pair of you seemed - intimate.'

Fear creeps cold up my back, but I do not show it. 'An acquaintance merely, sir. We happened to meet and, as our paths coincided for part of our journeys, she requested I escort her.'

'A true gallant!' He diverts his scrutiny to Charlie who stands, mouth agape, beside me. 'And now I find you in company with a young boy...'

'Charlie Stubbs, at your service,' pipes up Charlie. 'I bin a-helping Will with his business - Mr Garrick's business, that is.' A quick learner is Charlie!

'Very commendable.' Grey stoops, hands on knees, interested. 'And are you an actor, too, a colleague of Master Archer?'

'Nah, I'm just a pot boy. Will's my friend.'

'Indeed?' Grey gave a thin-lipped smile. 'You are a fortunate fellow, Master Archer, to have such an admiring young companion. Would that be Sir Francis Courtney's influence? You share his tastes, perhaps?'

His insinuation is clear. 'No, sir, I do not. Now, if you will excuse us...'

He steps aside. 'Of course, you have your master's business to attend to...'

'As, I presume, have you, sir.' Then, my anger making me reckless, I add. 'Since you are here, I guess you have bankers, such as Mijnheer Hendricksen, to see?'

His face hardens for a brief second, then takes on a vulpine smile. 'You are forward, Master Archer - but not so forward as to know who are your real friends - and who your enemies. Beware, lest too much confidence should lead to *madness*.' He pauses a moment, to assess if I take the significance of his emphasis. He dips to chuck Charlie under the chin. 'Take care of this young man, Master Archer - the city streets are dangerous places - as you know to your cost.'

Then, with the curtest of nods and one last mocking smile, he turns on his heel and launches himself into the mêlée of traffic, flitting like a carrion raven between carriages and coaches till he gains the portico of the Royal Exchange, where a dusky carriage bearing the arms of Sir William Hervey awaits.

I vent my anger on poor Charlie. 'I thought you said no-one followed!'

'Nor did they - on foot,' he protests. 'You said naught about fine gennelmen in coaches!'

'He is no gentleman - but say, did you see that coach at London Wall?'

'To be sure, one very like passed me before turning

up Finsbury. Ten minutes later it returned, leisurely-like and turned down Bishopsgate. 'Tis but a cat's fart from there to 'Change. Who is he, Will?'

'Nathaniel Grey - Hervey's creature.'

Who, I have little doubt, is now on his way to report me to his master.

As I must do to mine.

At the Bedford Coffee House Mr Garrick is in his usual place by the window. But today he is not reading the newspaper. He is deep in conversation with a man I do not recognise.

As soon as he sees me, Garrick leaps to his feet and bids me join them. He turns to his companion. 'James, allow me to introduce young Will Archer, an actor of no little talent and, like you, a seeker after justice.'

The stranger looks up. Dark eyes in a frank visage. For a moment he scrutinises me, then nods and smiles, giving the impression I have passed some test. He holds out his hand and grips mine firmly. 'James Lacy, one-time actor with Mr Fielding's company, and upholder of free-speech... Delighted to make your acquaintance, Master Archer.'

'The honour is all mine, sir.' The name, I now recall, is familiar. 'I have read your pamphlet upon the Licensing Act.'

'A vindictive piece of legislation, Master Archer, designed to curb the right of every citizen to speak his mind. Yet our self-styled Prime Minister may soon, God willing, have his comeuppance!'

I am aware that Lacy is a vociferous opponent of Walpole, not only for his proscription of theatres, but also for his alleged abuses of power. After my brush with Sir William Hervey and his creature, Grey, I am keen to know more of their master. 'His comeuppance? How so, sir?'

'There are those within his own party that would have him out. He is old and grows indolent. Yet it is events abroad that will prove his downfall. He has little appetite for war, believing it bad for trade. But the common people take it ill that dago pirates board our ships with impunity. They would have him prosecute the war against Spain with more vigour.'

'And war costs money...'

'Indeed it does, Master Archer - money that Walpole would not have the country risk.'

'Is that such a bad thing, James?' I know Mr Garrick to be generous to me personally, but among others he has a reputation for parsimony. 'Whatever may be said against him, Walpole knows the value of money. He came to power on the back of the South Sea fiasco, did he not? When the country was almost bankrupt after years of war?'

Lacy is dismissive. 'That was twenty years ago, Davey. The country has moved on, but Walpole has not. That is why he faces opposition even within the Whigs. Carteret is the coming man and he supports war. Not only against Spain - for there are other stirrings afoot in Europe.'

'The Prussian cub, Frederick? He is no threat to us, surely?'

'Do not be too sure! He thought to march into Silesia unopposed. But the new filly in charge of Austria showed more spunk than he allowed for. And the French, scenting rich pickings in the disputed territory, are set to join the fray. If they do, their route lies straight through the Low Countries and into Hanover - our revered monarch's homeland! Do you think King George will stand for that?'

'So England may have to go to war, like it or not?' say I. 'And Walpole - if he survives - must find the money from somewhere?'

'You have hit it, Master Archer! The only thing that keeps Walpole in power at the moment is that he has the favour of the King - but that will not last long if he opposes war when Hanover is threatened.'

Lacy's words make me think. If Walpole needs money - and large amounts - who better to approach than our allies the Dutch, well known as traders and merchants? And who better to start with than a banker like Hendricksen? Hervey's warning to stay away from the Mijnheer, and Grey's presence at the Exchange begin to make sense - they don't want a cub like me upsetting their delicate negotiations...

'Tell me, Mr Lacy,' I say, 'is there any substance to the rumours that Walpole has set up a department of government that has no name - a sort of secret service whose purpose is to bring about things, er - unofficially?'

Lacy regards me narrowly. 'There is much talk of Walpole's spies and agents, but tangible proof is hard to come by. Yet reputations are destroyed, opponents miraculously converted and people mysteriously disappear...'

'And if Walpole falls, these spies and agents would fall with him?'

Lacy smiles grimly. 'Ah, there you show your naïveté, Will. Such an organisation tends to take on a life of its own, independent of its creator. Walpole may well have found it expedient, but those who run it now will regard it as indispensable - there are those at Westminster who will ensure its survival.'

I glance across at Garrick and see that he's thinking the same as I.

Lowering his voice, he leans closer to Lacy. 'Sir William Hervey?'

The flash of alarm in Lacy's eyes is enough. 'A man to stay clear of, Davey. And dangerous to talk of...'

It is clear that Lacy prefers the conversation to pursue less contentious paths, so he and Garrick revert to talking theatre. In normal circumstances, gossip of the management deficiencies of Fleetwood at Drury Lane, the triviality of Rich's Covent Garden or the lure of Sheridan's Smock Alley Theatre in Dublin, would easily engage me. But after what I have just heard from James Lacy, my mind is a-buzz with conjecture.

I know now why Hervey warned me off. If Hendricksen is a possible financier for potential war, my investigation into Harry's death is an irritant. Like a blowfly hovering about the meat of Hendricksen's riches, I must be swatted away. His threat to use my past to disgrace me - Grey's implicit threat to Charlie, barely an hour ago... Is it Hervey I have to thank, too, for the attack on me the other night?

Once I allow this thought rein, speculation gallops. What about poor Joe, the street boy? Or even Hendricksen's own sons - one disgraced, another murdered...

No. Surely no-one would be so ruthless just to clear the way to the old banker's money...?

Besides, if Hervey really has dealt so decisively with Nicklaas and Hendrick Hendricksen, why has he not done the same with me? Why go through all the rigmarole of warnings and threats?

As Garrick and Lacy chatter away beside me, and the usual hubbub of the Bedford washes round me, my mind goes back to the interview with Hervey. Underneath the apparent affability that Sir Francis had advised me to be wary of, the cold authority had been unmistakable. Yet in certain looks I thought I had caught - what? - appraisal? - challenge? It was almost as if he expected something of me... Something, perhaps, that the Hendricksen brothers wouldn't provide, and that simple, insignificant Joe couldn't?

'Come, Will, we must be on our way.'

Garrick has risen. I join him in taking our leave of James Lacy. But he has noticed my distraction.

Once outside, he says, 'You are pensive, Will? Is it the business of poor Harry?'

'Not entirely, sir.' It is difficult enough to bring my thoughts to order - let alone explain them to another. 'You would not take it amiss if I were to walk awhile - alone?'

I sense his disappointment. All the same, he says, 'As you wish, my boy. You will be home in time for dinner? I would not have you abroad after dark again.'

Reassured by his continuing concern, I part from him and we go our separate ways.

Debts

My mind preoccupied, I let my feet take me where they will, and find myself in the Strand among the beaumonde who flock here daily to the multitude of shops dealing in fashion and fripperies, everything that fine ladies and gentlemen could want in the way of perukes, pomades and the trappings of elegance.

A dowdy enough figure I make as I thread my way among peacock dandies. I know some of my humble rank come to admire and wonder at the gaudy cavalcade. But they do not impress me as they totter by on their high heels, flouncing their canes and simpering over each other, for I have seen another side of such shallow painted butterflies during my time at Mother Ransom's molly house. There, under the paint and patches, the fine clothes and affectation, I have seen both foulness and vulnerability.

A shrill, braying laugh from one popinjay startles me from my reverie. He greets acquaintances with wide-flung arms and kissing of cheeks.

What am I doing here? Can it be that, deep down, I harbour some hope of seeing Agnes, seeking remedy for her spirits in the distraction of silks and lace after the visit to Bethlem? Yet as I near Temple Bar even that frail hope flutters to extinction as the stench of the Fleet Ditch begins to pervade the air.

Suddenly, lightly, someone touches my arm.

'Master Archer - Will?'

The sudden pang of hope is soon dashed. It is not

she, but Tom Parsons. He looks haunted, eyes fearful with daylight phantoms, his face white and drawn.

'Why, Tom, what ails you?'

With timid desperation, he draws my arm through his and, with an anxious glance over his shoulder, hurries me onward. 'You come most opportune, dear friend. Come, let us walk.'

I cannot say I welcome such intimacy, but I can not repulse his obvious distress. So I allow him to hurry me along until by degrees his agitation and his pace show some abatement.

'You have been shopping in the Strand, Will?' His voice is brittle, shrill with feigned interest.

'I have been observing those who do.' I humour him. 'I cannot afford such prices. Smithfield and the Garden serve my needs - or Cheapside when I am in funds. Which is not often!'

My jauntiness does not seem to cheer him. Indeed, he seems not to remark it, for as we approach the Fleet Bridge, I feel him shiver and catch his fearful glance towards the stark, forbidding walls of the Fleet Prison.

'God save me!' He murmurs it so soft that perhaps he does not realise he has said it at all. But I hear it plain enough. And it helps explain his present agitation.

The Fleet Prison, where - like the Marshalsea over the river at Southwark - debtors are incarcerated.

I recall our earlier conversation, when he confessed his addiction to gambling. Not two hundred yards from where he accosted me is one of the most notorious gaming clubs in London, the Bacchus, situated in a huge underground vault beneath the Strand. Is it from there that he has come?

I place my hand upon his. 'You are faint, Tom. Come, let us put the ditch miasma behind us. It infects the air.' In truth, the Fleet Ditch is particularly malodorous today, but my concern, though genuine, is also a ruse to draw him out. We enter St Paul's churchyard and there, in the shadow of the great cathedral, he finally breaks.

'I have been *foolish*, Will, *weak* and *reckless*.' With each emphasis, he strikes his head so fiercely that I have to catch his fists to prevent further harm. 'That bastard Aikin!'

'He has been taunting you again?'

'He was at the Bacchus - he and his succubus, Foote. They challenged me to cards.'

'And you lost?'

'Of course I lost!' he cries. 'How could I not, with their goading and their foul innuendoes - oh, and all done so politely and like gentlemen. So civilly!'

All at once, emotion burns him out and he collapses. My hands, still about his wrists to restrain his self-belabouring, are called on for support as he slumps against me, sobbing. Suddenly he seizes my shoulders, anguish brimming his eyes. 'What am I to do, Will? He threatens to arraign me for non-payment of gaming debts - I shall go to prison!'

Gently, I release his hold and lead him to a bench beside the churchyard wall. 'Have you no resources?'

'None,' he says hopelessly. 'All lost - all gambled away - how could I have been so stupid!'

'Your mother, she is alive still. Would she not help?'

He looks at me despairingly. 'Of course she would. But how can I ask her? My father left her only a modest stipend. Besides, the shame... it would kill her.'

He shakes his head. 'No, Will, I am irredeemable. I had a fortune - and I squandered it. What am I to do?'

'Aikin knows you have nothing?'

'Yes - but that will not stop him. He will have me arrested.'

I am not so sure. I suspect Aikin delights in tormenting people, watching them wriggle, extending their agony. He'll prefer his plaything close at hand, to observe and goad, not locked away in prison.

'I do not think he will bring an action against you.'

'How can you think that? What is there to stop him?'

I can hardly tell Tom he's too tempting a victim.

I think quickly. 'His friend, Foote, may stop him. From what I hear, his finances are none too secure. If Aikin were to take action against you, much unwelcome light might also be shed upon Foote's difficulties.'

Hope flickers in his eyes. 'Oh, Will, do you really think so?' But just as swiftly, he is downcast again. 'He still has me in his power, though. He will humiliate me still.'

His self-pity starts to annoy me. His problems are nothing to those Charlie and I have overcome. His misfortunes are of his own making.

'You can remedy this, Tom. Take courage, man! Steel yourself against his insults - words, when all is said and done, are only words. From today you must endeavour to save and not squander money. I know not what you owe, but in time you will repay your debt and be free of him.'

'I will do it!' he cries eagerly. Then, before I can stop him, he clasps me to his chest. 'You are my saviour, Will Archer. I am eternally in your debt.'

'No more talk of debts, Tom!' I joke, prising him gently off me.

But he retains hold of my hand. 'With Harry gone, I thought I had no one to turn to. When he died, my world seemed empty. I loved him, Will. I want you to know that. And he - he...' He falters into silence. Then, after a moment he raises his downcast eyes. 'Now you have let me hope again.'

The ardour of his gaze is unnerving. 'I offer advice, that's all, Tom.'

'And - friendship?' Between his eyes, a small crease of dismay, pleading.

I get up from the bench, businesslike. 'You may count on it, Tom. But your best friend must be yourself - you alone can decide your fate.'

'You hearten me prodigiously, Will!' he exclaims, rising. 'Come - I am born anew! Whither are you bound? We will go together.'

Thus we continue along Cheapside and Cornhill until we part company, he to his lodgings, I to mine and all the while he chatters with a hectic gaiety that is almost as unsettling as his previous despair.

As I turn towards home I can't help thinking that though I have brought him some comfort, Tom Parsons may expect more from me than I am prepared to give.

Daylight is fading as I climb the stairs to my garret. But there is one more task that needs to be done. If, as I suspect, Hervey has been responsible for removing Nicklaas and Hendrick in his quest for the old banker's money, there is yet one more person who stands in his way. Agnes. But how to warn her without alarming her?

After rejecting numerous drafts, I settle on:

My Lady Agnes,
I suspect someone may be seeking to do you harm. Pray be not alarmed, but be vigilant at all times. Be alone only with those you trust and do not venture out without a companion. And be assured that, should you ever need someone to turn to, I am here.
Yr humble servant,
WA

I search out Charlie and give him the note, telling him he must deliver it only to the lady in person.

'Billet-doux, is it?' the young rogue jeers. 'Another secret assignation?'

'Mind your business,' I tell him, 'and be about it, sharpish!'

I give him sixpence to expedite his errand.

'Lawks!' he exclaims, gawping at such generosity. 'You 'ave got it bad!'

I watch him scamper off down the street and return indoors.

From Mr Garrick's parlour comes the sound of raised voices.

'No, I tell you! I have the greatest respect for you but I will not be dictated to by you!'

'Dictated to!' Macklin's roar is unmistakable. 'You are unjust, sir! Have I not many a time given advice upon your acting, that you have allowed to be right, and have adopted my advice?'

'I freely own it. But in this instance, you are wrong, sir.'

'I cannot credit your inability to see what talents Mr Foote would bring to the company! He shows promise as an actor and has a fine way with words.'

'A satirical rogue, I grant you, with an undoubted talent for mimicry - a talent that too often appears malevolent. His presence would sow dissension.'

'Mr Aikin recommends him highly.'

'Mr Aikin's recommendation is no recommendation.'

'You are impossible, Garrick!'

The door bursts open and a red-faced Macklin storms out, almost knocking me over.

'Ha! Here's your protégé, Garrick! Listening at doors, eh? Well, that's what you get when you take in street boys and prefer them to true-born gentlemen!'

He slams out into the street.

'You must excuse Mr Macklin, Will,' says Garrick behind me, 'rash words, spoken in anger.'

''Tis no matter, sir.'

'Come in, Will.'

I follow him into the parlour, where a fire burns cheerily in the grate.

'Your solitary walk has resolved your thoughts?'

'Somewhat, sir.'

Surprisingly, he does not press me further. He has matter of his own to impart. 'Sit down, Will. I have something to tell you.'

I do as I'm told as he takes a letter from the mantelshelf and sits in the chair opposite.

'I have received distressing news, Will. Not, I must own, unexpected, but none the less aggravating. Mr Giffard writes that it is highly likely Goodmans Fields must close before the season's end. It appears Mr

Fleetwood and Mr Rich are threatening legal action.'

'Legal action - against Mr Giffard? On what grounds, sir?'

'On the grounds that the theatre is in breach of contract. It was a condition of re-opening that we would present only musical entertainments - which, clearly we have not.'

'We have presented what the public would have us perform...'

'As our capacity audiences have testified - indeed, that is true. But if the audiences are flocking to us, it follows that they are deserting the Garden and Drury Lane.'

'Are Mr Fleetwood and Mr Rich likely to succeed in their attempt to close us down?'

'They have approached Sir John Barnard, the magistrate, who, as you know has made no secret of his animosity to us. Mr Giffard knows that if an action is brought, we will lose.'

'Then we are homeless?' I cannot hide my dismay.

'Not quite.' He smiles conspiratorially. 'I was not unprepared for such an eventuality. Had *Richard III* been received less warmly, we would not be in this situation. Goodmans Fields theatre is, regrettably, the victim of its own success.'

'Rather of your success, sir. It is to see you perform that people come.'

'You are kind, Will - and I am not being immodest in admitting the truth of it. Which is why Mr Fleetwood at Drury Lane has offered me £500 per annum to appear next season at Drury Lane.'

Five hundred pounds! It is a huge amount - as much as Quin, who has been acting for over forty years, is said to earn. Mr Garrick is very astute in financial matters, but is he deluding himself? How often has he talked of Fleetwood's extravagances - his lavish town house, his several coaches, his alleged bevy of mistresses - and rumours of actors salaries in arrears, costumes and effects being impounded? Yet now he is considering working for him...

'And will you accept his offer?'

'I have told him I will consider it. But there must be provisos - if he is to have me, I shall reserve the right to recommend others, too.'

'I trust Mr Aikin will not be one of them?'

'No, Mr Aikin will not, Will. I am surprised you need to ask.'

I tell him of the threat to Tom Parsons.

'That boy is a fool unto himself,' says Garrick irritably. 'Yet he is unmatched in pathetic roles. I should be sorry to lose him.'

'So should I. He was very close to Harry Henderson and I am sure he has not yet told all he knows in the matter of his death.'

'Ah, Will, still searching after justice...' He returns to his main concern and his tone becomes solemn. 'I regret, Will. I cannot ask Mr Fleetwood to take you on as an actor. Fine as you may become, you are yet green - and there are others more experienced...'

My heart plummets. Here it is - I am to be thrown back onto the streets... Where will I go? I have nowhere. Since escaping from Mother Ransom's, my life with Mr Garrick has been a felicity whose end I have never dared to contemplate.

'I am most grateful for your past kindness, sir,' I murmur, choking, 'but if I must leave here...'

'You must prepare yourself, Will,' says he with infinite sadness. 'If I accept Mr Fleetwood's offer, you must say farewell to your attic, to this house that has been your home.'

He sees my distress. Cocking an eyebrow, he continues briskly, 'We all must - Drury Lane is too large a distance. I have already made enquiries about accommodation nearer to hand and more suited to my promised income. And I fully intend to take Mrs Wiggins, Susan, Charlie and yourself, of course, with me. You shall be my manservant, a kind of valet-cum-footman-cum-butler.' He pauses, as if struck by doubt. 'Provided, of course, that this is agreeable to you, and you have no other plans?'

Other plans? Agreeable to me? I have much to do to prevent myself falling weeping upon his neck as Tom Parsons recently did to me! Instead, I give him heartfelt thanks and take the stairs two at a time to my lowly attic.

Snow

Next morning, I awake to a milky obscurity. My attic windows are thick with ice, luminescent, pearly blind eyes against the outside world. The frost, threatening for days past, has finally struck in force, ushering in snow overnight like a silent felon, leaving the city smothered.

My room is icy cold, my extremities numb, and my normal clothes no guard against the cold. Hastily pulling on my breeches over my night-shirt, I creep downstairs to where Harry Henderson's trunk of clothes lies, unmoved since Charlie and I retrieved it from his lodgings and Agnes bequeathed it to me. Today I feel the need of undergarments and fine wool.

Though I choose the soberest shade of green, it doesn't prevent Mrs Wiggins from standing back, hands on hips and surveying me as I enter the kitchen for breakfast.

'Lord save us! Who's this dandy?' she crows.

Susan strokes the jacket and tests the thickness of the shirt between finger and thumb. Then as Mrs Wiggins busies herself at the range, she slyly inserts her hand inside my waistband. 'Linen drawers, too! What a fine gentleman!'

I squirm, embarrassed, one eye on Mrs Wiggins' back, as Susan's fingers explore further. I discover for the first time the restrictive nature of undergarments. Susan laughs and returns to her tasks as I discreetly adjust the damage she's wrought.

Two minutes later, Charlie bounces in, teeth chattering, and makes for the warmth of the range. 'Not too close,' scolds Mrs Wiggins, 'you'll get chilblains.'

'A rare biter out there, Mrs W,' he gasps between shivers. 'Pump's frozen and snow over shoes. Horses steamin' like they wus on fire.'

'Here, Susan, see to Will's breakfast,' says Mrs Wiggins, taking Charlie's red hands between her own and chafing them vigorously.

Charlie notices me for the first time. His eyes widen. 'S'welp me! Oo's the toff?' He extracts one hand from Mrs Wiggins and knuckles his forehead. 'Hexcuse my shiverin', yer Honour, but I bin out in the cold, cold snow, a'freezing mi cullions off...'

'Language!' scolds Mrs Wiggins.

'Very droll,' I reply and turn my attention to my bacon.

After a few moments, Charlie releases himself from Mrs Wiggins' ministrations and sidles over to me. 'If that's still Will Archer under the posh duds, I've a message for 'im.'

'Hand it over, then.'

''Taint written.' He helps himself to a slice of my breakfast and licks his greasy fingers with a leer. 'Give it me by mouth, she did.' He waggles his eyebrows lasciviously.

I glance over my shoulder. Susan is elbow deep in the sink, humming to herself. Mrs Wiggins is clattering pans. I bunch his shirt collar in my fist and drag him close, hissing, 'Out with it, pickle!'

Charlie grins. 'The lady says thank you kindly for your concern.'

'Is that all?'

'Unless you want the buss she gave me for you...' He puckers his lips.

'She kissed you?' I push him away.

He falls about with laughter.

'Your face!' he yelps. 'Of course she didn't, you looby. My ears, you have got it bad, ain't you?'

My foolishness at his goading still rankles as the company gathers later that morning at the theatre. News of our impending demise has already circulated. But chill and bereft as the theatre now seems, I am intrigued to see that gloom is not universal amongst those present.

Septimus Drake, looking more than usually melancholic, seems wearily resigned. Like any ageing but prudent actor, he will have a little put by, and sufficient contacts to give prospect of some sort of engagement next season.

I doubt that any such fortune, meagre as it might be, awaits old Garbutt. His reputation for difficulty and unreliability is well-known. Random employment in the provinces, monologues in alehouses are the best he might hope for. Then penury and the workhouse. It's clear he sees it too, for even this early in the morning, he reeks of drink.

Ned Phillimore and Kitty Blair, however, are in unaccountably cheerful spirits. He beckons me over and, with a quick glance to see that we are not overheard, he says with barely muted glee, 'Give us joy, Will! Kitty and I are off to Dublin to be Mr Sheridan's pair of ingenues. The Liffey calls!'

I have heard complimentary talk of the Smock Alley

Theatre. Thomas Sheridan, its enterprising manager, completely rebuilt it in 1735, transforming it from little more than a bear garden and brothel into a well-respected theatre, the centre of Dublin's cultural life. Since then, Sheridan has wooed many English actors to cross the Irish Sea. Dublin, apparently, is like a little London and Smock Alley is fast becoming as desirable a place to work as Drury Lane or Covent Garden.

I wish Ned and Kitty every success. 'I am very pleased for you both.'

'There may yet be further cause for congratulation,' says Ned, glancing teasingly at his companion. 'Miss Blair has allowed me to pay my addresses to her.'

'You could not wish for a better man, Miss Blair,' say I.

She flutters her eyelashes coquettishly. 'Nor Ned for a better woman, Master Archer, I am sure you will agree?'

'That goes without saying,' I reply gallantly. In private, I wonder if Kitty Blair will be satisfied with Ned. He's a fine fellow, but he lacks the one attribute, money, that I suspect she prizes above all others. I hope Ned won't be disappointed.

I have no leisure to indulge such doubts, however, for John Aikin strides in, casting scornful looks at those already assembled.

'So, here we all are,' he scoffs, 'rats scuttling about the sinking ship! Our revered captain not here, I note.'

'Mr Garrick is on his way,' I tell him.

He pointedly ignores me.

'I'll wager the old bear and the captain's moll won't show their faces,' he jeers to one and all. 'Too high and mighty for the likes of us. Too busy ingratiating themselves with other managers, no doubt.'

'No fear of you doing that, eh Aikin?' retorts Ned Phillimore. 'Calling Macklin an old bear? I'd be careful if I were you. Biting the hand that feeds, and all that.'

'I don't need his patronage.'

'Unlike your friend Foote?'

Aikin gives Ned a venomous look, but says nothing. The dart, I see, has gone home, but Ned is not an adversary that Aikin cares to cross.

Tom Parsons has crept in quietly during the foregoing exchange and is keeping out of Aikin's way. He is pale and heavy-eyed. He catches my eye briefly and glances away, blushing.

Garrick arrives in muffler and greatcoat, accompanied by Peg Woffington, fur-clad from head to toe.

His speech to the assembled company is brief. He tells of the impending lawsuit. Speculates upon how long we may have left. January he feels will be secure. February - possible. But he suggests people should make plans to seek alternative engagements from March.

At the end, Septimus Drake shakes Garrick's hand with lugubrious politeness. Garbutt, however, shambles unsteadily out without taking leave of anyone.

I turn to find Tom Parsons at my elbow.

'What will you do now, Will?'

I tell him of Mr Garrick's offer. 'And you, Tom?'

'I must return to my mother in Twickenham,' he says dejectedly. 'I have nowhere else.'

'Be not so glum. There, you will at least be out of Aikin's way.'

Aikin is at this moment complaining volubly to Mr Garrick. Peg Woffington is making little attempt to hide her disdain as he pleads servilely for Garrick's favour. But Garrick simply shakes his head until at last Aikin turns on his heel and flounces away.

As he leaves he throws a look of outright malice in my direction and favours Tom with a gloating sneer.

'We are well rid of him,' says Garrick coming over to us.

'And all such,' adds Mrs Woffington. 'Unnatural brute.'

'Unnatural, madam?' I ask.

'You are such an innocent, Master Archer,' she laughs. 'Mr Aikin loves not the fair sex, or had you not noticed?'

Out of the corner of my eye, I observe the colour rising to Tom's face.

'From my observations, madam, Mr Aikin shows scant love for any creature, male or female.'

'Very true, Master Archer. I stand corrected.' She smiles radiantly. 'But, from what Davey tells me, I must soon learn to address you as Will, as we are like to be under the same roof, you and I?'

I blink, not immediately understanding. Under the same roof? Mr Garrick did not mention that Mrs Woffington was to become part of our new household. I look to him for confirmation, but he has taken Tom aside, perhaps to tell him he will intercede for him with Mr Fleetwood.

Her smile broadens at my hesitation. 'I see he has not told you. You are shocked...'

'Not at all, ma'am,' I reply gallantly. 'It will be an honour.'

'Ah, Will, you are such an innocent!' She leans close. 'Have a care of Aikin, though. He said some very nasty things about you to Mr Garrick just now.'

'I pay no heed to Mr Aikin's malice, Mrs Woffington.'

'That is brave of you. But do not ignore him, neither. Vipers are dangerous when trodden on.'

I thank her for her advice. When she and Garrick leave, arm in arm, I turn to Tom.

'Mr Garrick has given you good news, Tom?'

He shrugs, disconsolately. I find my patience growing thin.

'So what ails you still?'

'Have even you forgotten, Will? 'Tis Harry's funeral today.'

To my dismay, with all that has happened, it has slipped my mind.

Whilst old man Hendricksen will not welcome our presence, I feel it is only right that I agree to accompany Tom - if only to let Harry's spirit know his friends have not abandoned him.

By the time Tom and I arrive at the Dutch Church in Austin Fryers, the sun is shining in a clear blue sky. The air around our ears is crisp as the snow that sparkles white on spires and tombstones. It is a fairy-tale world, transformed and magical. Not in the least funereal.

Already a crowd has assembled, black-clad, solemn. Friends and business associates of the family judging from snatches of conversation that drift by us as Tom and I take up a discreet position near the churchyard wall. The hearse and the close family mourners have not yet arrived, so I have leisure to cast my eye over the scene. A goodly number of those assembled are similar in feature to old Hendricksen - squat, dough-faced Netherlanders - relatives or fellow-countrymen? Others, erect and fashionable, reek of wealth - his fellow bankers, no doubt. Their mourning clothes are not scuffed or shiny at elbow like ours. Their voices are suitably hushed and respectful but I doubt their regard for the deceased is as genuine as that of Tom and myself. We may not have known Harry Henderson well, but I am sure he found more affection and friendship in his last months with us than with any here today.

A crunch of wheels in the snow announces the arrival of the hearse. Four black-plumed horses are reined in beyond the churchyard wall and the black bulk of the carriage creaks to a halt. As the horses paw the trampled snow, their flanks steaming, snorting clouds of vapour into the cold air, the coffin is slid from the hearse. It must be carried from the churchyard gate into the church and thence to the grave which yawns black amidst the snow.

The onlookers doff hats and bow their heads as the casket, its bearers' upper bodies obscured by the black pall which drapes it, proceeds like a slow, many-legged insect between rows of tombstones. Behind it, three figures - old Hendricksen in the centre, supported by a black-veiled Agnes on one side and - I cannot help gasping in surprise - Nicklaas Hendricksen, his face almost as pale as the surrounding snow.

Beside me I hear Tom's sharp intake of breath. He has never seen Harry's brother before and here, in the harsh bright light of the winter's day, the resemblance is uncanny. He grasps my arm and, fearing he may swoon, I put a supportive arm around him. He whimpers soundlessly as slowly the crowd falls in behind the procession passing into the church.

I am all for leaving as the last few disappear into the shadowy porch, but Tom pulls my arm. 'Come, Will,' he says, 'we must see him through to the end.'

We slip in to the back of the Church, unremarked. The service is in Dutch. The words may be incomprehensible but their solemnity is evident and beside me Tom weeps silently, brushing aside his tears with fierce sweeps of his cuff.

At last the congregation rises and the coffin is taken up again. Once more it proceeds, a lugubrious sable caterpillar, up the central aisle and out towards the awaiting grave. As it passes, I see Agnes's black-veiled head turn and am sure I detect the faintest inclination in my direction. If so, it is the only acknowledgement of our presence, for old Hendricksen plods hunch-shouldered beside her and Nicklaas, still ashen-faced, stares stonily ahead.

After the dimness of the Church, the sunlight reflecting from the snow is blinding. The Pastor is already intoning the words of interment as Tom and I slip once more into the shelter of the churchyard wall.

The hearse, with its four sable horses has departed. In its place, the Hendricksen Landau with Menninck, the dumb coachman, sitting inscrutable on the box.

At a discreet distance, well-to-do carriages line the road ready to carry the bankers back to their world of business after the inconvenience of the funeral. Among them I note, with a faint thrill of unease, one with an all-too-familiar crest. Sir William Hervey was not in the congregation - why is his coach here?

But I have no time to speculate further. The coffin is lowered into the grave and Hendricksen throws a handful of earth upon it. Gradually the crowd begins to disperse.

As some gather about old Hendricksen to offer their respects, I see Agnes lead Nicklaas aside. Unhurriedly but unmistakably she heads in my direction, keeping tight hold of her companion's arm, politely fielding condolences from departing guests as she passes through the assembly. Nicklaas allows himself to be led, a bewildered smile hovering on his lips as he nods dazed acknowledgement to respectful sympathisers. I cannot begin to think what a trial all this must be for him.

My own companion, Tom, seems little less bemused. He cannot take his eyes off Nicklaas as the pair approach. It is as if he has seen a ghost.

'Master Archer.' Her face half seen through the dusky material, her soft voice sending shivers through me. 'You risk Mijnheer's displeasure, yet still you have come - that is noble of you.'

'It is for Harry's sake that Tom and I are here.'

She turns her gaze on Tom. 'You, too, are in Mr Garrick's company, sir?'

I make the necessary introductions.

'And you also knew Hendrick, Mr Parsons?'

'Indeed, Madam - Harry and I were... We were - friends.'

As he falters into silence, it is clear that his hesitancy has conveyed more than his actual words.

'Ha!' barks Nicklaas, and for a moment I see contempt in those normally vacant eyes. 'Hendrick had need of such friends!'

'Charity, Claas,' Agnes reprimands him. 'He was your brother.'

Nicklaas looks downcast as a rebuked child.

Tom finds his voice again. 'You are very like him, sir. The resemblance is most striking.'

'A little more than kith, but less than kind, sir!' Nicklaas finds the quotation highly amusing. 'Sorry to disappoint you.'

Tom is clearly disconcerted by young Hendricksen's sudden shifts of mood. He does not know his history.

Agnes places a restraining hand upon her companion's arm.

'You must forgive Nicklaas, sir,' she says to Tom. 'The occasion is very stressful for him.'

'As indeed it is for us all, Miss Mayer.'

She starts at the interruption. Another has joined us. But her dismay is nothing to my own.

'We meet again, Master Archer,' says Sir William Hervey, 'under unexpected - and unfortunate - circumstances.'

The sad smile is one of condolence, but I am left in no doubt as to his real meaning. Here I am, caught in a situation he expressly warned me against.

'Sir William,' I murmur nonplussed.

'Master Archer and his friend are here at my invitation, Sir William,' says Agnes serenely. 'They knew Hendrick in his last months - probably, to my regret, better than his own family. I regarded it as only fitting they be allowed to pay their respects.' Then, with a cool temerity which leaves me speechless, 'Their presence here is therefore less surprising than your own, if you will allow me to say so. I was not aware that you had any dealings with my deceased fiancé.'

Hervey acknowledges the affront with a tight smile. 'You speak true, madam. My dealings are with his father, Mijnheer Hendricksen. I am here to show my respect for his grief. And to acknowledge your fortitude, Miss Mayer, in your loss. You appear to be bearing it with extraordinary courage.'

'You are too kind, Sir William. But we women have more strength than perhaps you give us credit for.'

'I do not doubt it.' Then, with a low bow, 'Your servant, madam. And yours, Master Archer. I look forward to renewing our acquaintance under more congenial circumstances.'

As he goes, I see another figure waiting beside his coach. It is Nathaniel Gray who, as his master joins him, shakes his head slowly from side to side. Even at this distance I can see the mockery in his face.

Agnes lays a gloved hand upon my arm. 'You are acquainted with that odious man, Will?'

'Would I were not.' I glance nervously at my companions. Tom seems unable to wrench his eyes from Nicklaas Hendricksen, while he, in turn, gazes vacantly about him. Nevertheless I lower my voice. 'The letter I sent, warning you...'

'It was about him?'

'He is not a man to be crossed.'

'Dear Will, I applaud your concern - but put your mind at rest - I know Sir William Hervey better than you imagine, and I assure you I regard him as no sort of threat.'

'You would do well not to underestimate him.'

Her laugh tinkles, cold as the surrounding air. 'Oh, I

do not, Will - I do not. Now, If you will excuse us, I see Mijnheer is ready to go. Come Nicklaas.'

Obediently, he follows her back to where old Hendricksen waits. I watch the three of them go towards the Landau which is now almost the only carriage remaining. As they approach it, a disreputable looking figure slinks into view from behind. Agnes stops, appears to entreat the old man who dismisses her pleas with a wave of his arm. He acknowledges the newcomer with a curt nod and turns on his heel. Menninck helps him into the Landau.

The man seizes Nicklaas's arm and pushes him towards another vehicle, box-like with but one barred window. And it is then I recognise him. The man is Jack Sampson, the surly Bedlam warder, and he is clearly there to escort Nicklaas back to the madhouse.

For a moment Agnes detains him and they converse briefly. Then, Sampson offering his hand, she angrily brushes it away and goes to join old Hendricksen in the carriage.

Sampson, his mocking smile apparent even at this distance as he insolently salutes her, hustles the bewildered Nicklaas to the madhouse van.

Frost Fair

At breakfast next morning, Charlie bursts into the kitchen, jumping like a firecracker.

'There's people walking on the river,' he cries excitedly. 'Down by London Bridge, the water's frozen. They say there's going to be a Frost Fair. There's hucksters already a-linin' up their booths on the bank...'

Breathless and lost for words in his elation, he falls to pummelling me. I fend him off as Susan laughs. Even Mrs Wiggins cannot forbear to smile.

'Peace, you madcap,' chides Susan. She hands him a chunk of bread spread with beef dripping, well peppered against the cold. 'What say you, Will? Shall you and I and Charlie go down there this afternoon?'

It is Sunday, her afternoon off, when she and I are wont to walk in the park and marvel at the nobs. More often than not, in clement weather, our excursions culminate in some secluded bower where my little soldier is called up for action. 'Tis full three weeks since our last outing, and I can see from the sparkle in her eye that she's as eager to engage him in another outdoor skirmish as am I. But if Charlie comes with us...

Susan glances at him as he devours his fat treat and gives me a big wink to put my mind at rest. Clearly she's thought of a solution.

So it is that, at just a little after two, we all three set off towards the river. The afternoon is bright, but towards the west the sky looks bruised with the promise of more snow. We are well muffled against the cold, Susan in her woollen cloak, whilst I wear a fine wool coat from Harry's chest and feel quite the dandy.

Below the Tower of London the river runs sluggish, choked with great blocks of ice. Only a narrow channel, hardly wider than a country stream, snakes down the middle.

Beyond the narrow arches of London Bridge, however, where blocks of ice have lodged against the piers and dammed the flow, the river is solid. The ice here must be six inches thick at least and is already crowded with people laughing and chattering as they gingerly trust their feet to the precarious surface. Enterprising stall-holders have already set out their wares - sweetmeats, trinkets, even an ox roasting on a spit. Dozens of small boys whizz past, playing chase, pulling sleds across the ice from Old Swan Stairs to Southwark on the far bank, filling the air with their delighted cries.

Charlie's eyes are wide with wonder. Susan snuggles close, stroking the soft wool of my coat. Together we thread our way through the crowd, sensing the excitement of new experience. Under our feet the ice creaks and I cannot help but think of the water below. Beneath patches clear as glass, I glimpse the slide and slither of flattened bubbles large as dinner plates and begin to feel giddy as a green sailor. I feel my whole world tilting...

Suddenly Charlie is shouting. 'Hold fast, you sneakin' dipper!' He leaps towards me and hauls a skinny urchin from behind my back. 'Don't you see 'oo yor a-nickin' from?'

A grubby face looks up at me, wide-eyed with fear. Then recognition dawns.

My ice-nausea fuels my anger. 'You again!'

I make a grab at his ragged shirt but Charlie intervenes. 'Steady on, Will. Natty di'nt mean nothin', did yer?' He digs his companion in the ribs. 'Say somethin', yer clodpole.'

'Sorry, guv,' mutters Natty.

'It's yer fancy coat,' says Charlie. 'Mistook you for a gent, lord knows why! Anyhow, you owes Natty 'ere an apology - you should be thankin' 'im, not cloutin' 'is 'earole...'

'For picking my pocket!'

'Nah - come on, fair do's - 'e did 'elp save yer life when you was clobbered that night.'

Natty looks up with a shy smile.

I grunt reluctant acknowledgement. 'Thanks for that.'

'Come, Will,' says Susan who has observed the encounter with amusement, 'you can do better than that. Give him a sixpence. There's a pie stall back there. The lad looks half-starved.'

As I delve into my pocket, she whispers in my ear, 'And I might have a treat for *you* as well.'

I give Charlie two tanners and bid him and Natty investigate the other stalls after they've enjoyed their pie. 'Be back here before nightfall,' I tell him. It is already past three. The light will start fading within the hour. Time enough for Susan and I to find a secluded corner to exercise my little soldier.

She, in fact, has already noted a convenient spot as we wandered about the fair. Ducking behind the line of stalls, we squeeze past mounds of ice piled against stone buttresses into the gloom of a bridge arch. Here, against the rough stonework, we fall to kissing. Her cold afternoon skin smells of kitchen soap, her lips and mouth sweet as a warm posset.

Her deft fingers unlace me and she stifles a giggle as she encounters the unaccustomed underwear, kneading me into frenzy through the linen until I can bear it no longer, my little soldier standing so stiff he hurts.

I give over stroking her breasts and wrench my drawers and breeches down to my knees, letting my subaltern spring to attention against my stomach. Then, up with her petticoat - she wears no drawers - and he plunges into the heat of action.

So lusty an account does he give of himself that we cannot forbear crying aloud in admiration of his endeavours. But, mindful of the echoes set up by our acclaim, we must cover mouths with our hands and stifle our ecstasy. Thus the battle rages until, both sides breathing heavy with excitement, Susan pushes me away, forcing my lieutenant to disengage. After a brief hand-to-hand tussle, he discharges his shot in a series of far-reaching volleys, that draw gasps of admiration from Susan and of elation from myself.

Entwined in each other's arms, panting still, the heat of our encounter drains away. Gently, Susan strokes my retreating soldier, murmuring, 'Well done, my fine fellow - but no babbies yet, thank you very much.'

The chill of the afternoon creeps about my naked buttocks and I pull up my drawers. Susan, too, adjusts her dress. The gloom under the bridge has thickened into darkness and beyond the ice-sculpted arch we see the flicker of torches.

We emerge into a demoniacal twilight, torch-lit

grinning faces dancing against the darkness, flames reflected in the glassy surface underfoot - smoke from the ox-roast and the steam of breath from countless mouths billowing grey as the reeks of hell.

If anything, the crowd has multiplied and we are carried along through the jostling, shouting throng until we arrive at our appointed meeting-place with Charlie.

He is not there.

We wait for five minutes - ten. Around us, the mob surges, intent on enjoyment. There is still much to delight us - but inside me the smallest seed of unease slowly sprouts.

'Come,' says Susan at last, 'he's probably gone home - or off with his pal.'

'That's what worries me... I would not have him in the company of pickpockets.'

'Nay, Will, you're not his keeper. Charlie's got an older head on his shoulders than you give him credit for. He'll come to no harm.'

And so, half-an hour past the time appointed for him to meet us, she persuades me to set off for home.

After the glare and bustle of the ice-fair, the streets are dark and unusually quiet. Susan and I stay close, holding on to one another, treading carefully over the rutted snow. And at every measured footstep, my anxiety increases.

I think of how I first found Charlie huddling, half-starved, a shivering child of the streets - and saw in him what I might so easily have been if fortune, in her admittedly capricious way, had not favoured me. I think how devoted he is to me, how intimate the bond between us... His failure to turn up at the appointed time is so out of character that I cannot help but worry.

Suddenly the fear of harm overwhelms me. I choke back a sob.

'Why, Will, what ails you?' Susan is all concern.

I essay a laugh. ''Tis nothing. Just wait till I get my hands on the addle-pate!'

But when at last we reach Mr Garrick's lodging, all thought of Charlie is swept away.

There is a note awaiting me. It is from Agnes.

Dearest Will, she writes, *I write in haste. Something dreadful has happened and there is none other I may turn to. Tomorrow I shall persuade Mijnheer to let me visit the Frost Fair at noon. Please meet me there. As we may be observed, our encounter must appear fortuitous. I pray you, do not fail me. A.*

Her hastily scribbled words set my heart and mind a-racing. I cannot deny my elation at her summons - and her addressing me as Dearest! - but what event can be so dreadful that I must be her only recourse in distress?

Has aught happened to Nicklaas, or old Hendricksen?

Or has her bold exchange with Sir William Hervey at the funeral rebounded upon her?

Having, as I suspect, disposed of Hendricksen's two sons in order to secure his fortune for Walpole, has Hervey now turned his attention to Agnes? Is her life in danger?

One thing is certain - I shall get no rest tonight.

To still the turmoil of my emotions, I set out for the Ship Tavern, hard by the theatre. Perhaps poor Joe, the street boy, and the surly watchman were not the only ones who witnessed comings and goings on the night of Harry's murder? It is a long shot, but far better I occupy my mind in some pursuit than sit brooding in my garret.

I change into my own old, shabby clothes. Harry's fine wool coat would only draw unwelcome attention in such a place as the Ship. Once outside Mr Garrick's door, I unfasten my queue and ruffle my hair, scoop dirt under my fingernails and smear my hands and face. Then, suitably unkempt, I set off towards Goodmans Fields.

It may be Sunday, but the night-time streets are no less populous for that. The Sabbath means little to the low life of London. Nearing my goal, the going underfoot becomes easier, the day's snow turned to muddy slush by the passage of countless feet.

The Ship is cramped and smoky, a warren of dim-lit rooms each with its huddle of ill-kempt bodies hushed or raucous, buzzing with talk and furtive, fumbling encounters. A warm blast of sweat and stale beer meets me as I edge my way in. A few look my way, some assessing, some hostile, but most do not spare me a second glance.

As the landlord takes my coin and hands me a tankard of ale, I casually remark, 'Odd goings-on at the theatre over the way last week, I hear?'

His eyes flash momentary suspicion, but he is ready to talk.'The dead man, you mean?'

'Aye - topped 'isself, didn't he?'

'So they say.'

'Know 'im, did yer? A reg'lar?'

The landlord frowns. 'What's it to you?'

'Nothin' - just interested. See anything of it, did yer,

that night?'

But this is a step too far. He leans close. 'I saw nothing. I minds me own business. And if you knows what's good for yer, you'll do the same.'

From an adjoining room comes a shout of, 'Holla, Ned! Two of stingo and a six-and-tips for Patrick.' The landlord, with one last glower, turns his back on me.

I take a seat in a dark corner and apply myself to my drink, covertly scanning the other customers.

After a while, I'm aware that I, too, am being observed. An ugly youth, his face scarred by acne, leans on the chimney breast. As I catch his eye, his lips part in a half-smile, revealing a snaggle of brown broken teeth.

I lower my eyes, unsure of his purpose. But only moments pass before he sidles across.

He indicates the space beside me. 'Yer don't mind, do yer?'

He takes my half-shrug as acceptance and seats himself on the bench. 'Bit o' company don't come amiss, eh? George Gedge.' He offers a grimy hand. 'And you?'

'Will - Will Archer.' No point in lying. There's little likelihood of my being known.

'Pleased to make yer acquaintance, Will Archer.' He leans close, confidential. His breath has a stable reek. 'You ain't the law, is yer? Only I couldn't help overhearing you talkin' to old Ned about the murder the other night...'

I am uncomfortably aware of his thigh, hot against my own - but if that's what it takes to get the information...

'Murder?' I say, puzzled. 'I 'eard it was suicide.'

'That's what they'd like yer to think.'

'But you think different? Saw something, did yer?' I try to keep the eagerness out of my voice.

He grins - not a pretty sight. 'Aye. I was on a promise with Bess Ballard. She'd had a skinful and was up for a romp so we went along the alley, the two of us...'

'And?'

He shoves his empty tankard towards me. 'Be a pal, eh, and I'll tell yer.'

I order two more pints of porter.

'Well?' I say after he has taken a long, leisurely draught.

'Well, Bess had just sported her dairy and was a-loosening my breeches to give my pizzle a bit o' the old hornpipe jig when I spied someone sneakin into the back door of the theatre.'

'A man?'

'Aye, difficult to tell at a distance, but he walked liked a man. Then, hardly had I got my hand up Bess's smicket when another two shows up.'

'Two more men?'

'I don't rightly know. It were dark, and they was all muffled up. Besides, Bess was hotting up...'

'You didn't see anyone else?'

'I didn't see nothin for a while because I was otherwise engaged, wasn't I? The old hair-splitter was well away into cock-alley... But then, just as pego was about to shoot his load, there was one devil of a screech. At first I thought it was Bess - she's a rowdy whore at times! Near put me off my stride, it did. But no, it weren't her a-screeting – it was a'comin' from over at the playhouse. I screws my head round just in time to see some kid belting off round the corner.'

Joe, the street boy.

'Was he one of those you saw go in earlier?'

'Nah, the others was all dressed up. He was all ragged.'

So Joe must have crept in whilst Gedge and his paramour were at it. Had Agnes slipped in unnoticed, too? But what of the other men - were they Harry's killers? And had they left before Agnes or Joe arrived?

'You didn't see anyone else come or go?'

'Not then, because Bess heaves me round and slams me against the wall a-pumping up and down, intent on getting her share, seeing as I've already 'ad my bit of pleasure. But once she's dismounted and we're 'avin' a bit of a cuddle and a draw on me pipe, there was comings and goings a-plenty. The kid comes back with the watchman in tow. Five minutes and they're out again, the watchman haulin' the youngster after him. Then, near on half an hour later, just as I was leavin' for home, the watchman's back again, with a couple of gents this time.'

Garrick and Macklin. So Gedge must have left before Charlie and I arrived.

We chat a while longer, during which time I glean that no-one else saw more than he. Then, before his familiarity becomes oppressive, I take my leave and head back to Mr Garrick's house. By now it is nearly two-o'clock in the morning and a sharp frost is crusting the trampled snow. I take care not to let my thoughts distract me from dangers underfoot and in the shadows. I will not be surprised again as I was after leaving Agnes. Only when I am once more in the safety of my garret do I give myself leave to mull over what I have learned.

Patchy and unreliable as Gedge's story is, it has thrown new light on the events of that night.

One man, presumably Harry, followed by two others... Infuriatingly, Gedge did not observe them closely enough to provide an adequate description.

Hervey's men? Or someone with a more personal grudge?

The next thing I know, it is morning, and Mr Garrick is calling me. However tumultuous my thoughts on Gedge's story and my imminent tryst with Agnes, exhaustion has claimed me and I am late for rehearsal.

Marriage

Whatever I may think of Aikin's character, I cannot deny his power as an actor - in certain roles.

As I watch from the wings I think how well the pent-up grievance and desire for revenge in the character of Tomazo suits him. Lying in wait for DeFlores, his voice oozes discontent around the empty theatre:

I cannot taste the benefits of life
With the same relish I was wont to do.
Man I grow weary of, and hold his fellowship
A treacherous, bloody friendship, and because
I am ignorant in whom my wrath should settle,
I must think all men villains...

To think all men villains must be a sad state indeed. Or is it I who am too trusting - too willing to see the good rather than the evil in others? Even Aikin - sneering, scathing Aikin - surely has some redeeming quality? Has he, like Tomazo whom he plays with such conviction, suffered some great loss that he holds the fellowship of man treacherous? And are Tom Parsons and myself included in that fellowship?

My reverie is broken by Macklin elbowing me aside to make his entrance.

It is our last rehearsal before we perform tomorrow evening. The production is ragged and Mr Garrick's temper is short. Already he can sense the critics distilling their venom. But the show will go on, if only to reward all the work the company has put into it.

Unless some unforeseen disaster prevents it.

As the play approaches its closing scene my heart quickens for my final cue. In my role as Antonio, I have acted the madman, declared my love to Isabella, spurned her when she dons the disguise of a madwoman herself, and now am about to confess my folly.

Yes, sir, I was chang'd too, from a little ass as I was to a great fool as I am; and had like to ha' been chang'd to the gallows but that you know my innocence always excuses me.

My innocence, or rather inexperience, as an actor does not excuse me yet another irritated exclamation from Garrick as I stumble over my lines. It is not my first mistake. I have already had barbed comments from Aikin and Macklin, and even Ned Phillimore has joked about my gaucheness, so by the time Mr Garrick begins on the Epilogue I am feeling thoroughly miserable. To my mind, the unaccustomed briskness of his delivery signals his displeasure:

All we can do to comfort one another,
To stay a brother's sorrow for a brother...

If only I could be sure of such comfort! As it is, I feel I have let the whole company down, not least Mr Garrick who reposed such trust in me.

And what an irony that my debut should be in *The*

Changeling, a play in which no-one is what they seem, where everyone adopts a disguise to hide their true purpose, for during the last three hours it has become only too evident that any attempt to disguise myself as an actor has been less than convincing!

The last thing I need is Aikin approaching me as the company disperses. Under their hooded lids, his eyes gleam with malice.

'How gratified Mr Garrick must be with his protégé. When the wits of the town feast upon you, I trust he'll be as eager to rescue you as he was to exalt you. My only hope is that my repute is not sullied by such mediocrity.'

My hackles rise. 'Little fear of that, sir,' I reply. 'Your repute is already well known. Mine at least may yet improve.'

His mouth twists in a triumphant sneer, pleased that I have risen to his taunt. 'You would put me down, Master Archer? Have a care, sir. I will not be affronted.'

'The affront was yours, sir, in the first place.'

For a moment, he assesses me, a half-smile playing about his mouth. My open defiance has caused some subtle shift in his demeanour towards me that I am at a loss to explain. He says softly, 'You display spirit, Master Archer - you would engage with me?'

His eyes seem to drill into me. What is he at? Is he calling me out - or has he some less honourable purpose? I stand firm under his scrutiny. 'I would not, sir - not in any way.'

He reddens momentarily, then sniffs and tosses his head. 'Very well, Master Archer. You have made your decision - an unwise one, I may say. I trust you will not live to regret it.'

'How, sir? Unwise?'

But he is gone, a mocking half-smile still on his lips, and I sense Tom Parsons next to me.

'Was he talking of me?'

'No. His insults were for me only.'

'Oh, Will, I'm sorry.' Tom grasps my hand and would put his arm around my shoulder, but I shrug it away, too wound-up to bear his self-serving pity.

It is time he was honest with me. My agitation makes me bold. The time for dissimulation is past.

I confront him. 'Tom, when we spoke the other day of Harry, you were understandably upset. You told me in the warmest terms how he defended you from Aikin, and how you loved him for it. I ask you now - was that love more than simple gratitude? Were you and Harry, in every sense, lovers?'

His eyes widen in shock at my directness. I see denial flit across his mind. Then something else - relief? He gulps and looks down. 'I - I loved him, yes. You know, Will - you understand... You will not tell on us...? Now he's gone I care not what becomes of me, but I would not have Harry's memory traduced...'

'Never fear, Tom. Your secret is safe with me. You have my word.'

'So kind and gentle he was, Will. I never thought to find love - but he...'

I see tears mist his eyes and think how vulnerable he is, how artlessly he reveals himself.

And if his emotions are so transparent to me, I wonder if others, less sympathetic than I, have observed them too – and perhaps used them for their own ends?

'It wasn't because you owed him money that Aikin demanded favours, was it, Tom?' I say. 'It was because he guessed about you and Harry and threatened to expose you unless you submitted to his demands... Am I right?'

Anger flares in his eyes and through stiff lips, he mutters, 'He was jealous, Will. He wanted to destroy us... He took every opportunity to taunt and goad us - insinuating in front of others - never quite to the point of revealing our relationship, but enough to put more pressure on me, hoping I would at last submit to his foul advances. But Harry kept me strong, and that infuriated Aikin.'

Enough to murder...? I have dismissed the idea of Aikin killing Harry through professional envy - but does this new jealousy make his motive stronger?

'You remember what you said the first time we talked after Harry's death? You accused Aikin of hounding him to commit suicide. If I tell you that I don't believe Harry took his own life but was murdered - do you think Aikin could have done it?'

'Oh, he could have - I don't doubt it! - and would have, given the opportunity.' Grimly, he exhales. 'But, Will, you cannot know how much it pains me to tell you this... I know it not to be true - Aikin did not kill Harry.'

'How can you be so sure?'

'The very night that Harry died, Aikin and Foote were with me at the Bacchus. We played until the early hours.'

I put my hand on his shoulder. 'I'm sorry, Tom. That is noble - to exonerate him you hate so much. Especially after you've told me the truth about you and

Harry.'

He takes my hand. 'You understand, Will? Do you, truly? And you do not despise us?' His eyes are eager. 'Surely only one who feels the same...? You and I - could we..?'

Gently, I detach his grasp. 'No, Tom,' I say softly. 'You may count me a friend, but not a lover.'

He looks so disconsolate that I cannot forbear from offering him a crumb of hope. As well as the libertines at Mother Ransom's there were several unhappy souls whose one desire had been for a quiet life with a companion of their heart. If one such could be found for Tom...

'Don't be downcast,' I tell him. 'I said you may count me a friend, and I hope I can prove a true one - I may have the means to bring you to one who shares your desires...'

'Could you, Will? Is there indeed such a one?'

'More than you would credit, Tom.'

He wrings my hands in thanks, but I have no time for his gratitude. Agnes awaits me at the Frost Fair.

There is no heat in the mid-day sun, but the chill in the air seems less - or is it just the prospect of meeting her?

The Fair is as much a-bustle today as it was yesterday evening – but the crowd is different.

Gentry, few of whom were there last night, wary of shadows and mayhem in the flickering torch-light, now amble, preening, in the brightness of noon. The banners may be as garish, but the hubbub is less raucous.

Hucksters at their stalls court notice with eloquent gestures rather than shout their wares. It is almost as refined as a mêlée at Vauxhall Pleasure Gardens - except that ragged urchins dart amidst the colourful throng.

Seeing them reminds me of Charlie. Still not returned when I left for rehearsal this morning, he may, for aught I know, now be warming himself against the fire in Mrs Wiggins's kitchen, but the worm of anxiety still gnaws and I shall not be easy until his ear is near enough to cuff for thoughtlessness.

The smell from a pie-stall reminds me that, in the rush to rehearsal, I missed breakfast this morning. The savour of gravy is tempting a sixpence from my pocket when I espy Agnes at a ribbon stall. My stomach grumbles protest as I abandon base appetite and thread my way through the crowd towards her.

'Why, Master Archer!' Prettily, she feigns surprise as I come up behind her. 'What an unexpected pleasure. I had thought you busy with preparations for your forthcoming performance.'

'Indeed, Madam, my morning has been thus engaged. But, my afternoon being at leisure, I thought to sample the delights of the Frost Fair - it being an uncertain feast, so to speak, dependent upon the continuance of the weather...'

Fitting in with her pretence of a chance meeting, I'm prattling foolishly - but mention of a feast sets my stomach a-growling once more. I feel myself blushing.

She hands a bunch of ribbons to the stall-holder. 'These, I think.' Then, as the transaction is completed, she turns with a questioning smile. 'You will do me the honour to walk with me, Master Archer? We may admire the attractions together.'

'My pleasure, Madam.' I bow and offer my arm,

which causes a bubble of my innards that I attempt to suppress. Without success.

Agnes looks at me mischievously. 'Something tells me you are hungry.'

I smile, embarrassed.

'Come,' she says, taking my arm, 'there is a sweetmeat stall yonder. I have no appetite at present for savoury stuffs – but honeyed cakes and sugared buns are all my fancy.'

Though I would prefer a hearty meat pie, I settle for a currant bun and a piece of apple pie. Agnes selects several delicate sugared cakes. We walk towards the middle of the river, where the crowds are less. There is no place to sit, so we pause mid-river and eat.

Abjuring further conversation she displays surprising appetite, devouring the cakes with what, in another, I would consider unseemly haste. Then, hunger sated, she licks the last traces of sugar from her lips.

'Now, Will, enough of formality. We are not overheard out here. The clandestine nature of this meeting is unfortunate, but necessary - I need your help, Will.'

My mouth is full of pie. 'Of course,' I mumble, 'anything that is in my power to do...'

She holds up a hand. 'Hear me out, Will. You remember I told you that the principal reason for my presence in Mijnheer Hendricksen's house was because I was affianced to Harry?'

I nod acknowledgement.

'Well, now that Harry has gone, so has my reason to stay.'

'Old Hendricksen will not cast you off, surely?

Where can you go?'

'As for that, I have a distant aunt in Holland who has a small property in Antwerp which is mine whenever I require it. No match, of course, for Mijnheer's house, or for what our family once had - but enough for a spinster lacking both fortune and prospects.' She turns and gazes wistfully across the frozen river. Under our feet, I am aware that the ice is wet, less crisp than last night, more glassy clear above the swirling dark beneath. 'If only it were so simple,' she sighs. 'But Mijnheer would have me stay...'

'That must be a good thing, surely?'

'Oh, Will, my innocent boy! It is not from the goodness of his heart - there is a condition to my remaining, and that condition is that I should marry...'

'Not Nicklaas?'

A short, reckless laugh. 'No, not Nicklaas - Mijnheer would have me marry himself. That he may yet produce an heir who will not bring disgrace to the Hendricksen name.'

'But he is an old man!'

She shudders. 'Exactly, Will. The thought of his old flesh on mine...'

''Tis not to be borne!'

'Which is why I must beg your aid, Will. Mijnheer would have us marry in three days time. Before then, I intend to steal away. But there are things I am loth to leave - jewels, clothes - the last remnants of my dowry. I cannot carry them myself...'

'Fear not, Agnes - what would you have me do? Name it.'

'Today is Monday. Tomorrow, late at night, I shall order Menninck to bring the carriage, on the pretext of an urgent summons from Bedlam - some harm befallen to Nicklaas. He is accustomed to obeying without question. Mijnheer retires by half-past nine at the latest. That will allow you time to come after the performance and help me carry my few last chattels. As the river is still impassable here in the city, I shall direct Menninck to drive us all the way to Gravesend where I shall take the Rotterdam packet...'

'But will Menninck not suspect? He is loyal, you said, to Mijnheer...'

'So he is. But he also understands my situation, and though he be dumb, he is not insensible to my distress.'

'But if he informs Mijnheer of my part in the affair...?'

'How? He cannot speak and is unable to read or write. Why else do you suppose Mijnheer reposes such trust in him? But, if you are afraid, Will...'

'My only fear is for you, Agnes, for your safety.'

'In that case, will you do it?'

'You may rely on me. I shall be at Hanover Square, without fail, at eleven tomorrow night.'

Disaster

I creep back into Mr Garrick's lodgings unnoticed, desirous to avoid his further displeasure after this morning's disappointment. The gloom of encroaching evening shrouds the house, echoing my mood. From the parlour I hear voices - Mistress Woffington and my master, low, muted - and tread past carefully.

In the kitchen, Susan listlessly scrubs the table while Mrs Wiggins sleeps in her rocker, her mouth ajar, glutinously snoring. Susan looks up as I poke my head round the door, gives a silent shake and grimace indicating that Charlie has not yet returned, and returns to her scouring.

I retreat upstairs.

As I enter my dim attic room, a gleam of white attracts my attention. It is a scrap of paper on the boards just inside the door.

Picking it up, I read: *If you would see the brat again, be at St Paul's churchyard at nine. Come alone.*

All at once, the room lurches and I sink onto my bed. It is several moments before I can muster my thoughts. I re-read the note again and again, striving to find more meaning than those few words can deliver.

Anger churns within me - if they have harmed him...! And behind the anger a growing disquiet - why St Paul's churchyard at night, that haunt of jades and mollies? Is it a reference to my own past, or an attempt - a threat - to debauch the child?

I leap down the stairs to the kitchen. 'Has anyone

been asking for me?' I ask Susan.

'And who should that be?' she retorts with raised eyebrow. 'Will Archer, the talk of the town is he that the beau-monde must all be inquiring after him?' But then she sees my concern. 'What's the matter, Will?'

'Has anyone been here this afternoon?'

'Why, only the world and his wife - Mr Garrick has not had a moment...'

'Who, can you tell me, Susan?'

'First there was that old actor, what's his name? Voice like a parson...'

'Drake?'

'Aye - that's the one. Then Ned and Kitty - they're to be wed, did you know, and off to Dublin?'

'Yes, I know - any other of the company?'

'Well, Mrs W. sent me out on an errand around two, but when I come back, there was that old bear, Macklin, at the door with Mr Aikin and another gent...'

'Pasty-faced, plump?'

'That's him.'

'Foote - his friend.'

'Then comes Mr Giffard...'

'The owner of the theatre? I thought he was out of town...'

'Well, he's back - and no more than a couple of minutes and there's a right to-do - raised voices, shouting... Then I heard some of them storm out...'

'Who?'

'I was at the sink - 'twas only the sound of their boots and the slamming of the door - but then a while after, as I was emptying the slops in the area, I hear Mr Giffard and Mr Garrick up in the street and looked up to see them talking to some queer little cove all in

215

black. Refined voice he had, oily. And then Mrs Peg arrived.'

'And you never saw any of them near my room?'

'From the kitchen! No, except when I went out to the shop, or was emptying the slops, I saw nobody, only recognised their voices.'

'All members of the company, apart from the stranger who was talking to Mr Garrick and Mr Giffard.' I muse to myself. 'He was all in black, you say? Anything else you noticed about him?'

But Susan has lost patience with my interrogation, and refuses to answer any more until I tell her what is wrong, which, she being as fond of Charlie as I, I cannot bring myself to do. In any case, Mrs Wiggins is stirring and preparations for dinner will soon be under way. Promising to let her know when I myself know more, I leave her sulking.

Yet from what she's told me, the stranger in black sounds uncannily like Nathaniel Gray. What business he should have with my master I am at a loss to fathom.

It is Garrick himself who enlightens me. As I come from below stairs, he emerges from the parlour. His irritation of this morning is gone and he greets me, smiling.

'Will, shall you dine with us this evening?'

'That would be kind, sir, but I would not intrude...'

'No intrusion, Will.' He ushers me into the parlour where Mrs Woffington rises from her chair by the fire. 'Peg and I would welcome your company. Won't we, my dear?'

'Of course.' She gives me a sly smile. 'You will be glad of a kind word or two, am I not right, Will?'

'You refer to this morning's mortification, ma'am? I can but apologise most heartily to Mr Garrick.'

'No need, Will. It happens to us all.' There is a mischievous glint in her eye. 'How else are we to improve as actors if we are not dissatisfied with our first performance? I have already reprimanded Davey for his over-loud tutting which I am sure only increased your discomposure.'

'Truly, Will, you were not nearly so bad as you think,' agrees Garrick, clapping me on the shoulder. 'And you have had other things on your mind of late. Is there news of Charlie?'

My gratitude at Garrick's forgiveness encourages me to show him the note.

A line creases his forehead. 'This was put under your door this afternoon, you say?'

'Susan tells me you had several visitors, sir?'

For the next half hour we go over who among them might have slipped upstairs to my room and confess ourselves baffled that any should have any reason, or be so malicious as to abduct a twelve-year-old boy.

But Garrick makes no mention of the stranger in black.

At last I ask, 'There were no others beside members of the company and Mr Foote?'

Garrick shakes his head, remembering. 'None, Will... Ah! There was someone - 'twas as Mr Giffard took his leave. A small man, neat - well-spoken. But he did not come inside the house.'

'His business, sir?'

'He recognised Mr Giffard and paused to pass the time of day. He seemed to have knowledge of various members of the company... Was complimentary of our talent...'

'He gave no name? Nor any reason to be passing your door?'

Garrick smiles indulgently. 'My dear Will, a chance conversation that lasted no more than a few minutes... Would you have me interrogate every passing well-wisher? Why such interest? There is no way he could be the bearer of this note. Have you considered that your suspicions over poor Harry's death and your concern for Charlie may, perhaps, be leading you to see malice where none exists?'

He has reason. I have no evidence that the stranger was Nathaniel Gray - only an inner conviction... After all, at our meeting after the Bedlam visit, his threat to Charlie was more than implicit - if I had any more dealings with Hanover Square, there would be consequences. What else can Charlie's kidnapping be but reprisal for my attending Hendrick's funeral?

Mistress Peg places her hand on mine. 'What do you intend to do about this note, Will?'

'What else but do as it tells me, ma'am? I shall go to St Paul's. I would not have the boy come to harm.'

'And what of any harm to yourself? Should you not take someone with you?'

'That might risk the very thing I would avoid, ma'am - the writer specifically states I must be alone. Who knows what he might do to Charlie if I disobey?'

'All the same,' says Garrick, 'it might be better if someone were at hand... A member of the Watch to follow at a distance, perhaps? I could accompany him...'

'It is time I set off,' say I. 'You must do as you see fit, Mr Garrick, but I would prefer not to know.'

Taking my leave, I race up to my attic and don a caped coat from Harry's trunk, for during our talk I have heard rain begin lashing at the parlour windows. Then, head bent against the icy blast, I set my course for St Paul's churchyard.

The route through Cornhill, Poultry and Cheapside is so familiar that I traverse it out of habit, my thoughts all concerned with what might lie ahead. The roads, so populous in daytime with brokers at the Exchange, with traders, beggars and the like, with coaches and chairmen crowding the way, are at night eerily quiet. Those few abroad on this rain-swept winter evening stride as swiftly as the slush underfoot allows, heads bowed, shoulders hunched, avoiding human contact. Out of the shadows they loom and are gone.

I would cut through the lesser streets but that the uncleared snow and darkness make them dangerous. So I stick to the main thoroughfares, until the bulk of St Paul's looms black against the leaden sky.

Here, the denizens of the night change. No longer do huddled figures hurry past. Now shadows peel from the dark of arches or from the shade of trees, inviting trade. Little enough to be had on this unwholesome night. But this only makes them more bold, encouraged perhaps by the fact that I must pause each time to discover if the importuner is the one who has summoned me hither. I lose count of the number of grasping hands I shrug off, the number of pleasures unnamed or shamelessly offered that I refuse, until I penetrate almost to the very walls of the Cathedral, still seeking Charlie's kidnapper.

Under cover of the walls, the rain is less but activity

more. Couples take the place of soliciting whores. As I pass, I hear their furtive grappling, the grunts and moans, the sharp intake of breath. Every other gloomy alcove, dripping bower or moss-grown tomb seems to writhe with copulation.

Repellent as it is, my spirits rise, for here a child in company with a man will pass unremarked. There will be several such among the unseen shadows, men too afraid or impecunious to visit a molly house buying street boys' mouths or arses for a few pennies.

Suddenly there's an outraged screech and a man barges past, hitching his breeches as he runs. He is followed by a whore, hair flying. 'Come back and pay your dues, you poxy bastard son of a bitch!'

She trips on a root and goes sprawling as the man makes his escape, laughing.

I stoop to help her up, but she thrusts aside my arm. Close to, I see the lines on her face, the sores that are already eating away her nose. 'Keep yer mitts off of me, unless you're goin' to pay fer the privilege.' Her breath, through blackened teeth, stinks of onions. As she heaves herself to her feet she looks at me for the first time and her mouth leers into seduction. 'You're a pretty boy, though - I'll give you a good time...'

I side-step the hand that reaches to squeeze my crotch and make my escape.

Circumnavigating the cathedral, I come round to the south side. The rain, less persistent now but colder with sharp stinging hailstones among the drops, gusts in sudden squalls from the river. There are fewer couples on this side, only the most hardy, or desperate, willing to brave the cold. But I have gone no more than a few paces when a dark figure resolves itself from the night and blocks my path.

'Archer!' The voice is hoarse, little more than a whisper muffled by a scarf which hides the lower half of a face already shadowed by a tricorn hat. Even so, disguised as it is, there is something vaguely familiar in its tone.

But I have no time to reflect, for as soon as I stop I am seized from behind and my arms pinioned. A gloved hand prevents me from calling out.

The figure in front turns, beckoning me to follow. I have no choice. My captor bundles me forward, kneeing me in the back and kicking my feet to urge me on.

Thus we proceed down a steep, narrow way towards the river until we emerge on a riverside wharf. Behind and to either side in the gloom stretches a broad way which must be Thames Street. Ahead is the open river, frozen still, on which the occasional squalls patter like grapeshot as the ice strains and creaks. My captor thrusts me forward on to a wooden pier that juts out over the ice.

On either side are steep drops to the mud banks of the Thames.

Many is the story of poor unfortunates, their bodies claimed by the sucking mud, who lie hidden for years until the tide uncovers them. Am I to add to their number? I struggle against my restraint, uttering muffled protests through the hand clamped over my mouth. But then reason penetrates my panic. The water is frozen - so, too, must the mud be.

And, even as I think this, I begin to make out a shapeless bundle lying at the end of the pier. A bundle which, sensing our approach, begins to wriggle and squirm.

The figure which has preceded us aims a kick at the trussed-up boy. For, now we are close, I can see it is indeed Charlie, his wrists and feet tied, his mouth gagged. With a twist of his body he avoids the foot and lands a double-footed kick on the ankles of his tormentor.

'Bastard boy!' curses the figure, reaching down and hauling Charlie to his feet.

And immediately I know who it is.

Lurching forward, and stiffening my arms painfully behind me, I take my captor off his guard. He takes his hand from my mouth to help secure my arms again, and I take the opportunity of his panic to kick out backwards. It is a pleasure to feel my foot connect with the flabbiness of his belly. His hold on me releases as he staggers back, winded.

In front of me, the figure throws Charlie aside and leaps towards me. As we grapple, I tear the scarf from his face and my suspicions are confirmed.

'Aikin! What in God's name...?'

But I get no further, for Foote - who else could it be? - clamps me again from behind and takes me off-balance. Both of us fall heavily upon the wooden boards. But this time Aikin is not taken unawares. He closes in on us as we struggle, punching me till I submit.

He kneels astride us, panting. 'So, Archer - I have you where I want you at last. No Garrick to save you here.'

Beneath me, I hear Foote protesting. Aikin steps back and pulls us both to our feet. 'Hold him firm this time.' He retreats a moment and then hauls Charlie closer. 'Let the brat see how brave his hero really is, eh?'

From his pocket, he draws a short heavy club. 'See how well you play your part tomorrow with a broken rib or two, eh, Archer?'

'Is that what this is all about?' I pant. 'Jealousy?'

Aikin puts his face up against mine. 'Me? Jealous of you?' he sneers. 'You flatter yourself, boy. You're not an actor - you're just an upstart that Garrick's soft on. There's nothing personal in this. I'm doing this for the honour of the profession.'

'And is it honour dictates your lackey here must hold me while you cudgel me? Is that the bravery you'd have the lad see?'

His gaze does not waver, nor does his face retreat as he hisses. 'Foote - stand aside!'

'John...'

'Do as I say.' As soon as Foote releases his hold, Aikin grabs my wrist. 'You have spirit, Archer. I'll say that for you. If only you had been more amenable... It could have been you and I, Will... ' I feel the cudgel in between my legs. Almost tenderly, he lets it slide against my balls. 'A pity I'll never know - your prick – is it as pretty as your face, eh? What am I missing...?'

And now it is his hand, not the wood, that strokes while his face is so close I can feel his breath, sickly sweet and insidious as his whisper.

Suddenly I understand how Tom Parsons must have felt – but I am not Tom...

I hold his gaze, half smiling, and submit to his lewd caress. He is not the first man to handle me thus. My time at Mother Ransom's taught me to dissemble pleasure. Not difficult - for a young man's virility through instinct will often rise of its own accord. As happens now.

I see puzzlement in his eyes as he feels my growing firmness. 'You do not recoil from me, Will...? Indeed, the opposite - can it be that you...?' His voice betrays uncertainty – and hope?

I play to my advantage. Coyly, I lower my eyes. 'How, John, could I have ever aspired...?'

I bring my free hand to caress his cheek, let my lips brush his...

At first he resists, still unsure, but then I feel him yield. His body moulds itself to me and fiercely his lips fasten on mine.

And this is the moment I choose to knee him in the balls.

As he bends double, I seize the cudgel, wrench it from his grasp and in one slicing movement, swing it round to crack against Foote's knee as he starts forward. He screams in pain and collapses, clutching his leg.

Flinging aside the club, I am ready for Aikin as he staggers upright, his face a mask of fury, and we lock arms with one another.

He is stronger than I gave him credit for. Fop he may be, but there is sinew beneath the silk. He fights with the fury of thwarted desire, but also with the desperation of one unused to single combat.

Ordering Foote to release me was an act of bravado which I shall make him regret. Used to having others support him, he has not the skill to overpower me, lunging and grabbing without method. My greater nimbleness prevents him gaining a permanent hold on me.

Yet I, too, am finding it difficult to lay solid hold on him. Thus we wrestle for I know not how long, each of us gripping, losing hold, striving to land the one decisive blow that will subdue the other.

Out of the corner of my eye, I'm aware that Foote is slowly getting back to his feet, testing his injured leg. And that Charlie, rolling over and over in his bonds, is attempting to follow our ungainly struggle.

Suddenly the boards are no longer under me. Without realising it, we have edged ever closer to the end of the jetty where it projects into the river.

Now, as Aikin seizes my arm, dodging to avoid my blow, he loses his footing and drags me over.

We fall, arms flailing, through the sodden night. Landing winds us both. The ice groans under the impact and I am almost sure I feel it heave under us.

Rolling over, I make a grab for Aikin but he scrambles away, sliding spread-eagled. I clamber to my knees, sure now that the surface beneath me is pitching. Before me, Aikin has risen shakily to his feet, still half bending, his hand on the ice for balance.

With a kind of horror I hear the ice crack and tear. Dark snakes wriggle towards Aikin as he totters. The whole ice surface bucks and rocks, sending him staggering drunkenly. I see terror in his face. Then, as a huge section breaks off, he slithers, clutching frantically but hopelessly until he is pitched into the dark waters beneath.

A moment later he surfaces, spluttering. 'Help me!' His scream is strangled as once more he disappears below the surface.

Beyond him, towards the middle of the river, huge blocks of ice are tumbling slowly, inexorably in the gloom. Nearer the bank, however, the ice is still holding.

Above me, I am aware of Foote's terrified face peering over the edge of the jetty.

'Untie Charlie,' I yell, scrambling out of my overcoat. 'He is light. With his aid we may yet save him.'

Gingerly, I creep over the creaking ice towards Aikin, who is still floundering, coming to the surface and submerging again. How long can one survive in such freezing water?

His struggling is causing the ice under me to rise and fall with the swell, but still I inch forward, trying to ignore the cracking around me.

Next time he comes to the surface, I can see he is almost done.

I fling my coat towards him. 'Take hold of this,' I shout.

He scrabbles desperately, but it eludes his grasp, five inches short of his clutching fingers. He claws at the edge of the ice, maintaining a tenuous hold. 'For the love of God, Archer...!'

'Stay still - we're coming to get you.'

There is less than ten foot between us. Already smaller chunks of ice are breaking off but one thicker section provides a possible causeway. I direct him towards it.

And now Charlie is beside me.

'Spread out on your belly,' I tell the boy, passing him the coat. 'Throw this as far as you can towards Aikin. I'll keep tight hold of your foot.'

Charlie mutters under his breath, 'Let the bugger drown, I would.' But still he does as I tell him.

Gradually, we spread ourselves as far as possible towards Aikin who clings desperately to the edge of the ice, grasping with alternate hands as his grip slides. His face is deathly white and I can hear his teeth chattering as he shivers uncontrollably.

At last Charlie manages to slide the coat within his reach. With a supreme effort, Aikin heaves himself almost to chest height on the ice and lunges.

With a terrific crack the ice under Charlie's nose sunders. He scrambles back relinquishing his grasp upon the coat. Aikin, his lifeline useless, pitches back into the depths, my coat slithering after him.

I haul Charlie back from the brink as all around us cracks multiply. Desperately, we both scramble back to the frozen mud bank. Only when we both feel solid ground under us do we look back.

Now even the edge of the river is breaking up. Slabs of ice, large and small, are detaching themselves and turning to flow sluggishly down-river. Nearer the middle of the channel, the flow is swifter as the river re-asserts itself.

Of Aikin there is no sign.

For the first time I feel how cold I am. Charlie, too, is shivering and I realise that I have my arms about him and am hugging him to my chest.

Slowly, stiffly, we climb across the mud-flats alongside the wharf.

Above us Foote staggers, limping along the pier, following our progress.

As we climb towards the road, I see two figures hurrying towards us. I recognise Mr Garrick. So, he has followed. And he has brought the Watchman.

It is to the Watchman that Foote lurches,

gesticulating, brushing Garrick aside.

'Arrest him, officer!' he cries. 'That man has just murdered my friend!'

Clink

In spite of Garrick's protestations, the Watchman takes me in charge, securing my wrists and ordering me to accompany him to the lock-up.

Harry Dobbs, an ex-soldier he tells us, with a limp from a shattered right leg, is younger than the old dolt who had charge of poor Joe. As he marches me to the Bridewell he is willing to listen to all parties but obdurate in his duty.

Garrick is eloquent in my defence. 'Will is not the villain here. He is the victim. It was the dead man, in league with this fellow - ' (Foote is skulking along beside us) ' - who lured him here - doubtless with the intention of doing him harm. They had abducted the boy...'

'That's right, yer honour. Trussed me up, they did,' pipes up Charlie.

'You wasn't trussed when we arrived,' states Dobbs.

'That's because 'e untied me.' Charlie flicks a derisory thumb in Foote's direction.

'And why would he do that, eh, if it was 'im tied you up in the first place?'

'Will ordered 'im to.'

'And why would he take orders from him?'

Foote breaks in, fawning. 'He had already viciously assaulted me, officer - almost broke my knee. I was in fear of what further violence he might do to me. Especially after I saw him push my friend off the jetty...'

I twist in Dobbs's grasp to confront the villain. 'He fell, you lying cur, and pulled me after...'

'And what was you doing to get pulled in as well, young feller?' growls Dobbs, pulling me back.

'They were fighting, officer. Archer attacked my friend - totally unprovoked.'

'You frog-marched me down to the river and held me for Aikin to beat me up... You call that unprovoked!'

And so, exchanging claim and counter-claim, we arrive at the watch-house where Garrick after more fruitless reasoning with Dobbs concedes that I must stay. But he at least persuades him to let me sit awhile before the paltry fire while he takes Charlie home and sends him back with some dry clothes.

Once they've gone, Foote seizes the opportunity to damn me with his own account. But Dobbs holds up a ponderous hand. 'Save it for the Magistrate tomorrow, sir. I've had my fill of you. Go home and see to that knee you say is so badly injured.' Dobbs, with his permanently damaged leg, has not failed to notice the fleeting nature of Foote's affliction.

Foote, affronted, departs with bad grace, leaving me and Dobbs alone. The watchman fetches a threadbare blanket and drapes it round my shoulders. I thank him.

'For mi own sake, not yours. Dereliction of duty to 'ave you die o' cold afore the beak passes judgement on yer in the morning.'

'Will it be Mr Fielding?'

'Might be - might not.' A gruff man of few words, Dobbs is disinclined to talk further.

As I sit shivering before the meagre fire I recall Fielding's concern on finding the body of Joe. If he is on the bench I am sure I will have a fair hearing. But I've heard of other magistrates who, eager to dine, rush through their cases and are less scrupulous at eliciting the truth, resulting in many stories of innocents condemned through false testimony.

Foote is a persuasive speaker and his account may hold the day. It will be my word against his, for neither Garrick nor Dobbs arrived in time to see what transpired. And how much note will the court take of a twelve-year-old boy - the only other present? A boy who says that he was kidnapped, who says that he was tied up, for neither of which is there any evidence but his own words. A boy whose loyalties clearly lie with me.

And who will believe I was lured there, rather than went of my own accord to pursue my animosity to the dead man? There is no more evidence for this than for Charlie's abduction, for the note was in the overcoat with which I tried to save Aikin – the coat which now lies with him at the bottom of the river.

Garrick may bear witness to the existence of the note and others of the household may testify to Charlie's absence. But their evidence can be hearsay at best - and what use is such a defence against the fact of one man injured and another dead?

A solitary flame struggles briefly and expires in the dull embers and I realise it is my own foolhardiness has brought me to this pass. Nor is it just I who faces disaster. Others will suffer as well.

Mr Garrick, whose production I have wrecked. *The Changeling* cannot possibly be performed with one actor dead and another arrested for his murder.

And, what is worse, I have dashed Agnes's hopes.

Who can help her escape a loveless marriage now that I have failed her?

When Charlie returns with a change of clothes, a warm blanket and some cold meat and bread, he does his best to lift my spirits.

'Cheer up, Will,' he tells me. 'Things is never as black as they looks. That's what I kept tellin' myself when those two bastards got me.'

With a pang of guilt, I realise that, with events moving so quickly, I have hardly given Charlie's ordeal a second thought.

I lay my hand upon his arm. 'They didn't harm you, did they?'

'No more'n a few bruises - lodged like a lord, I was!'

He tells me how, after leaving Susan and me at the Frost Fair, he went off with his pal Natty and they met with the rest of the gang.

Time passed, drink was taken and night fell.

'Next I knew we was waking up in the gang's current lay - ware'us down the docks - an' the day's well gone. So I thought I'd better get a shift on and high-tail it back 'ome. And that's when I was took.'

I can imagine the scene. Aikin, still smarting after his clash with me after rehearsal, encounters Charlie hurrying home and sees an opportunity for revenge. Giving him a message, supposedly from me, to meet at an address in Whitechapel, he offers to walk with him part of the way and, meeting Foote, the pair overpower him and bundle him to Aikin's lodgings.

'They tied me up,' Charlie continues, 'and I 'eard 'em hatching a plan to get back at you. Then they up an' left me...'

'That must be when they visited Mr Garrick and put the note under my door.'

'Come it gets dark, they're back and hauls me down by the river while they goes to get you... You goin' to eat that meat, or what?'

Although he has been captive for little more than half a day, he has probably had nothing substantial to eat since he left Susan and me at the Fair. I share the viands that Garrick has sent. Having eaten his fill, he belches and gives a huge yawn. I realise that it must be nigh on one in the morning, well past Charlie's bedtime. Dobbs, who has been listening to our conversation rises to do his round. He offers to see Charlie on his way after he has locked me in.

'Don't want you bein' nabbed again, do we, young feller-me-lad?'

'You believe my story then?' I ask him.

'Makes no odds what I think. 'Tis the beak you needs to convince.'

But a glimmer of hope lightens my foreboding as he turns the key of the cheerless cell of the Bridewell.

I doze but fitfully, my repose disturbed by recurring images.

A coat slithering across the ice as if alive. Aikin's terrified face, which dissolves into Agnes's tearful visage.

At times I feel myself flailing, sliding over ice, falling endlessly. I shout in despair, yet there is no sound.

Several times I jerk into consciousness, my body drenched in sweat as dark figures - faceless, fearful - intone doom-laden words that inspire terror but are without meaning.

And faces - Aikin, Agnes, Harry, Grey - merging one into another and resolving into my own. And, half heard, half sensed, a mournful litany: *I am not what I seem...*

I awake to the sound of the key in the cell door. Knuckling my eyes, I see the bulky figure of Dobbs framed in the doorway.

'Is it time?' I ask.

'Collect your things. You're free to go.'

At first I misunderstand him. 'You're taking me to the Magistrate's Court?'

'I'm taking you nowhere, lad. Didn't you hear me? You're free to go.'

'Free?'

'Aye, you're not to be charged. Now move yerself, my shift's done. I've a wife waiting.'

In a daze of disbelief, I roll up the blanket that Garrick sent and tuck it under my arm. I hold out my hand to Dobbs. 'Thank-you.'

He does not take it. 'For what? I ain't done but my duty. I took you, locked you up and held you overnight. My orders this morning is you're to be let go. 'Tis them above what gives the orders - I only does what I'm told. So, be off with you.'

I walk out of the Bridewell into the cool morning. All around the world is dripping. Trees weep tears from bare branches, roofs dribble melting snow and, underfoot, channels trickle. The sun hangs pale in a pewter sky as the earth thaws. The London streets, muddy, smoky, grey, have never looked so beautiful to me.

I hurry back, but as I near Mr Garrick's house my

pace slackens. Will he be as pleased to see me, the author of *The Changeling's* collapse, as I shall be to see him and give him thanks? For I have no doubt that he has been busy since my arrest pleading my case with Mr Fielding , the Magistrate.

He greets me with amazement. 'Will? But how...?' Delighted, he ushers me into the parlour where breakfast is laid.

'Your diligence on my behalf has been rewarded, sir.'

'My diligence? In what way, Will?'

I feel the first twinges of doubt. 'You have not prevailed with Mr Fielding for my release?'

'I have not seen Mr Fielding these ten days.' Again he takes my hands in his. 'I am most heartily glad to see you, Will!'

'And I to see you, sir - I cannot apologise enough for confounding your plans.'

'What plans are those, Will?'

'Why, the production, sir, that must be cancelled...'

'Pshaw, Will! What difference does one day make. 'Twas like t'have been so lambasted 't would have had but the one performance. Y'have done both Middleton and me a service!'

'But all the work the company have put in...?'

'Consider, Will - would you rather your efforts were foiled by chance or subject to ridicule? I know which I'd prefer. But, come, sit and take breakfast with me, and tell me all.'

As we eat, I recount all that has passed since I left him and Mrs Woffington yesterday evening. When I have done, he sits back and regards me curiously.

'I admit that when I left you in that dismal place last

night, Will, I feared for you. A charge of murder, I thought, was certain. So tell me how you come by such a happy deliverance.'

'I wish I knew, sir. I supposed it was yourself had worked on my behalf... All I know is that the watchman, Dobbs, received orders this morning to release me...'

'That villain Foote, perchance, has withdrawn his accusation...?'

'I hardly think that likely.'

'You did not question Dobbs about it?'

'He would not say. Only that *them above gives the orders.* He merely did as he was told.'

'And they, whoever they are, gave orders for the charges to be dropped?'

'Not quite. Even if dropped, a suspicion of guilt remains. Dobbs was very specific: I was to be let go without any charge being brought.'

'Clearly, you have powerful friends, Will.'

It is a conclusion I have already come to – there is but one friend to whom my freedom is of the essence, and money is a powerful persuader...

The only question that puzzles me is: How did Agnes learn of my imprisonment that she has worked so swiftly for my release?

Disbanding

Gathered in the theatre preparing to receive last minute notes before tonight's performance, the company are stunned by Garrick's announcement that the production is cancelled.

As they mutter in surprise, he holds up his hand. Immediately they fall silent.

'It is natural that you inquire the reason for the cancellation and I shall satisfy your curiosity. Last night, Mr Aikin suffered an - er - accident which unfortunately proved fatal.'

There is an audible gasp of horror from Kitty Blair. Ned puts a consoling arm about her shoulders, but even his face registers shock.

'In the dark, he ventured upon the frozen river, unaware that the ice was unstable. It broke beneath him. His body has not yet been recovered. These are the simple facts of the matter.' Garrick's gaze sweeps the upturned faces. 'You will all be as aware as I that a second death following so soon upon that of Harry Henderson is like to spawn rumours. Should any of you hear such rumours I trust that your loyalty to a former colleague will enable you to disregard or, better still, refute them. With the future of the theatre in such a parlous state, it behoves every one of us to do our utmost to ensure this tragedy does not become a subject for scandal.'

He goes on to tell us that, with the cancellation of *The Changeling,* the production of *Pamela* which ended its run only a week ago will be revived at the end of next week. Time enough for roles to be refreshed and Aikin's part to be re-cast. This news is greeted with murmurs of approval. *Pamela,* adapted from Mr Richardson's novel published only last year, has been one of the season's main draws. It will be satisfying to perform something familiar in the run up to Christmas, for none of us knows what the new year will bring.

'So, Will, you look to have been in the wars?' It is Ned Phillimore commenting on the cuts and bruises on my face. 'I hope the other fellow fared worse!'

Unwilling to explain the true cause, I shrug off his all-too-apt jest with a laugh and change the subject. 'Say, Ned, shall you go to Dublin before the end of the season?'

'I had thought to go after *The Changeling*. Kitty and I had squared it with Mr Garrick. But if the theatre is to close, 'twould feel like rats deserting the sinking ship. No, although Mr Sheridan promised to find parts for us if we went earlier, we are not definitely booked, Kitty and I, until April. So you have not seen the back of us yet. Sorry to disappoint you.'

'Would all disappointments were so welcome!'

He leans in closer. 'How goes your investigation into Harry's death? Do you think this latest tragedy is linked? Might Aikin have taken his own life in remorse for killing Harry?'

'I do not think so, Ned. 'Twas no secret Aikin and Harry disliked each other - but who among the company *did* Aikin like, or who liked *him*? You saw how news of his death was received just now. Initial shock at the manner of it, but then indifference. I cannot think of any among us who will grieve overlong for him. So very different from Harry who, although secretive, is still much missed.'

'By some more than others, I think,' says Ned with a glance over to where Tom Parsons is chatting with Septimus Drake, 'and yet, if your supposition is correct, someone here murdered him. Do you still hold to that belief?'

'That he was murdered, yes. But whether by one of our company, I am now inclined to doubt.'

'How so?'

'Aikin was the only one who would seem to have motive. Yet there is proof he did not do it. He was elsewhere at the time.'

'Yet you are sure Harry was killed. If not by one of us, by whom? And why?'

'On the night he died, he was seen going into the theatre. Shortly afterwards, two men followed. I do not know for certain who they were, but I think it was they who killed him.' I lean closer. 'I do not believe Harry was killed as a result of any personal animosity. I believe it to be because he got in the way of a very powerful man.'

Ned's face is a picture of incredulity. 'And can you bring this person to justice?'

I shake my head. 'I doubt it. He is one of the most powerful and feared men in the land. Nothing I could say or do would touch him. The most I can hope for is that I may find the truth of the matter - to satisfy myself and those who knew him, and to lift the slur of suicide from his name.'

'And may one know the name of this tyrant?'

'For your own sake, Ned, it is best you remain

ignorant. I have already crossed him and live in constant fear of reprisal. I would not draw you into my danger.'

He looks with greater awe at my injuries. 'Did he do that to you?'

Hervey, I am sure, would choose far more subtle methods, but I do not disabuse Ned . 'It is the kind of thing I might expect,' I tell him.

He lays a hand on my shoulder. 'Take care, Will. Consider whether the living are not more important than the dead. I would not lose another friend...'

I essay a smile. 'No fear of that, Ned. My life may be dear to you, but it is dearer still to me!'

No sooner has Ned rejoined Kitty than Tom Parsons is at my elbow.

'That matter we talked of...?'

He does not remark upon my bruises, so wrapped up is he in his own concerns. With the events of the past day and night, the promise I made to him has slipped my mind. But now, with my evening's assignation with Agnes only hours away, I would be rid of his imploring eyes.

I tell him to meet me in half an hour at my lodgings, dressed to meet a gentleman. Then I hurry home to find Charlie.

I despatch him with a note and tell him to make haste. He returns with a reply only minutes before Parsons arrives in a coat that, though sober hued, displays his figure to advantage. I have raided Harry's trunk again and am clad in shades of grey.

Tom is wound tight as a watch-spring with excitability and apprehension. He grins nervously. 'We could pass for two lawyer's clerks, Will.'

'That will be no great harm, considering the gentleman I am about to introduce you to.'

'Is he - is he a nobleman?'

'He has a title and houses in both town and country - but noble is not the first word that springs to my mind,' I reply sourly. 'He has, however, connections and patronage which may do you some good.'

Following the route that Charlie and I traversed only a week ago to Hanover Square, we pass it by on its southern edge and head towards Grosvenor Square.

Irritatingly, throughout our journey, Tom's nervous anticipation displays itself in such a ceaseless flow of inconsequential chatter and constant fidgeting that I am hard-pressed to keep my composure. It is with relief that we arrive at our destination.

Sir Francis Courtney, though wealthy, is not sufficiently so to lord it in Grosvenor Square itself where leases cost in excess of three thousand pounds. Mrs Wiggins once told me - though how she comes by such information, I do not know - that its west side alone boasts a dowager duchess, a duchess, three earls and a lord.

Sir Francis's town house, towards the western end of Upper Brook Street, is nevertheless imposing, its four storeys coldly etched in the winter sunlight.

A footman in plum livery opens the door. He is young and tolerably handsome and wears his uniform with a jauntiness untypical of a servant. Doubtless a former favourite who now serves Sir Francis's acquaintances at soirées. His knowing smile as he brazenly inspects Tom and me confirms it.

'Sir Francis is expecting us,' I say.

'Indeed he is.' His voice is pure east-end and his

wink is complicit. 'Lookin' forrard to it an' all. Foller me, gents.'

He leads us upstairs to a first-floor parlour. This is the first time I have been in Sir Francis's house and I have never seen such a profusion of statuary and oil-paint. Scantily clad figures cavort on every wall and naked marble youths yearn in every niche and corner. Beside me, Tom's eyes are wide with wonder. He thinks he has come to heaven. To me it is merely a more elegant version of Mother Ransom's.

As it is not yet turned noon, Sir Francis receives us in dishabille - a loose silk robe, heavily embroidered, turban and kid slippers.

'Will, my dear, such an unexpected pleasure.'

I see him start as he notice the fresh injuries to my face, but then he regains his composure and flicks an elegant wrist at the footman. 'Robbie, a dish of tea for my guests.'

The footman retreats as Sir Francis motions Tom and me to two armchairs opposite the sofa on which he reclines. Once more he glances at my bruises, his visage clouding momentarily, then turns his gaze on Tom who perches, dumbstruck with awe, upon the edge of his seat. I perform the necessary introductions and begin to broach the purpose of our visit.

'The last time we met, sir...'

'You were uncharitable, as I recall.'

'Indeed I used some harsh words to you, for which I apologise. Neither of us were, I believe, at our easiest on that particular day.'

'Understandably so. Has - has anything more come of that meeting? Your - your injuries... They are not...?'

'No sir. They are unrelated. But Tom here knows

nothing of either that meeting or my injuries. Nor need he. We are here upon another matter entirely.'

'How very intriguing. Say on.'

'When you came to Mr Garrick's lodgings, sir, you were kind enough to praise my modest acting talents.'

'Not modest, Will. You do yourself a disservice.'

'Tom here might disagree. He is indeed an actor of rare skill and pathos.'

Sir Francis nods thoughtfully. 'Yes, I believe I have noticed you before, Mr Parsons. In *Richard III* was it not? You played the doomed young prince with affecting poignancy.'

Tom blushes. 'I thank you sir,' he murmurs. 'You are too generous. It is the kind of role, alas, that I seem fated to play - in life as well as on the stage.'

Sir Francis raises a quizzical eyebrow.

'Tom undervalues himself, Sir Francis. He has had setbacks of late. Come, cheer up,Tom. What will Sir Francis think?'

'I ask your pardon, Sir Francis. I am in low spirits at the present time. If it were not for Will's encouragement, I do not know what I would do. He has been my saviour.'

Sir Francis looks at me meaningfully. 'Warm words, indeed. What *can* you have done to earn them, Will?'

'It is not so much what I have done, sir. Rather, with your assistance, what might be done.'

'A riddle, Will! You intrigue me mightily.'

'Let me be brief, then. You recently hinted that I might do well to cultivate the patronage of a man of - er, *sensibility*. I would enlist your aid to seek out such a one - not for myself, but for Tom.'

Sir Francis raises a finger to his lips and fixes me

with a steady gaze. 'Direct, Will, very direct. And you, Mr Parsons, are you a man of *sensibility* also?'

Tom, looking like a frightened rabbit, blurts out, 'I seek only someone who will love me, sir, and whom I can love in return.'

Sir Francis grimaces in distaste. 'A trifle *too* direct, Mr Parsons, But I take your meaning.'

At this moment, there is a gentle knock at the door and Robbie enters with the tea tray. He rearranges small tables, pours tea into cups, lays them before us, then prepares to go.

'Stay, Robbie. We have need of your advice. Pray stand, Mr Parsons.'

Hesitantly, Tom rises to his feet and I wonder what game Sir Francis is about to play, for I see a smile flicker upon his lips as he eases himself from his seat.

Rustling silkily, he perambulates around Tom, examining him from every angle like an art connoisseur examining a new purchase. Tom blushes fiery red under the scrutiny. Robbie is clearly enjoying the spectacle. His eyes glint with mischief.

With his forefinger, Courtney tilts up Tom's chin and examines his profile. I start to protest but am silenced with a peremptory wave of his hand.

'What think you, Robbie? Which of our modest gentlemen might take a fancy to Mr Parsons here?'

Hands behind back, Robbie joins in the assessment. 'A delicate-looking gennelman. Wistful air about 'im. Mr Connolly's type, perhaps? Or Sir Peregrine? They're partial to the waif look...'

The pair of them continue for some minutes, suggesting or dismissing names as I grow increasingly uncomfortable. Tom, however, seems oblivious of his humiliation, his face flickering with pathetic hope at mention of each new name.

At last Sir Francis says, 'It is decided. I have a soirée on Tuesday next, to which shall be invited a number of the gentlemen we have considered. You, Mr Parsons, shall of course be the centre of attention...'

I can hold back no longer. 'Sir Francis, I would not have Tom be made a common show...'

'Tut, Will - you insult me. Common indeed! These are some of the finest in the land - men of means and title. Discreet men who seek a confidential companion, not a plaything to cast away when they are done with him.' He sees the doubt still evident on my face. 'Come, Will. I know you hold my tastes in no high regard, but I am nevertheless a man of honour. I seek to harm no man in pursuance of my pleasure and would coerce no-one - as you, yourself, have reason to know. For all your low opinion of me, have I ever shown you less than respect?'

I have to admit the justice of his remarks. Without his intercession with Mr Garrick I do not know where I would be today - begging on the streets, probably, or dead. And when he accompanied me to Westminster Hall, I believe his concern for me was not entirely due to his own fear.

'Very well, sir. If Tom is agreeable...?'

'Oh yes, Will.' Tom seizes my hand. 'I can't thank you enough.'

Sir Francis claps his hands. 'Then all are satisfied!' He gathers his silk robe about him. 'Now, if you will excuse me, I must dress. The town awaits! Robbie, be so kind as to show our guests out.'

Robbie ushers us out with studied deference. 'He's

not a bad old stick, y'know,' says he as we descend the stairs. 'Generous to them he likes. That's 'ow I come to be 'ere. When I growed a bit big for his tastes - know what I mean? An' 'e often talks about you, sir. Real soft spot 'e 'as for you, Mister Will Archer. Can't see 'im doin' this for many another of his acquaintance.'

As Tom and I step out into the chill winter afternoon on Upper Brook Street, I feel absurdly grateful to Sir Francis. Yet the gratitude is tinged with the suspicion that a price may yet be exacted for his favours.

Flight

With Tom Parson's business done, all my thoughts for the remainder of the day tend towards my nocturnal assignation with Agnes.

Shortly before ten, I don clothes fit for the night's adventure and prepare to make my way to Hanover Square.

Skirting the parlour, whence comes the sound of muted voices and Mistress Woffington's stifled laughter, I pause by the kitchen stairs. Even from here, I can hear the snuffling snores of Mrs Wiggins, and imagine Susan at her mending, her needle illuminated by the one dim candle, and Charlie curled up by the embers of the dying fire.

Some inner voice urges me to descend the stairs, confide in them, tell them what I'm about to do... They are my friends, my family almost - they deserve to know.

But I stop myself. They would, I know, only try to dissuade me from so rash an enterprise, prevent me from going... And that same small voice inside me tells me they are right - until I remember Agnes's face, the plea in her looks and words. I know that I must not fail her.

I creep to the front door, open it carefully and close it soundlessly behind me.

The night is dark and overcast, a sliver of new moon only occasionally visible between muffling clouds. The few people around at this late hour hurry by, heads down against the cold, intent on home. I pull my coat about me and set off briskly for my destination.

Along Cornhill, near deserted now that 'Change business is done for the day. Through Cheapside and St Paul's coming alive with taverns and the citizens of the night. Past the theatre in Drury Lane, disgorging theatregoers into chairs and coaches.

Further west the streets are better lit and the way less crowded. My pace slows but, at the same time, my heart begins to pound in anticipation.

Hanover Square is deserted. Entering from the north side, I see one or two workmen's carts, shuttered for the night, dark islands in the centre of the square. Beyond them, the lights from steps and windows hang starry on the blackness.

Outside number forty-three I see movement. Hendricksen's landau has just pulled up. I recognise the squat bulk of Menninck on the box.

I increase my pace. If Agnes has summoned Menninck early, it must mean she needs my assistance immediately. But, as I approach, I am stopped in my tracks. Two figures emerge from the coach. Two men who hurry into the house while Menninck sits impassive at his post.

Old Hendricksen and a manservant? It would seem the most reasonable explanation. *But surely the old man would be slower, a servant more deferential?*

Intrigued, I move closer. I do not approach the door, for if it was indeed old Hendricksen, I can think of no reason to explain my presence. Instead, I retreat down into the front area of the neighbouring house, taking care to keep in the shadow of the entrance steps away from the window. These grand houses all have sunken yards to either side of their front doors which give access to the basement rooms for servants. From here I have a clear view of the front of number forty-three.

The landau still stands there, Menninck staring impassively ahead, apparently with no intention of moving. The horses snort gently and paw the ground. In the light from the steps I see that they are steaming in the cold night air. Whatever journey they've been on, it's been enough to make them sweat.

A light flickers in a window on the first floor. I guess it is the chamber adjoining the room where old Hendricksen received me when I came to tell him of his son's death. Suddenly the light is dimmed as a curtain is pulled across the window.

My attention is momentarily distracted as, across the square, a hackney carriage pulls up and the driver alights from the back to help out a lady and her gentleman partner.

Mounting once more upon his box, the driver waits as the gentleman escorts the lady to her front door where, upon its being opened by a maidservant, he formally kisses her hand, bows and takes his leave.

A young beau escorting his lady home from the theatre, doubtless. From across the square I watch him re-enter the hackney carriage and hear the sharp rap of his stick upon the carriage roof. The driver flicks the reins. Horse and carriage trot away and out of the square.

As the silence settles back, I become aware of muffled voices, apparently raised in argument, from next door. I crane my neck to see round the railings, but can see nothing. As suddenly as they started, the voices cease.

A few more minutes pass and I begin to feel the cold penetrating my coat.

Then, suddenly, light floods the pavement, picking out the waiting landau in sharp relief, causing the nearer horse to roll its eyes and stamp its hoof. Agnes hurries down the steps to speak to Menninck and I seize my opportunity to announce my presence.

She does not see where I have come from and she turns in alarm as I utter her name. But then her face breaks into a smile of relief.

'Ah, Will. I knew you would not fail me. You come most opportunely.'

Seizing my hand, she pulls me into the house. In the hall are several boxes, piled haphazardly upon the floor.

'Help Menninck load these in the carriage.'

I am suddenly aware that the coachman is behind me, blocking the door. I stand aside to let him shoulder the largest trunk.

'The old man - he is abed?' I ask.

Agnes is fastening a fur-lined cape about her neck. She starts at my question and for a brief second I glimpse some unreadable emotion in her eyes. Then, 'Fear not,' she says, 'he will hear nothing.'

I take up two leather valises and carry them into the coach. When I return, Agnes takes my hand and leads me upstairs. 'Menninck will see to the rest.'

Bypassing the reception rooms on the first floor, she leads me up a second flight and into a room in which a candelabra burns. I see four newel posts and silken drapes. A heady perfume hangs in the air.

I step back to the doorway, nonplussed. Why has she brought me here – to her own chamber? I feel the heat of uncertain anticipation colour my cheeks.

'Nay, Will, be not so bashful. Have you not been in a lady's bedroom before?'

'I - I, er...'

'Here, take this.' She thrusts a large carpet-bag at me. 'And these.' Two lacquered jewellery cases.

Then, scooping up several gowns from the bed she shoos me downstairs. I obey, chagrined, my relief tinged with disappointment.

Once all is safely stowed in the landau, she tells me to follow her upstairs once more.

This time we stop on the first floor and enter the room where earlier I saw the light.

From a table she takes a pistol and hands it to me.

'Put this in your coat, Will. There may be highwaymen, and we must be prepared.'

I take it, unsure, discomfited. 'But, Agnes, I have never used a pistol...'

From an armchair in the centre of the room, a figure rises.

'Then now is the time to learn, Master Archer.'

My mouth drops open in shock.

'Mister Nicklaas?'

I look to Agnes for explanation. She lowers her eyes apologetically.

'I'm sorry, Will, I should have told you. Nicklaas is to accompany us.' She takes my hand and speaks with renewed passion. 'You must see, I could not leave him here? He is so much improved, 'twould be cruelty beyond measure to leave him in that dreadful place with none to visit him. You must see that?'

I bring myself to nod. 'If that is your desire...'

'It is, Will, it is.'

'Then I will assist you as I promised.'

'You spoke true, Agnes. He is indeed a paragon,' says Nicklaas. 'Let me shake your hand, Master Archer.'

Taking my hand in both of his, he pumps it energetically, laughing like a schoolboy. His manner of speaking seems to confirm Agnes's assessment of his improvement – there is little of the madman about it. But this uncontrolled laughter...?

Gently Agnes prises my hand free. 'There is but one more thing needful...'

Until now, she has been decisive, eager with the excitement of it all, but now I sense an anxiety in her that was not there before.

'Nicklaas!' Her voice is nervously loud. I look up anxiously - if the old man should hear... 'Go down,' she orders him. 'Wait for us in the carriage.'

He obeys, meek as a child. She waits until he has descended before taking my hand once more. Her face is pale. Her hand shakes. 'Will,' she murmurs, 'I'm sorry. Believe me when I say I wish I had not involved you in this...'

Before I can open my mouth to reply, there comes a sudden muffled explosion from above.

I glance at her, alarmed, and see my own shock reflected in her face. All colour drains from her cheeks and she clings to me. Her body trembles against mine.

Thus we stand, rooted to the spot, as seconds pass.

At last, with no further noise from above, I whisper, 'Mijnheer...?'

'It cannot be...'

I take her by the shoulders. 'Stay here,' I tell her. 'Trust me.'

'His is the room at the end of the corridor beyond mine. Oh, Will, take care.'

Leaving her at the turn of the stair, I ascend slowly to the second floor.

My eyes take a moment to accustom. Slowly the darkness is silvered by the pale moon through the skylight. Enough for me to find the heavy panelled door at the end of the passage.

No light shows beneath it, nor can I hear any sound as I press my ear to the wood.

Cautiously I turn the handle. It slips round noiselessly and I feel the door give as the latch disengages. For a moment I wait before gently easing it open, just wide enough for me to see into the room.

In the gloom, I make out the shape of a weighty four-poster bed, on which white sheets glow, palely translucent.

His dark shape is visible. He must have cast aside the coverlet. Is that what we heard - a book, perhaps, falling from the bed, sounding frighteningly loud in our highly-strung state?

On the pillow his head seems unnaturally large.

Easing the door open a fraction more, I step into the room. I have brought no light with me. Even if he is awake, he will not see the door opening. But I must set my mind at rest that he is sleeping.

I crane forward to catch the rhythm of his breathing - and realise there is none.

Is he lying awake, holding his breath, ready to spring upon me?

As I begin to step back I hear a footfall behind me.

Turning, I see Agnes in the doorway, hands raised to her face in horror.

She is the last thing I see as a blow lands on the side of my head. A myriad of light shatters my brain before darkness engulfs me.

I turn my head and crimson pain erupts behind my eyes. I fall back, fighting to keep at bay the bile that burns in my throat. After a moment the pain and nausea subside enough for me to attempt to move again.

With extreme caution, I try to raise myself on one elbow. I am in complete darkness and the movement causes my head to thump, but I feel my mind gradually clearing.

Gingerly I touch the side of my head where the blow fell. It is tender and my fingers come away sticky with blood. I take two deep breaths and attempt to stand. The effort is too great. My head spins and I sink to my knees where I remain until equilibrium is restored, breathing slowly and deeply.

A thin shard of silver resolves itself into moonlight through a gap in the curtains. Slowly I crawl towards it and twitch the drape aside, letting in enough light for me to take in the configuration of the room.

I am still in Mijnheer Hendricksen's bedchamber. The four poster bed looms large in the centre. Around the edges of the room, the shadowy bulk of other pieces - chairs, a linen-press and a table with a candelabra.

If there are candles, there must be flint and tinder!

I ease myself to my feet. This time my head remains level and I take careful steps towards the table.

Half a dozen strikes and the tinder catches. I blow it gently to life and touch a taper to it, then light the five candles.

Holding it aloft, I fully expect to see the bed empty. Who else but the old man could have hit me?

But no. There he lies still, and the mystery of his unnaturally large head is revealed. A pool of blood lies like a halo about him. Dead eyes stare upwards. His thin lips are drawn back over stained teeth in a rictus grin. And where the left side of his head should be is a bloody mess of brain and bone.

This time I cannot stem the tide. I swivel round and vomit down the wall, clutching the table for support.

When finally the convulsions cease, I wipe my hand across my mouth and brace myself to look once more upon him.

The old man lies huddled on the bed. Beside him lies a blood-soaked pillow, its ticking ripped, its feathers exploded. Now I know why the explosion we heard was muffled.

And, as I notice the pillow, I notice something else also. On the floor, next to where I was lying, is the pistol that Agnes gave me.

A dead man. A pistol. And myself the only other person present.

The full horror of my situation rushes in upon me.

And simultaneously my thoughts turn to Agnes. What did she see over my shoulder that caused her such terror?

Has the killer of the old man now taken her captive?

I realise that for both our sakes, I must get out of here immediately.

I stoop to pick up the pistol, forgetting my recent blow on the head. Sudden giddiness reminds me and I slump against one of the bedposts until my head stops spinning.

When it does, I make for the door, only to find it locked. The murderer is clearly determined to establish my guilt and hinder any attempt by me to rescue Agnes...

I scan the room for any other means of egress.

Wrenching up the sash window I discover only a sheer two-storey drop to the pavement below. A dizzy enough descent even for someone not already nauseous.

Casting my eye again about the room, I see another door in the side wall.

It leads to a dressing room. In here the window overlooks the garden. On the floor below, a small balcony protrudes. A drop of no more than ten feet I guess. Too far to jump without possibility of hurt. But if I can hang on the sill of this window...?

Stowing the pistol inside my coat, I climb out. Supporting myself on elbows, I lower my legs, scrabbling against the brickwork for purchase, then transfer my weight to my hands till I hang at arm's length from the sill.

Taking a deep breath, I let myself drop. The impact jars my legs and I stagger, near knocking myself out on the balustrade, but otherwise, my landing causes no hurt - apart from setting my head swimming again.

Leaning against the wall to let it steady, I see that I am outside the reception room where first I met Agnes. Either I can take the steps from the balcony into the garden below, or make my escape through the room. The rear garden is enclosed and I don't know if there is any exit other than through the house. At ground level, such access is likely to be a solid door, whereas here on the balcony, it is through a glass-panelled one.

Which is, of course, locked. But the old man is in no state to complain of my breaking the glass. Shielding my face with my left arm, I turn my back on the door, draw out the pistol and launch the butt full force at the pane. It shatters. I swiftly knock out the remaining shards to form a space large enough for me to climb through.

Once inside, I head immediately for the door which I am relieved to find is unlocked.

But just as I am about to go out onto the landing, I hear a commotion downstairs.

Retreating into the room, pistol at the ready, I push the door almost shut.

Voices are coming up the stairs. I catch fragments of conversation. It appears there are at least three men.

''Twas from the second floor, yer honour ...'

'A gunshot, I'll stake my life on't...'

'We come fer you straight away...'

'You did right, my man. The Watch should be every citizen's first port of call... The second floor, you say?'

'Aye.'

'And the residents of the house - gone, you say?'

'An hour since...'

I peep through the crack of the door to see the Watchman and his two informants ascending the stair to the second floor. I wait till they are out of sight and slip swiftly out, taking the stairs down to the ground floor two at a time. The front door stands open. There appears to be no-one left on guard. Pulling my coat about my ears, I hurry out and down the steps into the street.

Walking quickly, I put number forty-three Hanover

Square behind me.

Out of the corner of my eye, I see another coach enter the square. I take no note of it until it draws close and stops beside me.

The window is lowered, and a familiar voice says, 'Get in, Master Archer.'

I look up, startled.

It is Sir William Hervey.

'Make haste, sir. The booby of a Watchman will be out in a moment and will raise the hue and cry. You would do well not to be about when that happens.'

The door swings open and, with sinking heart, I see Nathaniel Grey step out.

'Pray, take my seat, Master Archer. I will be but a moment.' He smiles mockingly and sweeps me a low bow. Then trots off towards the Hendricksen house.

Reluctantly I clamber into the coach, latching the door behind me. Sir William orders the coachman to drive on a little way to where he can observe the front door of number forty-three.

We sit in silence, until the Watchman and his two followers erupt from the house. They are met by Grey who, after showing them a document of some sort, converses quietly for a few moments, he doing most of the talking, they listening.

The watchman touches his hat respectfully, then turns on his two companions. Whatever he says clearly chastens them, for they turn on their heels and slope off without a backward glance. With a slight bow, Grey takes his leave of the Watchman and walks briskly back to the coach.

Once he is in and sitting next to me, Sir William raps upon the roof with his silver-topped cane and the coachman urges the horses to a fast trot around and out of the square.

Sir William sits back in his seat, with a self-satisfied smile.

'Well, Master Archer, did I not warn you to stay away from Mijnheer Hendricksen and his family? You see now the cost of ignoring my advice?'

'I own I was at fault, sir, but...'

'But you were acting from the noblest of motives - a damsel in distress. Ah, what it is to be young!'

'The lady may still be in danger, sir...'

'Indeed?'

His bantering tone galls me.

'Am I under arrest, sir. Have I escaped the Watch only to be taken by you?'

Beside me, I hear Grey snicker.

'Tut, Master Archer, so petulant!' chides Hervey. 'And such ingratitude. This is the second time I have had to rescue you. In truth, Master Archer, it would seem you court disaster.'

I cannot hide my amazement. 'The second time...?'

'Aye, Master Archer. But this is not the time for explanations. We have fugitives to catch. And they have an hour's start upon us. Our rather sedate landau must be exchanged for more speedy horses. I take it you ride, Master Archer? '

Pursuit

We soon draw up before a substantial town house. In my confusion I am unable to follow all the twists and turns of the journey, so if this is Hervey's residence, I have no idea of its location. Nor have I any clearer idea of what is happening, for my questions have received no straight answers. All I know is that we are to pursue the Hendricksen landau which was seen leaving Hanover Square over an hour since and in which Agnes and, for aught I know, Nicklaas may be at the mercy of the man who murdered Mijnheer.

By now, the night must be well advanced, past midnight at the least, for I do not know how long I was unconscious in the old man's room. But as soon as the coach comes to a stop outside Hervey's house servants issue forth and we stride into a spacious hall which is a hive of activity.

I am ordered to remove my outer coat and shoes. A greatcoat and riding boots are thrust upon me to replace them. Hervey and Grey undergo a similar transformation.

Then I am led through the house and out into a yard where, in the flickering light of many torches, half a dozen horses wait, ready saddled.

A groom helps me up onto a chestnut roan. It is many years since I have been aback a horse - not since my days as a boy in Yorkshire - and the unfamiliar sensation only increases the sense of unreality I have been feeling all evening.

The groom senses my unease and grins up at me. 'Never fear, master. Ruby's a gentle mare. Treat 'er gentle and she'll do the same for you.' His accent is rich with country vowels. He slaps the horse's rump affectionately.

It seems we are not to ride alone. Three others, Hervey's men, are already mounted.

'This is Master Will Archer,' Hervey tells them. 'Have a care of him. He is not to come to harm.'

They regard me, their eyes curious but their faces betraying nothing. None speaks. My own greeting dies in my throat.

At a signal from Hervey, we set off through an archway and narrow alley which opens onto a wide street that is unfamiliar to me. We could be anywhere in the city. And any attempt to recognise my surroundings is hindered by my efforts to keep my seat, especially as my companions set off at a quick jog as soon as we emerge.

The dark streets are near-deserted and still in places thick with trampled snow. But where the way is clearer, our pace increases to a brisk trot and I have much ado to keep up. The others, more used to regular riding, adapt their bodies to the rhythm of their mounts. I, not having ridden for nigh-on ten years, and that but a carthorse hack, bump ungainly up and down in the saddle. Ruby is a thoroughbred. She may be a gentle beast, but I sense her equine scorn - and she can't prevent the chafing.

Gradually, though, I gain confidence and, by the time we leave the London streets behind, Ruby probably feels that at last she has a rider on her back instead of a green novice.

By my estimation we have been riding for near three-quarters of an hour when we come to the first turnpike.

One of Hervey's men dismounts and raps loudly at the door of the tollhouse.

As the heavy-eyed keeper emerges and collects the dues for our six steeds, Hervey leans down. 'A coach has passed through here - how long ago?'

'There's bin a fair few since last evening.'

'A landau. Dark livery. Coachman a man of few words.'

'There was one such, not more than an hour-and-a-half since. Surly devil - ne'er spoke a word. Just threw the money at me...'

'And the passengers - how many?'

''Twas hard to see. The windows was tight shut. More'n one, though.'

Hervey holds a crown between his fingers. 'Would this help your memory - two? - three? Or more?'

'Three, I think. And one a lady.'

Hervey flips him the coin and the man swings open the gate with deferential haste, knuckling his forehead as we pass.

Out in the country and away from the city smoke, we can see our way more clearly. This turnpike road which leads from London to Canterbury is free of obstacles, its surface compacted hard from numerous vehicles. Our trot becomes a gallop and we make good time.

From the centre of the city to Gravesend is a good twenty miles. Three hours in a heavy horse-drawn coach. Much less on galloping horses.

By the time we reach the next toll-booth, two carts

laden with produce have passed us going the opposite way, heading for the early morning markets in the city, the drovers nodding with sleep as their beasts plod the familiar road.

The coach, we learn, is but half an hour ahead of us. We slacken our pace somewhat. We do not want to exhaust the horses and it is certain now that we shall overtake it well before it reaches its destination.

Hervey draws his mount alongside mine. 'When we close with our quarry, Master Archer, I would not have you involved in apprehending them. Let my men deal with the situation.'

I am offended. 'You would have me a spectator, sir - when a lady's life is in peril?'

'I understand your concern, but whatever danger there may be, it is not like to be lessened through any rash intervention by yourself. My men are experienced in engagements of this sort. Pray do not impede them with your impetuosity.'

'I hear you, sir,' say I, tight-lipped.

He leaves me and rides to the front of our band. After a brief consultation, two of his men spur their horses and gallop on ahead.

As they and the drumming of their horses' hooves fade into the dark, Grey comes alongside me. 'You would do well to heed Sir William's words, Master Archer. It does not do to be headstrong in these situations.'

'I have heard Sir William's words, sir.' I reply frostily. 'I do not need advice from you.'

His lip twitches and he continues. 'I was against bringing you on this expedition, Archer. If I had my way, you would be under guard now, awaiting our return. But Sir William would have you come. Do not give him cause to regret that decision.'

I turn to him. 'Mr Grey, I do not pretend to know what all this is about. All I know is that a lady whom I respect is in that coach in front of us, and that she may be in deadly danger. When we come upon it I shall, of course, endeavour to comply with Sir William's instructions - but whatever I do, you may be sure that my actions will be dictated by my sense of honour, not obsequiousness.'

If I wish to sting him, I fail. His mouth twists in a slow smile. 'Oh, Master Archer, how green! But I begin to discern something of what Sir William perceives in you. I hope you will not be too disappointed by this night's events.'

He falls back and I think I hear him chuckle. My neck burns hot with mortification even in the chill morning air.

For there is no doubt now that it is morning. Over to the east, on the black horizon, there is the slightest dusting of grey and around us dawn mist begins to roll, responding to a warmth that we cannot yet feel.

Suddenly, Hervey holds up his arm, bringing our remaining quartet to a halt.

Ahead, barely visible, no more than a darker shadow on the remnant of the night, is the coach.

Hervey signals to Grey and his other man to go ahead, leaving himself and me to bring up the rear.

For several minutes we follow, observing from a distance as the coach lumbers on. Its occupants are clearly unaware that they are being followed, for its pace remains steady, unhurried.

The horses, I guess, must be weary. Is it that

Menninck does not want to overtire them now they are so close to their destination?

Or is there some more sinister reason?

Is there, even now, a pistol pointed at the coachman's heart – or, worse, against that of his mistress inside the carriage?

In either extremity, he will not want to jeopardise her safety through reckless driving.

A picture the occupants rises unbidden to my mind - Nicklaas, bound helpless in a corner - Agnes sitting terrified while the murderer threatens her with the very pistol that killed the old man...

Then, out of the grey dawn in front of the carriage, two figures appear. The two horsemen Hervey dispatched earlier must have ridden fast across country, overtaken the coach and doubled back to confront it.

One holds up a hand, ordering the vehicle to stop.

And sure enough, the coach slows as Hervey's men come forward, one to each side of it. Then, just as they draw level, Menninck whips up the horses and they gallop off pell-mell, the coach lurching behind them.

My heart leaps in fear for Agnes as I strain my ears to catch the inevitable report of a pistol...

But none comes.

I pray the killer has been deflected by the giddy jolting of the coach.

Wrenching his bucking horse about, one of Hervey's men looses a shot at the retreating vehicle, and he and his colleague give chase. We, too, spur our horses, as do Grey and his colleague ahead of us.

The Dutch coachman, though, is driving like the very devil, veering the coach from side to side to prevent either of Hervey's riders overtaking him.

For several desperate minutes the chase continues.

Until, emerging from the mist, trundling slowly towards us comes another drover's cart.

Menninck wrenches the horses to one side. The carriage, jerked too suddenly askew, overbalances. For a dizzying second, it teeters on one wheel, then topples on to its side.

We hear the screech as it is dragged along... Then a splintering of wood - and the horses break free, dragging Menninck behind, entangled in the reins. In horror, I watch him bouncing like a rag doll until he rolls free and lies still.

The carriage horses, no longer encumbered, gallop a short distance further. Then, realising they're free, they slow and come to a halt, their flanks heaving as their snorting clouds the air.

The first of Hervey's men jumps off his horse and bends over the prostrate form of the coachman. After a moment, he rises and shakes his head.

Meanwhile, the second trots cautiously towards the fallen carriage which lies on its side, wheels idly spinning. As he gets closer, the door, now more like a trap in the topside, is flung upwards and I hear the shot I so dreaded. But as the the horse rears, whinnying in fright, it is its rider who topples and lies still.

Grey and the third of Hervey's men are still some thirty yards off. Hervey and myself yet further away.

We rein in our mounts and take cover. At the far side of the coach, the man near Menninck's body does the same.

From where we kneel in the scrub beside the road, we see a figure clamber from the wrecked coach. It is Nicklaas Hendricksen. Once out, he looks desperately around him, seems on the point of flight. But then a second man climbs out. He points a pistol at Nicklaas and turning his head, shouts something over his shoulder.

Shakily, a third figure begins to emerge from the vehicle. I start forward as I recognise Agnes. Even from this distance I see that her hair hangs in strands and her face is bloody. But as I am about to leap up, Hervey pulls me back.

'Stay, Will, you can do no good.'

So restrained, I have no choice but to watch the scene that plays out in front of me.

We are at too great a distance to hear what is said, but I see Agnes stagger towards Nicklaas. It appears she is trying to shield him, hanging about his neck. Behind her the man holding the pistol scoffs and gesticulates, pointing, inexplicably, to his own chest.

Then, in two strides, he is on her. He tears her away from Nicklaas and throws her aside. Once again he menaces Nicklaas with the gun. Nicklaas cowers, rooted to the spot.

Agnes, meanwhile, has crawled to the gunman and now clasps his knees in entreaty. All in vain. The man throws back his head in mocking laughter, points the gun and shoots. Nicklaas crumples lifeless to the ground.

This time I will not be restrained. I start running almost before I am on my feet. Half diving, half falling I stagger towards them only to see Grey dart from cover as I pass and hurl himself at my feet. As I thud, winded, to earth I hear the hiss of a bullet above me.

Raising my head, I see the killer running beyond the coach towards Menninck's body.

But as he nears the corpse, he alters direction. It is not Menninck he is heading for, but the horse belonging to the first of Hervey's men. At the same moment, the man himself rises from the grass and points a pistol at the murderer. He shouts for him to surrender.

Hardly pausing in his run, the fugitive fires. I see Hervey's man clutch his arm and watch his weapon drop from nerveless fingers. Without a backward glance, the killer vaults onto the horse and urges it into a gallop away from the road and into the trees.

Beside me, Grey orders Hervey's third man to go in pursuit. Then, getting up and dusting himself down, he reaches out an arm and helps me up.

'Well, Master Archer, you see where recklessness gets you - a bullet in the head, had I not been here to fell you.'

Hervey comes up. 'He will head back for London in the hope of disappearing in the stews and rookeries. But we shall have him, never fear. Now, for our horses - and you, Master Archer, may be reunited with your lady in distress.'

But even as he says it, we hear the sound of hooves and turn to see another horse galloping, this time away towards Gravesend. It is the one belonging to Hervey's man whom the villain shot as he clambered from the coach. And Agnes is riding it.

In amazement I turn to see a slow smile spread across Hervey's face. 'It appears the lady does not wish to be rescued.' He turns to Grey. 'Pursue her, Nathaniel. See that the right thing is done.'

I make to follow him. 'I shall ride with you...'

'No, Master Archer, you will not.' Hervey's tone is

curt and brooks no dissent. 'You will stay here.'

Thus I am obliged to watch Grey ride off into the mist while Hervey directs me to tend to his man's injured arm, to stanch the blood and devise a makeshift sling.

The drover whose cart precipitated the calamity, meanwhile, has alighted from it and is now soothing the two runaway coach-horses.

Hervey orders him to free them from the broken shafts, then goes to check on the man who was first shot. Having ascertained that he is indeed dead, he directs me and the carter to load his body, together with those of Nicklaas and Menninck on to the cart.

Meanwhile, he himself climbs into the overturned coach, emerging a few moments later with leather valise and a brass-bound deed-box which he straps to his horse's saddle.

When all is done and the two coach-horses hitched loosely to the back of the drover's cart, I help Hervey's injured man up to sit next to the drover. Then, with Hervey leading the way and me, in a daze of fatigue and incomprehension, bringing up the rear, our sad procession sets off back to London.

It is past mid-morning as we reach the outskirts of the city. Many a curious eye is cast upon the carter's grisly load, and several passers-by cross themselves and glance fearfully at Sir William's set features before hurrying about their business.

Approaching London Bridge, Sir William reins in his mount, signals to the cart to go on ahead and waits for me to come alongside.

'Go home, Will, back to Mr Garrick's lodgings. Get

some sleep. You have stabling for the horse?'

'A yard. But Charlie will get water and oats. And a blanket.'

'My coach will call for you tomorrow at noon.'

'What do I tell Mr Garrick?'

'Whatever you like, Will. The truth if you so wish.'

I am so weary from lack of sleep and sore from being so long a-horseback that I am near to tears. 'What is the truth, sir? I can make no sense of what has passed this night...'

Sir William clasps my arm. 'You are tired, lad. Go home. Rest. Tomorrow, I give you my word, all will be made plain.'

Then, trotting ahead, he gives instructions to the carter. I watch them trundle slowly on, then turn a tired Ruby towards home.

'Gawd a' mercy!'

Mrs Wiggins throws her apron over her face and rushes back indoors as my mount and I loom over her.

Her place in the yard is soon taken by an astonished Susan and a wide-eyed Charlie. His jaw drops at sight of the horse.

'Fuck me!' he gawps, earning a routine clip round the ear from Susan.

Painfully, I ease myself from the saddle and dismount.

Now that I'm home, all I want to do is sleep.

With eyes half-closing, I mutter something to Charlie about taking care of the beast, then with Susan's help, I manage to stagger up to my attic and fall upon the bed.

I am asleep immediately and only dimly aware of

Susan starting to pull off my boots before I lose consciousness.

When I awake, it is dark and I have no idea of the time. I lie, listening to the sounds of the City outside my window. Then, hearing movement from below, I conclude that it is yet evening. I have slept for the best part of the day.

And now that I'm awake, I realise that I'm ravenously hungry. I have had nothing to eat since last night's supper before I set off on my ill-fated mission to rescue Agnes.

Agnes! Where is she now? Having escaped Sampson, has she managed to board the Dutch packet? Or, appalled by the deaths of old Hendricksen and Nicklaas, might she have decided to return with Grey to see their killer brought to justice?

Is that what Hervey meant when he sent Grey after her with the instruction to see that the right thing was done?

Throwing back the cover, I sit up. And discover that I am naked. So Susan did not stop at the boots!

In the dimness, I see them standing in the corner, together with the greatcoat and my other clothes in a heap.

Searching out breeches and a shirt, I clamber into them, wincing in pain. All the skin around my buttocks and inner thighs is red raw. It will be days before I can walk properly.

Gingerly I make my way downstairs to the kitchen in the hope that even if supper is already finished, there may yet be some left over. And, indeed, as I am in the hallway, Susan comes from the dining room laden with dirty plates.

'Is there aught left, Sue?' I whisper urgently. 'I could eat a horse.'

'Good job that one's still in the back yard, then...!'

'Don't torment me. I'm famished.'

From inside the dining room comes Mr Garrick's voice. 'Is that you, Will?'

The man himself appears in the doorway. He casts his eye over my dishevelled state, the unlaced shirt, bare legs and rumpled hair. 'My, you look the worse for wear! Time, I think, to explain yourself.'

He sees my anguished look as Susan disappears towards the kitchen, and calls to her. 'Susan, put some victuals on a plate for Will and bring them to the parlour, would you?'

Together, we go into the parlour. He takes one of the two armchairs before the roaring fire and motions me to the other. I sit with great care.

He raises an inquisitive eyebrow and I explain the reason for my soreness.

'Yes, Mrs Wiggins told me of the horse when I returned home this evening. I thought it was the gin talking until I saw it with my own eyes. So - where have you been on this fine beast for the past twenty-four hours?'

I am about to start on my account of events when Susan comes with the tray. Garrick bids me slake my hunger and tells Susan to summon Charlie and Mrs Wiggins.

'I see no reason why we should not hear Will's adventures all together.'

And so, with Susan and Mrs Wiggins on the settle opposite the fire and Charlie at my feet, I tell, in between mouthfuls of cold meat and pickles, all that has happened since I left home at nine-o'clock last evening.

My tale takes near an hour in the telling, interrupted as it is by the women's gasps of horror, Mr Garrick's requests for elucidation at various points, and Charlie's demands for further descriptions of the dead bodies and the hideous visage of the murderer.

At last, Mr Garrick sits back with a sigh. 'I do not wonder you slept so sound this afternoon, Will. Such exploits would do well upon the stage!'

'I do not think that I shall sleep at all this night,' says Mrs Wiggins, fanning herself.

'I am sure you will,' says Garrick. 'But perhaps a warm cup for Will and myself before you do? And do you have some ointment that might ease Will's chafing?'

Mrs Wiggins heaves herself to her feet. 'I have the very thing, sir. A salve of sulphur and sal ammoniac, made from the best hog's lard. 'Tis a sovereign remedy for the itch, and I add a dram or two of lemon-juice to take away the smell.'

Thus it is, that, after a warming drink of chocolate laced with spirit, I am despatched to my room with a jar of Mrs Wiggins foul-smelling concoction.

Unstoppering it, I hold it up to the light of the candle and tentatively dip a finger. It is grey and greasy and the stink is indescribable.

With great reluctance, I strip off my breeches and squat to apply it.

It is in this position, naked legs akimbo, that Susan discovers me when she enters without bothering to knock.

Her hand flies to her mouth to stifle her laughter. 'Sure, is that your arse, or the fiery gates of Hell? Here, give me the stuff... I'll soothe the burning.'

She pushes me, none too gently, face down upon the bed and, after some minutes of ministration from her cool fingers, I discover that, for all the soreness in the adjacent regions, there is one part of my anatomy that has not suffered overmuch from my recent adventures.

Revelations

The next day dawns bright and crisp. Outside my window the whole world sparkles.

A slight foreboding of the meeting I must have with Sir William Hervey at noon nags at my innards, but otherwise my mood is unaccountably light. For some reason I cannot comprehend I feel elated, almost skittish.

It may be memory of my last night's encounter with Susan who with skirts tucked up and knees astride rode me with far more gentleness and finesse than ever I rode poor Ruby. Before, with unerring judgement, disengaging at the crucial moment, allowing me to fountain free.

Or it may be that Mrs Wiggins's potion, for all its noxiousness, has considerably eased my soreness.

Or, yet again, it may be that Christmas is but a week away and among the people I see below in the street cheery greetings abound and every face is smiling.

I anoint myself once more with the foul-smelling salve and then select the softest pair of the late Harry Henderson's linen drawers and a pair of silk breeches. Wool may be warmer but it is also coarser and at the moment I had rather my nether regions be cool than rubbed.

Down in the kitchen, I beg a bowl of warm water from Mrs Wiggins and lave my hands and face to remove the thickest of yesterday's dirt.

I am towelling myself after my ablution when Susan

breezes in with her basket from the bake-house. She, too, seems infected by the day's good humour. As she unties her bonnet she blows me a conspiratorial kiss. I return an equally conspiratorial wink just as Charlie bounces in, drawn by the smell of fresh-baked bread. He looks in mute appeal at Mrs Wiggins.

'No good making them eyes at me, boy.' She waves the knife with which she's hewing off slices of the loaf. 'Not if you've bin a meddlin' with that there beast out in the yard. Get those grubby paws under the pump afore you sit at my table.'

Taking this more as promise than threat, he shoots out and is back within moments, wiping his hands down his breeches. He climbs up next to me at the table.

'Goin' back today, is she, Will?'

'I should think so.'

'Pity. She's a gentle 'un. And she's took quite a fancy to me - nuzzlin' me and taking 'er feed soft as a whisper off mi 'and.'

I ruffle his hair. 'Sounds like you've took a fancy to her as well.'

Mrs Wiggins dumps a trencher of sliced bread and a pot of beef dripping in front of us, then returns to the range. She summons Susan. 'You made the master's tray up? His bacon's ready here.'

'Don't suppose there's a spare slice, Mrs W?'

'Less of your cheek, young man. Just because you goes a-chasin' fine ladies all over the countryside and wears silk britches of a morning, you think you can put on gentleman's airs!'

All the same, as Susan waltzes out to take Mr Garrick his breakfast, a couple of slices of bacon land on our bread.

'Spoils you, I does. 'Ave it now - but there'll be none for lunch.'

'Thanks, Mrs W.'

As I shan't be here for lunch, I don't much care. Feeling generous, I offer Charlie one of the rashers, only to see he's already taken it.

'Don' suppose we could keep 'er?' mumbles Charlie with his mouth full.

'Who? Mrs Wiggins?'

'No, you noddy - the 'orse, Ruby.'

'Not a chance.'

He returns disconsolately to his munching.

Prompt at noon, Sir William Hervey's coach arrives. Ruby's groom is perched beside the coachman and jumps down as soon as they come to a halt. He is to collect the horse and ride her back. I shout Charlie to take him through to the yard, knowing that he'll not escape until Charlie has examined him on every aspect of equestrian management.

The coach is empty. No Grey. No Hervey. It seems I am to ride in splendid isolation. I suggest to the coachman that I might ride beside him but he declines, perplexed.

''Twould not be fitting, sir - not for one of Sir William's acquaintance.'

I open my mouth to protest I am no such thing but think better of it and reluctantly take a seat within. There, as the coach rattles off, I have ample time for thought.

Hervey's absence does not surprise me. Men such as he send for whom they want, they do not come in person. But to send no emissary displays massive confidence that I cannot disobey his summons.

In that, at least, he is right. Yet as the London streets pass by the coach window, I persuade myself that my obedience to his command arises not from fear but from the need to discover the meaning of what has happened in the last two days.

I only hope that in the forthcoming meeting, he is prepared to satisfy that curiosity rather than baffle me further.

The journey to Westminster takes near half an hour. The streets are crowded and our progress slow. But at last the coachman reins in his steeds before the great doors and Grey's familiar, though unwelcome, head appears at the window. I must confess I am surprised to see him - and looking so composed and dapper - considering I last saw him riding off in pursuit of Agnes. Has his business with her been so soon concluded? And has he brought her back with him? Will she, too, be at Westminster?

To little effect I study his face for answers. He is his usual urbane, inscrutable self, with only the merest hint of a sneer beneath the deference.

'Good day, Master Archer. I trust you are recovered?'

'I thank you, sir, I am. And yourself? Your journey back from Gravesend was not too arduous?'

'Tolerable - informative and profitable.' Then, having dropped this nugget to spark my curiosity, he turns on his heel. 'Now, we must not keep Sir William waiting.'

It seems an age ago that Sir Francis Courtney led me between these panelled walls. Since that day, much has happened that I am at a loss to understand, yet today I tread these corridors with more self-assurance than I felt then.

I enter the high-windowed room overlooking the river with a sense of familiarity. No setting sun blinds me this time, only the bright even light of a winter's afternoon.

Sir William greets me with a firm handshake. Then his nose wrinkles.

'Without wishing to be impolite, Master Archer, what is that smell? I detect the whiff of the shambles about you. Have you been consorting with butchers?'

I smile nervously, blushing. 'Not butchers, sir, but only our cook. She gave me a preparation for the rawness I suffered a-horseback.'

'And does it prove efficacious?'

'It seems so. I must apply it night and morning for the week...'

He claps me upon the back and bursts out laughing. 'Zounds, Master Archer, you are even more courageous than I thought!'

Something about his square bulk and loud humour alerts me to Sir Francis's warning not to trust his apparent good nature. I remind myself that Hervey is head of Prime Minister Walpole's secret service, adept at creating an impression to put people off their guard.

'I regret if it gives you offence, sir. Shall I stand further off?'

'Nay, I am not so particular, Will, that I may not stand a little odour.' He turns to Grey, who has stood smirking all this time. 'Nathaniel, is all prepared?'

'He awaits your pleasure, sir.'

'Pleasure, eh? We'll see about pleasure!' He makes

to leave the room and bids me follow. 'Come, Will, I trust you are not squeamish?'

'In what respect, Sir William?'

From the corridor outside his rooms we head down a stone stairway. Grey is close behind me.

'There is someone I would have you see. He awaits below.'

I sense a cold grip on my heart as we descend. The wood-panelled walls give way to bare stone as we enter what I can only think of as a prison. On either side of a gloomy corridor lit by flaring torches are heavy, barred doors.

Hervey seems to sense my unease. He smiles grimly. 'Come, Will, it must be done. You cannot avoid it.'

A cold lump of fear forms in my gut. *What must be done? Am I to be interrogated - put to the torture?* My skin crawls in anticipation of imminent blows. I glance fearfully at the faces of my companions. They are set, impassive.

Arriving at a heavy wooden door with a metal grille at head-height, Hervey raps peremptorily.

It is opened by a tall, thick-set turnkey who stares at me impassively. *Is this the man they would have me see? My inquisitor?* I feel myself trembling as the man approaches me. But it is only to pass by me and go, at Hervey's nod, to stand outside the door.

Now I see that on the floor in the centre of the room sits a wretched figure. His head is bowed, his hands and feet bound.

As Sir William stands in front of him the poor fellow flinches, warding off the expected blow.

At the side of the cell Grey and I watch as, with the

tip of his cane, Hervey lifts the prisoner's chin.

'Look up, man,' he commands.

Sullenly the wretch obeys. His face, caked with dirt, is heavily bruised, his lip split. A thin ribbon of dried blood snakes down his chin, and his hair is matted with it. The burly turnkey who stands guard outside has evidently been at work before we arrived. Eyes, bright with hate, peer up at Sir William.

My heart goes out to the stranger. What has he done to be so abused?

'Do you not recognise him, Master Archer? Look closer.'

At mention of my name, the battered features seek me out and the lip curls back in a sneer revealing blackened teeth.

'Ha! The young gallant! What was't you told me, so high and mighty - *The lady has my protection, sir. She has no need of yours?* Where's that young lady now, eh, mi bucko?'

'Hold your tongue, sir, before your betters!' Hervey slashes the cane across his shoulders.

And now, as he cowers, I recognise him. Beneath the filth, beneath the weals, the face is that of Jack Sampson, the Bethlem warder.

'Betters!' he croaks. 'That jackanapes - that milksop gallant!'

Hervey plies his cane again. 'Peace, you blackguard!' He summons the turnkey. 'Here, Lancey, hose him down and bring him to th'interrogation room. He will tell us what he knows before he sleeps in Newgate this night.'

Lancey manhandles Sampson from the cell, and I turn to Hervey, a dozen questions on my lips.

But I must wait for answers until, having mounted the stone staircase to yet another part of the Westminster labyrinth, we are seated at a massy oak table in a sparse cheerless room. This at least boasts a window, albeit facing out to a blank wall, and has not the damp reek of a prison cell. It is oppressive nonetheless, its very walls redolent with the stink of inquisition.

Sampson, Hervey tells me, was apprehended in the early hours of this morning in the rookeries of Shoreditch, at a stewhouse in Old Cock Lane. It was the stolen horse that did for him. A beast of such quality could not pass without note in such an area, and someone has blown the gab to one of Hervey's spies.

What puzzles me still is how Sampson came to be with Agnes and Nicklaas yesterday. Was he the second man who alighted from the coach at Hanover Square last night?

'I do not understand, sir, why this rogue was there.. And why should he shoot his charge, young Hendricksen? And if it was also he who stunned me at Hanover Square and killed Mijnheer – where is the sense of it?'

'Good questions, Will. And ones to which I cannot yet provide an answer. But answers we shall have, and shortly, for I think I hear Lancey bringing him now...'

Sure enough, the scuffling sound outside resolves itself in the door being flung open and Lancey propelling a wet but relatively cleaner Sampson into the room. He thrusts him down on the chair at the opposite side of the table and takes a step back to stand behind it.

Hervey leans forward, elbows on the table, hands

steepled before him.

'Now, Sampson, you know you cannot 'scape hanging. Half a dozen witnesses saw you shoot dead both Nicklaas Hendricksen and one of my men, then wound another. You will gain nothing by prevarication.'

Sampson tilts back his head insolently. 'Why should I prevaricate? What's done is done. And I'd do it again, for such a prize.'

'What prize is that, sir?'

'Why, the lady - what else? I had her...' He throws a mocking grin my way. 'Yes, Master Milksop, I had her - the one you would so gallantly protect...'

I leap to my feet in fury. 'You liar! How dare you insult the lady so!'

Hervey stays me with an outstretched arm. 'Peace, Will! He says it but to goad you.'

Fuming, I sink back into my seat. 'You are a blackguard, sir.'

'Aye - and have been called worse, by better men than you.'

'Have a care, Sampson.' Hervey does not raise his voice. He could be in polite conversation with a friend. And he is all the more chilling for that. 'My young friend here has a gallant, fiery nature. But you will not find that in me. I require direct answers. Your jibes will not deflect me from my purpose and you may be assured, if you do not answer my questions, I have ways to make you answer. It is no matter to me whether you walk to Newgate tonight or are carried broken there...'

'Your threats are empty,' scoffs Sampson. 'I bear no remorse for what is done. Ask your questions and be damned!'

'Very well. How came you acquainted with the Hendricksen family?'

''Twas through the idiot son.'

'Nicklaas?'

'Aye, he was brought to the madhouse where I worked.'

'Bethlehem Hospital?'

'No - Clerkenwell. 'Twas a private madhouse at the top of Woods Close. The Dutchman was brought there by his father six months ago.'

I recall Agnes telling me how, visiting his brother, Hendrick was sickened by the condition in which he found him. I tell Hervey so. 'He was cruelly treated there - that's why they moved him.'

Sampson's lip curls. 'Is that what she told you?'

I bridle at his tone. 'You would doubt the lady's word, villain?'

'Nay, 'tis true he pined at Clerkenwell. The food and lodging were not of the best. But that was not the whole reason.'

'Explain,' says Hervey calmly.

'The lady was not his only visitor. He also had a brother.'

'Aye, Hendrick. Miss Mayer told me Harry was dismayed at Nicklaas's plight. She said he wrote to his father about it.'

'I know naught of that. But it does not surprise me. A namby-pamby boy was Hendrick...'

I am about to protest when Hervey lays a restraining hand upon my arm.

'Go on, Sampson. You say mistreatment was not the complete reason for moving Nicklaas?'

'Indeed 'twas not. At first, the lady would ask to see Dr Mudie - he was the visiting physician - to discuss the Dutchman's progress. But Dr Mudie was so seldom there - even for those who paid - that she sought me out instead.'

'To report on how the patient did?'

'Aye - and other things... asking me about myself, had I family, how did I like my job - and, as we became more familiar over time, confiding her own distress in a manner so pretty and affecting as to put fire in a man...'

'And Hendrick,' interjects Hervey quickly, sensing my bridling at the rogue's prurience, 'did he likewise?'

Sampson snorts contemptuously. 'Not him! I was beneath his notice.'

For the first time, Grey speaks. 'Were there occasions when Miss Mayer and Hendrick visited together? They were, I believe, betrothed to be married?'

'Ha! You would not have guessed it!'

'How so? Were they cool with each other?'

I leap to Agnes's defence. 'Miss Mayer confided in me that she did not love Harry - but I cannot see it has any bearing on the case...'

From Tom Parsons, I also know why Harry could not love Agnes, but I would avoid that being raked up here.

Hervey is irritated by my interruption, he casts me a stern glance. 'Allow me, Master Archer, to decide what does or does not bear upon matters. There is much that is as yet unclear. You would not be here if you had not decided to inquire into the circumstances of Hendrick Hendricksen's death. I believe Sampson may be about to provide the answer you seek. But I must insist that you remain silent, or I shall have you removed from the room.'

Thus rebuked, I sit back.

Sampson, meanwhile, gives a snort of laughter. 'Oh, that's easy! Who killed the young man - who strung him up to make it look like suicide? Why, I did! At the lady's behest.'

I am dumbfounded - speechless. I could not break Hervey's command to be silent even if I chose.

Sir William, however, appears unruffled. 'Tell us what happened, Sampson.'

I listen in horror as Sampson traduces Agnes's character.

Affected - as if a brute like him could have fine feelings! - by her unhappiness, he had offered to relieve her distress. In return for helping her avoid the prospect of a loveless marriage, she was to use Mijnheer Hendricksen's influence to secure him a position at Bethlem. The key to this was Nicklaas. She would insist that as Sampson had such rapport with his patient, he must accompany him on the move from Clerkenwell. On the night of the move, Sampson was to bring Nicklaas, who was lucid despite his debilitated physical state, to a meeting which Agnes would arrange with Hendrick. There, together with Nicklaas, Agnes hoped to resolve the matter of a marriage that neither party wanted.

'By murdering the proposed bridegroom - Hendrick?' says Grey cuttingly.

'That wasn't the original intention - but, as things turned out...'

'No evasions, man,' snaps Hervey. 'Did you kill

Hendrick Hendricksen on Miss Agnes Mayer's orders?'

'Not directly, no... But it's not as if she stopped me neither.'

As if transfixed, I listen to his account of that fateful night.

'The meeting didn't go well, y'see. Young Hendricksen had asked to meet in the theatre where he acted. While the three of them grumbled away on the open stage, I kept out of the way at the side. But I could see they wasn't none of 'em happy. The place upset the madman - twitching something rotten, he was - and it didn't help that there was a gaping great hole in the stage not two yards from where they was standing. From what I could see, Hendrick was insisting he'd go through with the wedding for her sake. Otherwise the old man would kick her out. She was in tears. So, when she and the madman took the lantern and went down to sit on the seats in the audience to comfort each other, I thought I'd solve the problem of her unwanted husband for her - I shoved namby-pamby boy down the trap in the stage. O'course, he yelled and that brought the two of 'em back up. By the light of the lantern, we could see him lying down below, moaning. "Sampson, what have you done?" she cries. "Don't worry," I tell her. "I'll fix it." So while they keeps out of the way, I takes the lantern, nips down below, finds a rope and strings 'im up. I'm just tying off the rope at the wall when I 'ears a shout from up above and footsteps running off over the stage. Then there's another yell, so I get back up and find 'er ladyship all a-flutter, talking of some beggar who's come into the place and run out again. She tells me to get Hendrick and says we must all get out before the lad calls the Watch. "Too late for that," I tell her, and shine the light down the trapdoor. At sight of the dead 'un, she near faints away, but I catch her. "Sampson," she moans, as she lies swooning in my arms, "you have done for us all!" It seems the vagabond lad saw Nicklaas when he ran out, which is why he yelled. So we get out quick and I take Nicklaas to Bethlem. But she insists on staying behind to see what happens.'

Even as he says it, I have the vision of Agnes accosting Charlie and me in the alley behind the theatre, and hear again her desperate plea to say poor Harry's death was suicide. If only I had heeded her, how many more deaths might have been avoided?

Suddenly I feel the need of air to clear my mind from all this evil.

I stagger to my feet.

Hervey looks up in annoyance but, seeing my pallor, signals impatiently to Grey to take me out.

Twenty minutes later, I am sitting on a stone bench in an enclosed courtyard. On each side rise high walls, their windows blank as sightless eyes. Grey, after thrusting me unceremoniously into the open air, has left me and returned to the interrogation.

After filling my lungs with great gulps of cold, clean air, the nausea in my belly has subsided and now I sit disconsolate with head in hands.

The truth, after all this time, about Harry Henderson's death brings no sense of satisfaction.

Yes, my suspicions have been proved right - he was murdered. Not by a jealous rival. Nor yet because of some secret service conspiracy. The two men that

Gedge saw going into the theatre that night were Sampson and Nicklaas - not, as I thought, men sent by Hervey. And his murder, far from being pre-planned, was committed on the spur of the moment.

It is some minutes before I can bring my mind to focus clearly. But when it does, I realise that there are other events besides Harry's death that I need answers to.

The death of the old man - Nicklaas's shooting... And why, in any case, was Sampson at Hanover Square that night?

Presumably Hervey is even now wresting the answers to these questions from Sampson But how much more will the villain malign the character of Agnes? What else will he maliciously accuse her of?

Hardly able to bear the thought, I rush back into the building, determined to face the scoundrel and give the lie to his slanders.

But the maze of passageways defeats me. So many panelled corridors, so many doorways all the same... If only I had taken closer note as Grey led me out...

At last, after many frantic minutes searching, I sink down, despairing, on the floor of yet another indistinguishable passageway.

And it is here that Grey finds me. His look is one of disdainful amusement.

'Why, Master Archer, you are proving elusive. I return to where I left you, only to find you gone... Sir William desires your company.'

'Has he finished questioning Sampson?'

'For the moment.'

But he is not prepared to say more. Our journey back to Sir William Hervey's room is made in silence.

There, Sir William is ensconced before a roaring fire. The afternoon is well advanced and encroaching dusk has brought a penetrating chill to the air.

'Come in, Will, sit down.'

'I must apologise, sir...'

'No need, my boy, no need. It takes a strong stomach to listen to such things. But we Yorkshire-men are made of sterner stuff, I hope - Nathaniel, a bumper of warm grog would not go amiss.'

Grey departs for a few moments and returns with glasses and a jug on a tray.

Once our glasses are filled, Hervey begins to tell what else he learned from Sampson.

'He was, of course, at Hanover Square that night.'

'Indeed, sir, I recall seeing two men alight from the carriage. I had thought it might be Mijnheer returning with a servant, but now I realise it must have been that miscreant and Nicklaas.'

'The mute coachman, Menninck, had just collected them from the madhouse, in preparation for their flight.'

'And did Sampson also murder the old man?'

'He did.'

Suddenly I see the image of Agnes at the bedroom door, her face stricken with terror at sight of something - or someone - over my shoulder...

'So it was he who struck me down?'

'Yes - with the express purpose of having you blamed for the murder of Mijnheer. Then they, all three, took flight - aiming to embark on the Rotterdam packet and be out of the country before the deed was discovered.'

'He did not reckon on my regaining consciousness

so soon...'

'Nor upon us keeping watch upon you for your protection.'

'My protection...? But I thought...'

Hervey laughs. 'You thought it was only to ensure compliance with my admonition to shun the Hendricksens?'

'I did think so, yes.'

Hervey raises his glass in mock salute. 'You are a headstrong young man, Will Archer, and obstinate in the pursuit of justice. That much was apparent at our first interview. I was under no illusion that you would meekly submit, so I decided to use you instead.'

'Use me, sir?' I inquire, offended.

Hervey shakes his head pityingly. 'You really don't understand yet, do you, Will? Just how much danger you've been in... Enlighten him, Nathaniel.'

I turn, perplexed, as Grey takes up the story.

'Know, Master Archer, that I pursued Miss Mayer all the way to Gravesend.'

I interrupt breathlessly. 'She is safe?'

'Safe in Holland I dare say by now. As are the documents she purloined - those I allowed her to keep.'

'Purloined? Allowed? Do you imply she has committed some crime?'

'Deception - theft - incitement to conceal a crime - accessory to murder... Do you wish me to go on?'

'I don't believe you. If she is in truth guilty of all these things you would not have let her go.'

'There was precious little point detaining her. Juries are loth to convict a well-born lady, let alone one who pleads her belly.'

The phrase is familiar to me, yet it makes no sense.

'You are saying she was with child - but how?'

'Rather you should ask by whom,' says Hervey. 'Not by Hendrick, for you said yourself that they did not love each other - and from what Sampson said, it appears Hendrick's tastes lay elsewhere. That leaves either Nicklaas - or Sampson.'

I cannot take it in.

Hervey beckons Grey to re-fill my glass as I struggle to come to terms with the revelation.

How can I have been so blind?

Slowly, things fall into place. The gossip Charlie relayed about her sickness every morning... Her craving for sweetmeats at the ice-fair...

And her extreme fondness for Nicklaas - not, I now see, merely tenderness for an unfortunate brother-in-law but desire for a longed-for husband. With dismay I recall their disarray when I burst in upon them at Bethlem, and Sampson's complicit smirk... Did that blackguard know even then?

Hervey lays a hand upon my knee. 'It is hard to comprehend, I know, but that is the substance of Sampson's testimony. Miss Mayer was in love with Nicklaas, the elder brother – a situation Mijnheer Hendricksen would never countenance. So much she imparted to Sampson and, once he thus had hold upon her, he did not hesitate to turn the screw...'

I see a flicker of hope. 'If Agnes was under such duress, she is surely not to blame..?'

'If it comforts you to think that, Will, I will not disabuse you. It will serve no purpose. The lady is of no further interest to us. We have what we wished for out of the affair.'

Possibly he wishes me to think he refers only to the

apprehension of Sampson as the killer. But I remember the conversation I had with James Lacy and Mr Garrick at the Bedford Coffee House not so many days ago. 'Of course! The documents that Mr Grey took from Miss Mayer give you control of Hendricksen's fortune - to prosecute the war in Spain.'

For the first time I succeed in astonishing him.

'My, my, Will Archer! You have even more perception than I gave you credit for.'

As his face breaks out in a broad smile, there is a tap at the door.

Lancey enters.

'The prisoner, sir. He awaits your convenience.'

'Very well, Lancey,' says Hervey, rising from his chair and summoning us to follow. 'We must do what must be done.'

The sky is the colour of lead as we emerge from a side door into Old Palace Yard. Evening is encroaching and in the distance thunder rumbles.

Hervey and Grey are dressed in furs as if ready for travel. I have only my coat and have been offered nothing other, so I presume I am not to accompany them. I clasp my arms about me. The cold is not as intense as in the last few days but the thick air of the city is heavy with the threat of rain.

A short distance away stands Sampson, guarded by one of Hervey's men. Beyond, half-beached, is a small rowboat in which I guess he is to be transported to Newgate. The river, although in parts still sluggish with partially melted ice, has channels clearer than the noisome streets.

In the dusk, the five completed arches of the new

Westminster Bridge stand gaunt in the middle of the river while, from wooden enclosures of deep-driven piles to either side, half-built piers stand proud. Already three years a-building, it is said 'twill be another seven before it is completed. Then London will have two stone bridges across the Thames.

A sight that Sampson will never see.

Hervey strides across to where the prisoner stands, shoulders bowed against the night.

'Well, Sampson, have you aught else to say before you take your final journey? Your life is forfeit, but there may yet be hope for your soul if you repent of your crimes.'

For reply, Sampson spits at Hervey's feet. 'Look to your own salvation, Sir William Hervey. My crimes at least are open - can you say the same for yours?'

Hervey grunts as if he expected no more. 'Take him away.'

The guard begins dragging him to the waiting skiff, but they have gone no more than a few steps when Sampson turns and yells over his shoulder, 'The child is mine, Milksop, not the madman's. Your lady whored herself for me! And what I have done has all been for her.'

I tense, bunching my fists, but Hervey stays me. 'See to him, Lancey,' he orders softly.

The retreating pair are almost on the water's edge where the small boat is pulled up on the mud when Lancey starts towards them, calling out.

The guard turns at the sound and, at the same moment, Sampson breaks free. Hampered by the clinging mud and his bound wrists, he staggers like a drunken man, floundering desperately.

He doesn't get far.

Calmly, Lancey raises his pistol, aims and fires. Sampson drops to the ground, his head shattered by the bullet.

I turn to see that Hervey and Grey are already making their way back to Westminster Hall. They show no reaction to what has just occurred.

Down at the river's edge Lancey and the guard, as if obeying previously given orders, unhurriedly retrieve the body and dump it in the boat, then row slowly off into the gathering dusk.

Outrage rises like bile. I catch up with Hervey in Old Palace Yard where his coach awaits him and seize his arm, spinning him round to face me.

'You never intended him to reach Newgate, did you?' I shout.

Grey has started forward, but Hervey waves him back.

His voice is cool as the surrounding air. 'Go home, Master Archer, and think on today's events. When you have had time to consider, you may view things differently.' Bidding Grey go first, he follows him into the carriage, then leans out of the window. 'It is a long walk home, Will, but I have taken the liberty of providing for you.'

As he speaks another landau trots into the yard. The door is flung open and Tom Parsons leaps down, his face wreathed in smiles. Behind him, seated inside, Sir Francis Courtney raises a coy hand in salutation.

Tom clasps me to his bosom with an ardour that I have never known him show before. Then, taking my arm firmly in his, escorts me to Sir Francis's coach. I allow myself to be led, my head in a daze. Over his chatter, I hear the departing rumble of Hervey's carriage.

As Tom bundles me up into Sir Francis's landau, there is a clap of thunder overhead and the first heavy drops of rain fall from the lowering sky.

Christmas

For several weeks the theatre at Goodmans Fields is dark. No use competing with the pantomime extravagances at Covent Garden and Drury Lane, with their low comedians, Italian singers, dancers and scenic transformations. Mr Rich rides supreme at Christmas.

In Mr Garrick's house, however, all is bustle. News has come from Mr Giffard that the theatre may have until March at the very least, and that, after the success of *Richard III*, he would like Garrick to attempt Lear.

Macklin, still smarting from Garrick's rebuff of Samuel Foote, is dismissive. 'The greatest of Shakespeare's tragic roles - and you but twenty-five years old... 'Tis folly, Davey. Or worse, hubris, in this your first season as a professional actor.'

They are seated before a roaring fire in the parlour over hot punch. I, as usual, sit attentive in the shadows at the edge of the firelight - my presence requested, I suspect, as merely an auditor to their wit.

'All the same, I shall attempt it, Charles, for Giffard's sake. It may be the last thing I do at Goodmans Fields.'

Indeed, for the last week, Garrick has started gathering his thoughts and possessions together, preparatory to our removal. Mr Fleetwood has definitely offered him a contract for the coming season at Drury Lane. 'At £500, Will, which is as much as Quin, the king of Covent Garden and a good twenty years my senior, commands!'

As a result, our Christmas celebrations, the last in this house, will be lavish.

For days downstairs in the kitchen Susan and Mrs Wiggins have been washing currants, soaking raisins in brandy, slicing and dicing all sorts of fruits and laying them out before the fire to dry. We are to have a rich Yuletide fruit cake and mincemeat pies.

In addition, a lovingly-constructed pastry case stands on the larder shelves, ready to receive goose, rabbit, chicken and quail for a stand-up pie, and Mrs W promises that the Christmas meal will start with her mother's recipe for plum potage.

Charlie salivates continuously like a starving dog and his head is sore from slaps for picking tit-bits.

Meanwhile, my master is telling Macklin that plans for a move to Bow Street may have to wait until the latter end of the year. 'I have had a letter from Mr Sheridan in Dublin...'

My ears prick up. It is where Ned Phillimore and Kitty Blair are booked from April.

'He would have Mrs Woffington and myself appear at Smock Alley for the summer.'

'And will you go?' I sense some envy in Macklin's growl. Being Irish himself, he may be wondering why no such invitation has come for him.

'I think I shall,' nods Garrick with a self-satisfied smile.

A satisfaction, I guess, that arises from the prospect of close companionship with Mistress Peg for at least two months in new - and possibly romantic - surroundings.

And I? Shall I accompany them to Ireland?

I own it would be a relief - to be away from the

scene of all the troubles of the last few weeks.

Since the night Sampson was killed, I have heard no more from Sir William Hervey. Nor have I had any news of Agnes.

And, whilst I now understand the circumstances of Harry's death, it has not brought me peace of mind. I have no sense of completion - for so many other things remain unresolved.

I still have no idea who attacked me after I left Agnes that night that seems so long ago now - or why.

Nor am I clear about who effected my release from the Bridewell after John Aikin's death.

And how did Hervey and Grey come to be at Hanover Square on the night old Hendricksen died?

The prospect of Christmas and Dublin is delightful but I cannot see myself enjoying it whilst these questions remain. And though I have no desire to see Hervey again, I suspect he is the only one who can provide the answers.

By Christmas Day the last of the snow has gone. The river flows free once more and Aikin's body is found, come ashore less than half a mile down-river. When informed of this, Foote, his supposed friend, declines any part in his interment so it is left to Garrick to contact his only relation, a brother, to arrange a fitting disposal of his remains.

Out of duty a few of our company - Garrick, Ned Phillimore and myself - attend his funeral, the only mourners apart from his brother. Thus John Aikin, little loved and little mourned, leaves this world.

It is a bleak occasion but we do not allow it to mar our festive celebrations.

On Christmas Day itself I politely refuse Mr Garrick's invitation to dine in the parlour where with the Yule log blazing brightly, he entertains Macklin, Peg Woffington, Ned Phillimore and Kitty.

Instead, I play one of the parts to which I must become accustomed in our new menage – that of butler, filling glasses to oil the wheels of conversation while Susan, in Sunday dress, serves out the feast.

Macklin is his usual overbearing self, relating tales of his theatrical success and urging Garrick to join him in setting up an academy of 'histrionic science' to teach the art and technique of acting. Mistress Peg disarmingly mocks his bombast without ever offending him, whilst Ned offers good humoured advice and Kitty simpers.

When at last, all replete, they retire to the parlour, I go down to the kitchen where for Mrs Wiggins, Susan, Charlie and myself our own Christmas dinner awaits.

Susan has fashioned crowns of coloured paper which, with much cajolery and laughter, she will have us wear before Mrs Wiggins presents us all with a bowl of her mother's famous plum potage. Hot and spicy, it paves the way for a slab of Mrs Wiggins's pie.

It is a remarkable piece of handiwork - the goose, the chicken and the quail, all boned and stuffed one within the other in a savoury aspic dotted with pieces of rabbit, and all enclosed in a pastry crust with such battlements and crenellations as almost to defy assault.

Mrs Wiggins, already ruddy with heat and hot posset, crimsons yet further from our praise and is in danger of tears until Susan puts another gin before her.

Then, as she rocks herself to sleep in her chair, Susan, Charlie and myself debate whether we have room for a piece of fruit cake.

'I'm as stuffed as Mrs W's squab chicken,' sighs Charlie. He lets out a long whining fart and dissolves into laughter. Susan and I join in, the unaccustomed rich food and drink making us giddy.

And so the afternoon passes in warm companionship. At length, we hear Mr Garrick's guests departing and Susan looks to the piles of dirty pans and crockery. With a sigh, she rolls up her sleeves and puts the kettle on the fire. I send Charlie to get water from the pump and then, as he curls up before the fire and snuffles into sleep, Susan and I set to with the pots.

Half an hour later, plates, salvers and pans are all clean and in their place. Mrs Wiggins and Charlie are fast asleep and from upstairs in the parlour come confidential murmurs and suppressed giggles from Mr Garrick and Mrs Peg.

Susan and I look at each other and without more ado creep upstairs to end our Christmas Day with one last festivity.

Enlistment

Early in January, two events occur which change my life.

The first is a letter from Agnes.

My dearest Will, she writes, *Can you ever forgive me?*

Since arriving here in Holland, the wrongs I have done you prey constantly on my mind and now I feel you deserve to know the truth.

You will have discovered by now that I was less than honest with you about my relationship with Hendrick. True, Mijnheer wanted us to marry, but we both knew it was impossible. Hendrick liked not the female sex, and I was in love with Nicklaas.

When you talked of the letters you found in Hendrick's room, you commented how cold and formal they seemed and I admitted that I did not love him. The truth is I hated him. Not because he deserved my hate - he was kind and gentle, I see that now - but because I was afraid.

On the night you and I met I was already with child - and that child was not, could not have been, Hendrick's. It was his brother Nicklaas who was the father.

Long before the intransigent Mijnheer had Nicklaas committed to the madhouse, we knew that we loved each other. As you so rightly said, Nicklaas was never mad - only reckless. And the more hopeless his plight became, incarcerated in that dreadful place, the greater our love grew. The child was conceived during one of my visits there - and that was also the occasion when I fell into Sampson's power...

God knows I regret that day! How could I have been so foolish!

I was so taken in by the villain's apparent kindness in allowing me to be alone with Nicklaas that I confided more than was wise - how I could see no hope for Nicklaas and myself as long as Mijnheer and Hendrick remained as obstacles to our love...

The paper drops from my hand. I sink on to my bed in disbelief as the significance of her confession hurtles in upon me. Can it really be true that Agnes herself planted the seed of murder in Sampson's mind?

Unwillingly, I take up the letter again.

Then one day the wretch walked in upon us... I shall never forget his look of smiling malice. 'A pretty pair of lovebirds,' he gloated. 'Well I, too, could fancy some of that, my lady.'

Nicklaas flew at him, but the rogue was too strong and beat him back. And then, seizing my wrists, he told us how it would be.

In return for ridding us of Hendrick, he would arrange for Nicklaas to escape so we could be together.

I was to arrange a secret meeting with Hendrick where Sampson would do the deed. Then, to cover our tracks, Nicklaas and he must be transferred to another, less secure madhouse. And in return - oh, Will, with how much self-disgust I write this! - I must submit to lie with him...

With sudden ferocity I slam my fist against the wall of my garret. The pain does little to dull the despair of knowing that Agnes is both guilty and yet a victim...

After a few moments, while my brain stops reeling and I feel tears wetting my cheeks, I know I must read on.

Believe me, Will, it happened but once. To recall it is to live again the foulness - but that was not the worst.

What I believed - and fervently hoped - would be the end, for him was just the beginning.

Learning that, after Hendrick's death, Mijnheer had proposed marriage to me himself, he saw a way to ensnare me completely in his evil web. He would kill the old man, too! He believed the old man's riches would come to Nicklaas – and, when he and I were safely married in Holland, to me.

When I told Sampson that I had asked you to guard me on my flight, he marked you down as a convenient scapegoat for the old man's murder, thus enabling him to accompany us in your place. His plan, once Nicklaas and I were married and the fortune secured, was to dispose of Nicklaas and have me all to himself.

Fortunately for myself, but tragically for Nicklaas, the plan went wrong when we were pursued by Hervey. Our coach overturned, Sampson shot Nicklaas, but I escaped. Before I could embark at Gravesend, however, Hervey's man, Nathaniel Grey, caught up with me and demanded I surrender all but a very few of the deeds and bonds I had managed to retrieve from the wreck of the coach.

I pause and re-read the last few sentences. It is clear that Agnes does not know I was there, or that I saw what occurred - the overturned coach, her pleading with Sampson, the killing of Nicklaas, and her flight from the scene.

I am relieved she does not know I witnessed her shame. But it is relief tinged with disillusion for her whom I can never think of in the same way again. With growing resignation, I read on.

Pray do not judge me too harshly, Will. I am a weak but not, I hope, a wicked woman. What I did, I did for love. In risking all, I lost all. In place of my honour, I have only shame. In place of a husband, a fatherless child. In place of riches, a mean house and a pittance to end my days.

All these I deserve - they are fit punishment for my wrongdoing. But the guilt that weighs most heavily on me is that, without thought for the consequences, I involved you in my schemes.

I have friends yet in England and it is with great relief that I hear Sampson has been apprehended and his plan to implicate you in Mijnheer's death has failed.

I cannot but be sensible of the regard in which you held me, and of the pain I have caused you, but you are young, Will, and have a noble heart. My hope now is that you can find it in that heart to forgive me – and, having forgiven, then you must forget me.

Your ever grateful,
Agnes.

Dazed, my feelings numbed, I sit staring into space, the letter fluttering from my nerveless fingers.

Evening gathers round me.

I am only wakened from my misery by Charlie clumping upstairs to tell me supper is ready.

With a weary smile, I follow him down, feeling suddenly older than my nineteen years.

Some days after receiving the letter comes the second life-changing event, a summons which, though expected, is nonetheless unwelcome.

Sir William Hervey bids me attend him at Westminster.

I do not know what further surprises he may have for me, but I am resolved to have the answers to those mysteries that still perplex me.

The view from the great window of his room is shrouded in thick mist, buildings at the far side of the river no more than phantoms.

As if to emphasise the chill outside, a hearty fire crackles in the grate, as hearty as Sir William's mood.

Wary, I meet his high spirits with polite formality.

His brow furrows. 'You are severe, Will? Has all the cheer of Christmas had so little effect? Can it be that you have not forgiven me yet for Sampson's death?'

'My forgiveness can hardly be material, sir,' I reply coolly. 'The villain was to die in any case. A day or two makes little difference.'

'Ah, there you are wrong, Will. A day, an hour, a minute - there is no accounting the damage may be wrought by an unguarded tongue.'

'It was expedient, then, to still it?'

'Indeed so.'

'Thus ensuring that the murders of Mijnheer Hendricksen and his sons might pass without comment? And his fortune and assets, retrieved by Master Grey from Miss Mayer at Gravesend, might pass unhindered into the public purse?'

Hervey raises a quizzical eyebrow. 'The lady, I see, has been in contact with you.'

'She has confessed all, sir. And I have forgiven her.'

Hervey purses his lips reflectively. 'You show great magnanimity - considering it was she who lured you to Hanover Square in order that you might shoulder the blame for the old man's murder.'

'That is monstrous suggestion, sir! It was Sampson's idea!'

Hervey sighs. 'Indeed, so he said...'

'You doubt his word?'

'A rogue to whom lying was second nature – why would I doubt his word?'

'You mock me, sir...'

'Believe me, no. Sampson's confession was perhaps the one good action of his whole life – seeking, as it did, to protect – however misguidedly – the remarkable woman who had seduced him.'

'Seduced him! Miss Mayer?' But my protest lacks force, for I cannot but recall the doubts I felt after reading Agnes's letter.

Perhaps Hervey senses my hesitation for he says, 'Can you promise to disengage your heart and think for a while only with your head, Will?'

'I will hear you out, sir,' I murmur.

And hear him out I do as he tells how Agnes, seeing fortune slipping from her grasp, planned to murder her unwanted lover, elope with her real lover and enlisted both Sampson and myself as her all-too-willing dupes.

When his tale is done, he sees my dejection. 'Do not reproach yourself, Will,' says he. 'You are young and sentimental – men of far more years and experience than you have succumbed to her charms.'

'Sampson, for one,' I mutter bitterly.

'Aye, and the old man, and both his sons. I cannot imagine that, once in Holland, Nicklaas would have survived long. Fortunately, Sampson relieved her of that task, too.'

One small shred of chivalry remains, which I cling to. 'But I saw with my own eyes – you saw it, too! - how she pleaded with Sampson to spare him!'

'To spare him? Or to dispatch him, with promise that she would then be his alone? Did she fling herself at Sampson's feet in entreaty for the victim, Nicklaas – or in submission to his killer?'

The realisation of my stupidity makes me angry. 'How could I have been so gullible! I would have done anything for her...!'

Hervey smiles sympathetically. 'Love is a powerful force, Will. It led Sampson, as I said, to confess in order not to incriminate her. Which is why I chose to be merciful...'

This is a step too far. '*Merciful!* To have your man shoot him in cold blood!'

'You would have had him hauled through the streets and thrash out his last minutes at a rope's end, soiling himself as the crowd jeered?'

'No – I, er...'

'A bullet – swift and clean. Expedient, as you said earlier, in preventing unnecessary complications. But also a kind of reward for his chivalry. I am, despite what you may think, a reasonable man.'

Smarting as I am from the enormity of Agnes's betrayal, I still find his smugness irksome. 'And was it reasonable, sir, to deprive the lady of all her inheritance?'

'Not quite all – Nathaniel left her sufficient for her needs. And in fact she had no legal right to any inheritance, for she was not yet part of the Hendricksen family...' Seeing me about to protest, he holds up his hands. 'Well, let us not debate the point. Suffice it to say, the money is ours - as promised by Mijnheer but two days before his death.'

Once again he succeeds in amazing me. I recall Charlie's talk of comings and goings at Hanover Square, of coaches and messengers from Parliament, but though I already guessed their purpose I am still appalled at the outcome. 'The old man disinherited his sons?'

'One son dead. Another mad,' says Hervey reasonably. 'After making sufficient provision for himself and his wife-to-be, and arrangements for the upkeep of his demented son, the old man signed over the majority of his fortune. Now that those provisions for wife and son are no longer necessary, we have it all - which, as a true patriot, I am sure he would not begrudge us.'

'A patriot? But he was Dutch, not English!'

'Exactly! Tell me, Will Archer - what do you know of events in Europe?'

'I know that Frederick of Prussia and Empress Maria Theresa of Austria are at war in Silesia and Bohemia...'

'Quite right - you are an educated young man and can read, and the newspapers are full of it. But some of us must not only *follow* events, Will - we must *predict* them. Intelligence tells us that the French who are currently in Bavaria will shortly be setting their sights on Flanders.'

I remember the conversation with Lacy in the Bedford Coffee House. 'But surely Prime Minister Walpole is set against war? The newspapers already berate him for appeasing Spain which seizes our ships. If he will not act against so direct a threat to England's interests, why would he oppose France marching into Flanders, which offers none?'

'Not to England, no - but to his Majesty...?'

'Of course! Hanover lies in their path.'

'Clever boy! And as his Majesty's visits to Hanover far exceed those to any region of his British realm outside of London, a threat to his homeland is an eventuality he is not prepared to contemplate - whatever Mr Walpole's views on the subject.'

Elated by this talk of world events, my initial reserve has melted. Hervey is speaking to me as an equal, man to man. I can't help basking in his encouragement. Yet one thing puzzles me.

'How then is Hendricksen's bequest patriotic?'

'Flanders, my boy, is controlled not only by Austria, but also by the Dutch Republic. A threat to Flanders, therefore, is a threat to the Netherlanders. At this very moment the Dutch, together with various German states, including Hanover, are raising an army against the expected French invasion. Our King would add English troops to their number. Hendricksen's money will go to supporting Dutch as well as English interests.'

I pause as a thought strikes me. 'Why are you telling me all this, Sir William? I am but a humble actor...'

Sir William looks aside and his mouth quirks into a smile. 'Ah, you come to the point at last! But I shall delay you a little more, Will, if I may. Long enough for you to ask those questions which I know you want to...'

'Questions, sir?'

'Like who attacked you that night on leaving Miss Mayer's coach - and who freed you from the Bridewell after Aikin drowned...?'

'Truly, I would know the answers to those questions, sir.'

Sir William sits back in his chair and steeples his hands. 'First, let me tell you a story. You will know by now that my role is - how shall I say? - unseen? The names of those in my employ appear on no government payroll, but their work nonetheless ensures that state and government run smoothly. My agents keep me abreast of affairs both foreign and domestic in a strictly confidential manner. And, to be effective, these agents must be drawn from all walks of life, especially those where they may be privy to unguarded conversations - such as, for example, may occur amongst those who flock to see Mr Garrick...'

He pauses with a look that seems to invite comment and, as the significance of his words sinks in, I blurt out, 'You are telling me that you have a spy in our company, sir?'

Faces flit before me - forthright Ned Phillimore, timorous Tom Parsons, drunken Garbutt and patrician Drake, even Mr Garrick himself... Surely it cannot be true?

'Who is it?'

'Ask rather who it was.'

All at once, Hervey's initial attempt to steer me away from my investigations into Harry's background makes sense. 'Harry...?'

Hervey shakes his head with a smile. 'Tut! Think with your mind, not your heart, Will.'

I am at a loss. 'I cannot think that any of my friends...?'

'Exactly!'

And now it is clear. 'Aikin!'

Hervey nods with satisfaction. 'John Aikin - from a humble family, but with aspirations to mix with society. And, more importantly, greedily ambitious. On the face of it, an ideal agent. Regrettably, the same flaw that fired his ambition also proved his downfall. Jealousy.'

'Jealousy of whom, sir?'

'Of those with more wealth and position - and of yourself, Will.'

'Me!'

'Yes, Will – your popularity, your good-nature, your closeness to Mr Garrick – all these stirred first envy, and then - desire.'

Suddenly the unreadable emotion I sensed behind Aikin's scorn in every conversation we'd had and that flash of disbelieving hope in our final encounter make sense.

'He *loved* me? I did not realise – his animosity blinded me...'

'Just as his feelings for you distracted him from his designated task, which was to observe and report on your investigation into Harry Henderson's death. Faced with your unresponsiveness to his desire, he resolved that what he could not have, he would destroy – and from that moment he ceased to be a reliable agent. First he attempted to hinder your investigation by disposing of the street urchin... '

'Joe?'

'Was that his name?' says Hervey, unconcerned. 'At all events, a pointless death resulting more from spite than from necessity. Then he attacked you on the night after your meeting with Miss Mayer and he abducted the boy, Charlie, whom he knew you were fond of.' He shakes his head sadly. 'He let personal feelings get in the way. Which is why I was obliged – against my usual practice – to intervene to remedy the effects of his malice.'

'It was you who had me released from the Bridewell after he drowned - to prevent any investigation into his death revealing his role in your secret service?'

'That is correct, Will. But it was not the only reason. It was in our interests to have you play your part in Miss Mayer's escape. With her out of the way, and in circumstances so hurtful to the old man's pride, he might have proved yet more generous. But Aikin's selfish desire for revenge nearly prevented that. His obsession for hurting you meant we did not know of Sampson's involvement. News of his presence at Hanover Square reached us only at the last moment. Which was why Nathaniel and I were obliged to rescue you in person. It was a close-run thing, Will. If it had not been for your resourcefulness in freeing yourself, I doubt we'd have achieved it.'

'I find myself indebted to you, sir,' I say humbly.

'Of that there is no doubt, Will. And debts must be repaid.' His glance flicks aside. 'You are to go to Ireland, I hear?'

Nothing in his knowledge surprises me now. 'That is Mr Garrick's intention, sir...' I reply warily.

'And I no longer have an agent in your company...'

I stiffen. 'You would have me inform on my friends, sir! I will not do it!'

He raises a placatory hand. 'Be not so hasty, Will. I have asked nothing of you as yet. It is just that there are rumours of discontent in Ireland. Nothing definite. But with affairs as they are in Europe, I would not have nasty surprises pounce in at the back door, so to speak...'

I gather my courage. 'I will not spy on my friends, sir.'

I sense a chilling of his mood. Hervey's smile is mirthless. 'Such high principles are all very well, Master Archer. But let me remind you that gratitude is as important a virtue as loyalty. I have gone out of my way to save your hide on more than one occasion. Mr Samuel Foote still itches to avenge his friend, Aikin's, death and, with Sampson dead, there is but one other suspect for Mijnheer's murder. If a former molly-house boy were to be accused...'

My cheeks burn with indignation as I spring to my feet. 'Aikin's death was an accident, sir, and you know full well I was wrongly implicated in Mijnheer Hendricksen's murder. As for the previous life you mention, I was never a willing participant.'

'Willing or not, the penalty for sodomy is a rope's end. As it is for murder. Have you such trust in our Courts of Justice, Master Archer, that you think they will be dainty over such fine distinctions?'

He regards me closely. Then his expression softens and his tone becomes cajoling. 'My apologies, Will, that was unworthy of me. You cannot be intimated, like Aikin and his kind. I have no option but to use such scoundrels, but they are my base coinage and I have need of true currency, too. You have shown yourself to be a young man of principle, honourable and loyal to your friends and those you love. Such qualities have a price beyond rubies. I would not have you lose them, for I believe you have a sure instinct for where and with whom to bestow them. I am not asking you to spy upon your friends, Will. Rather, I am asking that you make use of those qualities for a greater cause – the good of your country.'

I consider for a moment, eyes cast down, avoiding his gaze. I have no doubt that should I refuse outright he will carry out his threats. I already know too much - and I have the example of Sampson all too clearly in my memory.

And yet Sampson's death, for all it was illegally accomplished, was fitting justice for his murder of Harry and Nicklaas and of Mijnheer... If by agreeing to Hervey's request I can forestall such another villain...

I think also of Agnes Mayer and of how easily my loyalty and love were misplaced... But it is a lesson – though it shames me still - which I feel I have truly learned and if I, unlike John Aikin, can rise above personal desire to serve a greater cause...

I raise my eyes to his expectant face. A face which, even now, I know to be a mask. If I do not agree, he will destroy me - my choice is, in reality, no choice. It is true I keep my friends close, but will it not be circumspect to keep my enemy closer?

My reply, when it comes, is hesitant. 'If, as you say, sir, it is for the general good...'

He leaps to his feet before I have finished and claps me upon the shoulder. 'Splendid, Will. All I ask at this time is that you do not point-blank refuse me. I may not have cause to use you, but I give you my word that if I do, it will indeed be for our country's good and in no matter that will compromise your integrity.'

He seizes my hand and pumps it vigorously. 'Welcome, Will Archer, to your country's secret service. I trust our co-operation will be a long and rewarding one!'

Coming back through the hubbub of the New Year market, I reflect on the new beginnings in my own life. Changes that, two months ago, I could never have dreamed of. I can hardly believe that I, Will Archer, have ventured not only into the cells of Bedlam but into the halls of Westminster - and been in danger of my life on more than one occasion.

Nor can I yet comprehend the uncertain future that beckons – the voyage to a new country, Ireland, with a master who has my interests at heart - and the prospect of secretly serving another master who would cast me aside without a qualm...

Suddenly I sense a presence beside me.

Looking down, I see the grimy, grinning face of Natty, the pickpocket. His appearance at this moment seems strangely fitting - was it not he who started all this, the day that Harry Henderson was murdered?

'Wotcher, mate,' he says.

I cannot forbear smiling. 'Mates now, are we?'

'Well...?'

I make a show of considering. 'First you pick my pocket, then you help save my life, then you lure Charlie away to be kidnapped...'

He stops dead, hands on skinny hips, indignant. 'That weren't none of my doing!'

I ruffle his greasy hair. 'Just jesting - mate.'

Gratefully he punches my outspread palm and I rest my hand on his shoulder as we walk on. Around us, tradesmen shout their wares and customers haggle. The clamour of London engulfs us.

Then Natty stops, I feel him tense. His eyes fix on a gent at a nearby stall.

He glances up, half apologetic. ''Scuse me, Mister Will - business.'

He slides into the crowd and I find myself inwardly contemplating the straightforward candour of his villainy. Natty is what he is. And too many of those I've had to deal with over the past weeks have been a world away from what they seemed.

Deep in the world of acting, and rehearsing *The Changeling,* of all plays, I suppose I should have recognised such impostures. The counterfeit madman, the woman scheming to rid herself of an unwanted lover, the low villain so enslaved by desire that he will commit murder for her – all were there before me...

But when one is a character in the drama, how can one stand aside and view it as a dispassionate observer?

Yet now I am drawn back to what is unfolding in front of my eyes. Over at the stall I see Natty dart away from the gent. A brief moment – then the gent reaches for his handkerchief which is not there...

The hue and cry is raised! *Stop thief!* resounds about the market. Bodies from all directions hurl themselves in pursuit. Baskets are uptipped, fruit cascades and bounces from stalls. Outraged cries of vendors thicken the din of shouts and screams as the crowd pulses this way and that.

In the midst of the mêlée, the boy is fleetingly by my side again. He looks up and winks. I feel something thrust into my pocket as he passes.

Seconds later I see him saunter past the gent who, red-faced, gesticulates in recognition. With a cry of triumph, Natty is seized by the mob and upended, pockets rifled, every rag searched. Nothing!

Lacking evidence, he is reluctantly let go. With a fine display of indignation, he stalks off and is swallowed up by the din.

He will be back, I know, to claim his spoils and I smile to myself, briefly seeing us as others, if they notice us at all, must see us.

A mere boy and an almost man.

Two anonymous players in the multitude of humanity.

Natty, eight years old, experienced dipper.

And me...

Will Archer, nineteen - novice secret agent.

Historical Notes

Goodmans Fields Theatre

Goodmans Fields Theatre was opened by Henry Giffard on 31st October 1729, and the opening play was Farquhar's, *The Recruiting Officer*.

In 1736, either a performance of Gay's *The Beggar's Opera* or a political satire, *A Vision of the Golden Rump* (possibly by Henry Fielding) both heavily critical of Robert Walpole and the Whig government led to the Licensing Act of 1737. This Act of Parliament was a landmark event in the censorship of public performance and led to the ban on any play that criticised the government or the Crown.

David Garrick worked at the Theatre from 1740 – 1742, drawing in huge crowds.

Unfortunately, the success of Goodmans Fields Theatre led to its downfall, and the manager was threatened with prosecution under the Licensing Act. It was the death of the Theatre and it closed down in 1742 with a final nose-thumbing performance of *The Beggars Opera*, and was finally pulled down in 1746.

David Garrick

Garrick came to London in 1737 as a partner with his brother, George, in the family wine business.

His heart, however, was set on the stage and he began performing as an amateur in the house of Mr Edward Cave, who had converted a large room into a theatre. Here, he met other notable London figures, including the artist, William Hogarth. By 1740 he was already playing small parts in the professional theatre.

The big break came in October 1741 when his performance as Richard III became the talk of London. His new 'realistic' style of acting delighted audiences and earned him the attention of other rising stars such as Charles Macklin and Peg Woffington who became lifelong friends.

Pamela and *King Lear* were performed in the 1741-1742 season at Goodmans Fields, but *The Changeling* was not. It is used here for purely fictional purposes.

In Spring 1742, with the closure of Goodmans Fields, Garrick travelled with Peg Woffington to Dublin where they were the main attraction of the summer season at the Smock Alley Theatre before returning to London where Fleetwood had signed him up for a season at Drury Lane.

Fact and Fiction

I have tried, as far as possible, to be historically accurate in my depiction of 18th Century London and 18th Century language and to accurately reflect the manners, morals and atmosphere of the time. For this, I am indebted to a variety of online resources, not least *The Online Etymological Dictionary* and *A Dictionary of 18th Century Slang* which proved invaluable for double-checking words (like 'mate' and 'pal') which, though they sound modern, are actually centuries old. Other books I most frequently used are listed in the Acknowledgements section.

Some characters - David Garrick, Charles Macklin, Peg Woffington, Samuel Foote and James Lacy - really existed and any facts about their lives are, to the best of my knowledge, accurate. Their personalities and involvement in the events if this story, however, are my own creation.

All other participating characters are fictional, even if, like Sir William Hervey, they are said to work for or be related to actual historical figures.

Places, too – the theatres, the Bedford Coffee House, the Ship Tavern, Hanover Square, Bethlehem Hospital, Westminster Hall etc. – existed but are embellished by imagination.

Acknowledgements

Liza Picard
Dr Johnson's London
Phoenix Press 2001

Jean Benedetti
David Garrick and the Birth of Modern Theatre
Methuen 2001

William W Appleton
Charles Macklin – An Actor's Life
Harvard University Press 1960

Emily Cockayne
Hubbub – Filth, Noise and Stench in England
Yale University Press 2007

Catherine Arnold
Bedlam – London and its Mad
Pocket Books 2008

Julie Peakman
Lascivious Bodies – a Sexual History of the 18th Century
Atlantic Books 2004

A M Nagler
A Source Book in Theatrical History
Dover 1952

Made in the USA
Charleston, SC
06 August 2014